DEAD
END

Books by Nancy Mehl

ROAD TO KINGDOM

Inescapable
Unbreakable
Unforeseeable

FINDING SANCTUARY

Gathering Shadows
Deadly Echoes
Rising Darkness

DEFENDERS OF JUSTICE

Fatal Frost
Dark Deception
Blind Betrayal

KAELY QUINN PROFILER

Mind Games
Fire Storm
Dead End

DEAD END

KAELY QUINN PROFILER
BOOK THREE

NANCY MEHL

BETHANYHOUSE
a division of Baker Publishing Group
Minneapolis, Minnesota

Published by Bethany House Publishers
11400 Hampshire Avenue South
Bloomington, Minnesota 55438
www.bethanyhouse.com

Bethany House Publishers is a division of
Baker Publishing Group, Grand Rapids, Michigan

Printed in the United States of America

Library of Congress Cataloging-in-Publication Data
Names: Mehl, Nancy, author.
Title: Dead end / Nancy Mehl.
Description: Minneapolis, Minnesota : Bethany House, a division of Baker
    Publishing Group, [2020] | Series: Kaely Quinn profiler ; 3
Identifiers: LCCN 2019040908 | ISBN 9780764231865 (trade paperback) | ISBN
    9780764235566 (cloth) | ISBN 9781493422791 (ebook)
Subjects: GSAFD: Christian fiction. | Mystery fiction. | Suspense fiction.
Classification: LCC PS3613.E4254 D42 2020 | DDC 813/.6—dc23
LC record available at https://lccn.loc.gov/2019040908

Scripture quotations are from the New King James Version®. Copyright © 1982 by Thomas Nelson. Used by permission. All rights reserved.

The quotation of Deuteronomy 5:9 is from THE HOLY BIBLE, NEW INTERNATIONAL VERSION®, NIV® Copyright © 1973, 1978, 1984, 2011 by Biblica, Inc.® Used by permission. All rights reserved worldwide.

Cover design by Faceout Studio
Cover photo by Arcangel / Ryan Jorgensen

Author is represented by The Steve Laube Agency

20 21 22 23 24 25 26   7 6 5 4 3 2 1

I dedicate this book to my dear friend,
Debbie Dunagan.

The Bible talks about the kind of friend who is willing to lay down their life for you. Few people fulfill this scripture, but Debbie does. She is a true and selfless friend to many people, not just me, but I count myself blessed to be in that group. I thank God for bringing her into my life. I love you, Debbie!

PROLOGUE

Norman Webber offered his wife a tight smile as he dealt with yet another one of her awful presents. He felt like a fool walking back and forth in this abandoned rail yard. It was a beautiful spring morning, and he wanted to be out on the golf course with his friends. They were already there, but here he was, looking for treasure he would never find. What in the world had he ever said to make Rita think he wanted a metal detector for his birthday? When he'd opened the gift, she'd screeched with joy. If only she'd given him the golf clubs he'd hinted for.

Rita was a good wife, really, but in the thirty years they'd been married, she'd never given him one decent present. He had all kinds of weird things put away in a closet. A singing fish you were supposed to mount on the wall. A police scanner— not something he wanted to listen to when he got home from work. A key chain you could record a message on. He never could figure out what to say. Anyway, why would he want his key chain talking to him? Rita talked enough. He didn't need another voice telling him what to do.

The weirdest gift might be the antique anvil. He'd once mentioned that his great-great-grandfather was a blacksmith, and then Rita bought the anvil as a tribute to his long-dead relative. A sweet gesture, but who in the world needs an anvil? Where do you put it? Finally, he sat it on the floor next to his recliner. It took only three trips to the chiropractor to work out the strain he'd caused his back moving that blasted thing. At least now he had a place to set his beer can while he watched TV. Living with Rita was definitely made better with alcohol. Frankly, he might do better joining AA than the gym she got him a membership to for his last birthday.

The detector beeped, and he leaned down to dig in the dirt with a small folding shovel. Rita ran over to see what he'd found.

"What is it, honey?" she asked, a little breathless. Her blond hair was pulled back in a ponytail, and her cheeks were flushed with excitement. He held up the fourth pop can of the morning. "Another one of these."

She took it from him and put it in the trash bag she'd brought with her. "A lot of people used to work here. I know we'll find something really valuable if we just don't give up."

Norman wanted to point out that they might do better at an abandoned casino than a rail yard, but Rita had her hopes up, and he didn't want to disappoint her. He sighed. He really loved this crazy woman. At least life with her was never dull.

"I just know we'll find a diamond ring or something," Rita said in her high, childlike voice.

He turned to look at her. "If you want a diamond ring, I'll buy it for you. We don't need to be digging around in the dirt, honey."

She frowned. "But this is *hidden* treasure. We have no idea what we might find. It's exciting, isn't it?"

Norman looked at the bag with the pop cans. "Sure. Very exciting."

He squared his shoulders and went back to walking back and forth across the rail yard. As he reached the fence that encircled it, the detector went off again. Rita had finally quit following him, and she stood a few yards back. He lowered the metal detector to the ground and then pulled the small shovel out of his jacket pocket. When he knelt and began to dig, he was certain he was about to add to their growing pop can collection.

A few minutes later, he stood and turned to look at his wife. "I found that diamond ring you wanted," he said, feeling as if he was going to lose his breakfast right there.

Rita squealed and clapped as she started toward him.

Norman held up his hand. "Stay there, Rita. And call the police."

She came to a halt and stared at him with a look of confusion. "But there's nothing illegal about keeping that ring."

He sighed and dropped the shovel. "There is if it's still attached to someone's hand."

ONE

Chief of Police Everett Sawyer stood over the body they'd just dug up in the old rail yard north of the city. The medical examiner, Jim Arndt, knelt next to the dead woman, his gloved hands carefully inspecting the evidence. She appeared to be in her early twenties, and she had dark hair.

"How long has she been dead, Jim?"

"Gotta get her back to the office to be sure, but I'd guess she's been deceased three or four days. Maybe five." He shook his head and pulled up her left hand. "Engaged. Nice ring. Dressed nicely too. This gal must have a decent job. Probably came from a good family as well."

"How can you tell that?" The chief was used to working with the medical examiner's office, but they constantly surprised him with their expertise.

"Her teeth."

He lowered the girl's hand and then pulled on her lips until her teeth were fully exposed. Everett looked away. He'd been the police chief in Des Moines for more than twenty years, but dead bodies still bothered him. An old detective, now retired, once told him if you looked into the eyes of the dead, you were responsible for them. He felt responsible enough. He tried hard not to get personally involved in the lives of victims. But sometimes . . . This girl was young. Pretty. Engaged to be married. She deserved better than this.

"What about her teeth?" he finally asked, knowing Jim would wait until he did.

"Straightened. And not recently. She had parents who made sure she had braces."

Everett frowned. "We got a report about a gal who went missing a few days ago. I'm betting it's her. Can't remember the name right now."

"I can't give you a name either." Jim sighed. "No purse." He reached gingerly into one of the girl's pants pockets. His hand came up empty. Then he reached into her other pocket and slowly pulled out a folded piece of paper. He opened it carefully. "Marriage license application. Filled out but not signed by the groom."

"You got a name?"

"Rebecca Jergens. Twenty-three. Lives in town."

"Yeah, that rings a bell. But she signed it?"

Jim nodded. "Maybe she was on her way to meet her fiancé. Have him sign."

"Or maybe he's a suspect."

"Maybe." Jim drew out the word as if he didn't really want to release it.

Everett glanced at the couple who found the body and were now being interviewed by one of his detectives. They were obviously traumatized by their discovery. The man kept muttering something that sounded like *no more birthday presents*, but that didn't make any sense. Everett chalked it up to shock.

He took a step closer to Jim. "Something bothering you?"

"Yeah."

"What?"

"Red ribbons."

"What? Are you serious?"

Jim brushed the dirt off the victim's shoes to further expose a red ribbon. Then he reached for something next to the body and held it up. Another red ribbon. "It came off when your men pulled her out of that hole. I'm guessing it was around her hands."

The butterflies in Everett's stomach turned into wasps. "Some joker thinks he's funny." He noticed the victim's right hand was still covered with dirt. Jim hadn't examined it yet.

The men looked at each other. They didn't need to say anything to know they were thinking the same thing. Jim finally reached for the girl's closed fist. When he pulled it open, something fell to the ground. He carefully picked it up and held it out for Everett to see. A twisted piece of wire.

Everett felt as if the breath had been sucked out of his lungs. It took everything he had to clear his throat and speak. "Is that what I think it is?" He was praying it wasn't.

Jim looked closely at the object. Then he looked up at the chief and nodded.

"Of course, it's not him," Everett said, his voice unsteady. "He's in prison."

"I realize that. But how could this killer know about the angel? You never released that information, right?"

Everett had no answer for him. Twenty-one years had gone by since the serial killer known as The Raggedy Man had terrorized Des Moines. Ed Oliphant had killed fourteen women—that they knew of. He hunted at night, dressed as a homeless person, looking for women who might show compassion toward him so he could pull them off the street and into an alley or a deserted building. One night a little girl saw him drag a woman away. She told her parents about it, but they hadn't understood the seriousness of her story until later.

The little girl had described Ed Oliphant as a *raggedy man*.

When her parents were interviewed by a local paper, the media started calling the killer The Raggedy Man. Then in an article written to warn the public, a talented FBI behavioral analyst predicted this man would not only change his disguise but perhaps take on the persona of a law enforcement officer. That's exactly what he did. When they caught him, he was wearing a cop's uniform. After his arrest, it didn't take long to match his DNA to DNA found with one of the victims. And not long after that, they found his stash of keepsakes hidden behind a wooden wall panel in his house. He had a trinket from almost every woman he'd murdered.

Oliphant pleaded guilty to all the charges, saving the state from the expense of a trial. Currently, Iowa didn't have the death penalty, so he sat in prison serving life without parole, allowing taxpayers to house and feed him. That didn't seem right to him, but Everett couldn't do anything about it. At least Oliphant's reign of evil had come to an end. Everett had been the lead detective on the case, many times forced to look into the faces of family members who'd lost a loved one. It was the toughest thing he'd ever done. Not long before they caught Oliphant, Everett had a mild heart attack brought on by the stress of the case.

Thankfully, he recovered and was able to return to work, but those faces still haunted him. Honestly, he wasn't sure he could make it through another serial killer case.

"When are you going to transport her?" he asked.

"Soon. We'll look her over a little more closely when we get to the lab, and of course, we'll contact you after the autopsy."

"Holler when you're ready so my people can process the scene."

"I will. Don't want to miss anything. Especially with this one."

Everett was about to echo Jim's sentiments when one of his officers came up. Officer Malone's face was ashen.

"What in the world?" Everett asked.

"Uh, sir. We found another body." The young officer's voice was raspy with obvious distress.

"Another body?" Everett repeated. What was going on?

"Actually . . . there could be more. A lot more."

Everett's knees went weak. *Not again. Please, God, not again.*

TWO

FBI Special Agent Kaely Quinn scrolled through yet another online newspaper article. She'd been hunched over her desk all morning, checking out drug cases across the country. The St. Louis FBI field office had been working with local police to stop the distribution of a new and dangerous drug called flakka that first appeared in Florida and then spread to Texas and Ohio. Now, after several cases of overdose in Missouri, there was a push to find out how it had landed here and who was selling it.

Flakka caused excited delirium, which exhibited itself in hallucinations and paranoia. Users also seemed to exhibit superhuman strength, making it hard for only one or two officers to restrain someone experiencing an overdose. Flakka was akin to bath salts. Since the drug could be swallowed, snorted, or injected, it could be easily concealed in public. The police and FBI had joined forces with the DEA and the Federal Bureau of Alcohol, Tobacco, Firearms and Explosives in Fort Lauderdale. Kaely looked for the same thing to happen across the country.

She sighed audibly. What was missing in people's lives that led them to put their lives on the line for a quick high? Of course, she knew the answer. She'd once been searching for something to make life seem worthwhile too. Thankfully, she'd never tried drugs to fill the emptiness. She'd stayed away from all drugs and alcohol because she hated feeling out of control. Her fellow FBI agents had called her a control freak more than once.

Of course, when she'd found God, she realized that had to

change. Little by little, she was learning to trust Him, but trusting people was still a problem. She liked to refer to herself as a work in progress. Unfortunately, in some areas the progress part was pretty slow.

She stopped scrolling when she noticed an article out of Des Moines, the town where she grew up. Where her father, Ed Oliphant, had acted out the foul wickedness festering in his soul. She hadn't been back there since she was fourteen and her mother moved her and her brother to Nebraska.

The article said local police had uncovered several bodies in a rail yard near the city just over two weeks ago. The first victim they found, Rebecca Jergens, twenty-three years old, had been on her way to meet her fiancé, Paul Weigand, when she was killed. They'd planned to have a nice dinner at a local restaurant, where he would sign their marriage license application. When she didn't show, he tried unsuccessfully to reach her by phone. Finally, he called the police, who seemed to think Rebecca had simply changed her mind about the wedding. But her parents and Weigand wouldn't give up, insisting she would never run out on her fiancé.

Finally, the police began to search for Rebecca. Then a couple using a metal detector found her body. That led to unearthing even more gruesome discoveries.

The number of bodies discovered wasn't mentioned in the article, but surely the city, once assaulted with the evil her father brought, wouldn't have to endure another onslaught. She thought about calling the Des Moines PD, but even if they asked for help from the FBI, it wouldn't be from the St. Louis field office. The Omaha office covered Des Moines. Besides, if they knew she was Ed Oliphant's daughter . . . Well, she was sure they wouldn't want her anywhere near Des Moines. Kaely had changed her name twice, but her story still got out. After being kicked out of Quantico because word of her connection to The Raggedy Man was published in a Virginia newspaper—causing, her superiors said, too much distraction—she'd been transferred to St. Louis.

Everyone here knew about her family connection, but thankfully, the fascination seemed to have waned. Most of the agents kept their distance when she first arrived, but now the majority of them were friendly. A lot of that could be attributed to Special Agent Noah Hunter, a man she'd worked with several times now. He'd done a lot to convince their colleagues that Kaely Quinn was a normal person. Although she didn't always feel like one, she appreciated his effort.

In the past year Kaely had grown close to Noah—closer than she had to anyone since her father was arrested. But after a case in Nebraska six months ago, he'd suddenly become distant. She'd tried several times to fix that, but although they continued to talk and spend time together, their relationship had never returned to what it had once been. Kaely knew why he was angry. Noah felt she was too reckless, that she put herself in danger when she shouldn't. There was a lot of truth to what he said, but she didn't do it on purpose. She was driven to find justice—no matter what she had to do. How could she pull back with so much evil in the world? She wasn't going to change. Not for Noah. Not for anyone.

For a while, she thought their relationship had finally improved. Two months ago, their boss, Solomon Slattery, special agent in charge of the St. Louis office, had ordered her to take a vacation. He told her she needed to rest. Recharge. Although she didn't agree, she had no choice. Solomon sent her to stay in his cabin on the Lake of the Ozarks. Right after she arrived, she'd been pulled into helping with a local investigation. Once that was over, Noah joined her for the remainder of the two weeks she was there. They'd had fun, and Noah had seemed more relaxed around her. That was in June. But now, in August, Noah's aloofness had returned.

Solomon liked to pair them together as much as possible. He saw Noah as a protector, someone who would keep Kaely from going too far—not that it had worked. Her boss was under the delusion that she was his second daughter, a notion she'd tried to dissuade him from more than once.

She realized she'd been chewing on her pen—a bad habit. Her brother, Jason, had given her a set of pens with Scripture on them. This one read *I can do all things through Christ who strengthens me.* She set it next to her keyboard and scrolled down so she could finish reading the article. Then she locked her hands behind her head and leaned back, staring at the computer screen. Part of her wanted to know what was going on in Des Moines. Another part of her wanted nothing to do with it. Her memories were still too raw. Too painful.

When her phone rang, she jumped but then picked it up. Solomon.

"I need to see you in my office," he said in a flat tone.

Kaely was somewhat taken aback by what she heard in his voice, and she tensed. Could this be about Des Moines? He probably wanted her to hear about those bodies from him. Too late.

"Okay, on my way," she said before hanging up. She stood and grabbed her jacket from the back of her chair. When she slipped it on, she made sure the collar was down. Then she checked her hair. Her auburn curls were pulled back in a bun, but as usual, several strands had escaped. She wondered if she should stop by the restroom and fix that, but when Solomon called you to his office, you went immediately. She doubted he actually counted the minutes it took people to show up, but if he did, she wouldn't be surprised.

When she reached his reception area, his administrative assistant, Grace, smiled. "He's waiting for you," she said, gesturing toward a closed door. Kaely nodded and approached his office, trying to squelch an odd sense of apprehension. She quickly smoothed her slacks, then knocked before she heard Solomon call out. "Come in, Kaely."

When she stepped inside, she was surprised to see Noah there, sitting in a chair positioned in front of Solomon's massive desk. Another man sat next to him. Although she didn't recognize him, he seemed familiar, and she was almost overwhelmed by a sudden sense of foreboding. Why would she react that way to a stranger? It didn't make sense. She raised her eyebrows as she looked at Noah. A slight hitch in his shoulders told her he had no idea why they were there.

Solomon nodded toward a chair in the corner of the room. She pulled it up next to Noah, and quickly sat down, curious to discover the reason for their summons. She took a deep breath in an attempt to calm her jangled nerves.

"This is Police Chief Everett Sawyer from Des Moines," Solomon said.

Kaely's body stiffened. "I remember you now." Her voice sounded strange to her.

"I wondered if you would," Sawyer said. "It's been a long time. You were . . . what? Fourteen? Fifteen?"

"Fourteen," she said, trying to keep her emotions in check. She turned to look at Solomon. "Chief Sawyer was the lead detective working the case that involved . . . my father."

Solomon's bushy eyebrows shot up, and he turned to his guest. "You have a lot of experience with the Ed Oliphant case, then?"

"Yes. Probably more than anyone else."

"The FBI was called in to assist you," Kaely said.

Sawyer nodded. "And we were grateful. One of your profilers—

sorry, one of your behavioral analysts—came up with a profile so accurate it helped us nab him. I believe a lot more women would have died if it hadn't been for his help." He smiled at Kaely. "When I heard you'd joined the FBI, I was relieved. You didn't allow what happened to destroy you. Instead, you decided to fight back. It was a brave decision. Good for you."

Kaely felt her cheeks flush. Everett Sawyer had been there when she was questioned about her father, and she'd lumped him in with the people who'd frightened her after her father was arrested. She was confused and unsure about what was going on back then. It didn't feel real. More like a nightmare she kept waiting to wake up from.

"Thank you," she managed to say. She turned to look at Solomon. His weathered face gave the impression he was always a little worried about something, but today his lips were a thin line, and his crow's feet were deeper than normal.

Kaely waited for her boss to say something, but he was unusually quiet. Chief Sawyer refused to meet her gaze, sitting with his arms crossed. He was definitely defensive. The men's silence filled the room like some kind of noxious gas slowly poisoning the very air Kaely breathed.

"What's going on?" Noah finally asked, obviously as confused as Kaely was.

Solomon frowned at Sawyer as if he wanted him to answer Noah's question, but Sawyer didn't respond. Finally, Solomon took a deep breath and directed his attention to Kaely. "Have you heard about the bodies found in Des Moines?"

Kaely nodded.

Solomon clasped his hands together, his knuckles white with pressure. "The . . . the MO is . . . Well, the MO is the same as your father's. Strangled. The hands and feet tied with red ribbon."

Kaely frowned at him. "It's a copycat killer. Those facts were available to the public." She studied him for a moment. The tension she saw in his body and his expression hadn't lessened at all. There was something else. Something he wasn't telling her.

"Just say it," she said, feeling annoyed at his reticence.

He glanced at Sawyer and then took another breath. "They found a piece of wire in the hand of the first body found."

"What do you mean?" she asked, knowing exactly what he meant.

"It was a wire angel," Solomon said, his voice softer now. "Just like the one your father always left behind. Exactly the same. But that part of his MO was kept quiet. Never shared with the public."

"You're right," Chief Sawyer said. "We do have a copycat killer. But this guy knows more than he should."

"A lot of people had access to information about my father," Kaely said. "Anyone associated with the case. The police, the FBI. The ME's office."

"Under normal circumstances I would come to the same conclusion, Agent Quinn. But not in this case."

Kaely turned his comment over in her mind and found it incredibly naïve. Her father could have told someone in prison. "You said all the women had been strangled?"

"Yes. The bodies all showed evidence of strangulation. Broken bones in the neck. They all had red ribbons as well." He locked eyes with Kaely. "And they *all* had an angel in their hands. An exact match to the angels your father fashioned. Even the same kind of wire he used." He readjusted himself in the chair as if he were uncomfortable. "There's something else, though. Something we want to keep to ourselves." He cleared his throat. "The folks at the ME's lab found something missed at the scene. A piece of paper in the mouths of all the newer victims. In a plastic baggie."

Kaely frowned at him. "A piece of paper?"

Sawyer nodded. Kaely waited for more, but Sawyer hesitated. She was so tense that pain pounded in her head. "And something was written on it?" she asked, trying to force a response.

"Yes, but typed. It said, 'Deuteronomy 5:9: "For I, the Lord your God, am a jealous God—"'"

"'Punishing the children for the sin of the parents to the third and fourth generation of those who hate me,'" Kaely finished for him.

Sawyer's eyes widened in obvious surprise. "You know it?"

"Of course. If you were the child of a ruthless serial killer, wouldn't you?"

He ignored her question. "Look, because of the angel, we're convinced your father has something to do with this. Of course, he won't admit to it. Won't say anything. Not a word. It's like trying to talk to a brick wall." He shrugged. "We have no idea why the Scripture was added, but . . ."

"You think it's a message to me?"

Sawyer looked at Solomon, whose eyes were fixed on him as if he were trying to send the police chief some kind of mental message. He finally broke his gaze and turned his attention back to Kaely. "Des Moines authorities need to know if your father is directing someone to follow in his footsteps," he said. "Getting him to talk might be the only way to stop these killings."

"I still don't understand why you think he has anything to do with this," Kaely said. "He's locked up. It doesn't make sense."

"There's more. Quite a few bodies were buried in that rail yard. Some of them were new, but some of them were old. Twenty years old. And they all had a wire angel in their hands. The remnants of red ribbon. Their hyoid bones broken."

Kaely froze. "What are you saying?"

"I'm telling you we found more of Ed Oliphant's victims. And no one else could have told this copycat killer where they were."

"What are you talking about?" Kaely asked, unable to keep anger from her voice. "My father killed fourteen women. No more."

"I'm sorry," Solomon said, his voice low, "but they're definitely his. Everything matches up perfectly, and they were killed during the time he was active. They couldn't belong to anyone else."

Kaely couldn't believe this was happening. She turned to Sawyer. "Why are you here? What do you want from me?"

The chief seemed to be steeling himself for what he had to say. "We need you to talk with your father."

THREE

Kaely could only stare at the police chief, trying to understand what he'd just said. At first his words made no sense. Then as she realized what he was asking, her body trembled as though it had a mind of its own. She barely felt Noah reach over and touch her arm.

"You . . . you expect me to . . . interview my father? You think he'll share something with me he won't with you?" She stood. "You've got the wrong idea. My father doesn't care about me— or anyone. He's a psychopath. Ed Oliphant's world revolves around himself."

"We're out of options," Sawyer said. "We've tried everything. He just won't talk. Look, I realize this might not work, but we're grasping at straws. I don't have to remind you that women are dying."

Kaely pushed back a rush of anger. "I understand the implications, but he isn't going to break down and confess to me. I told you, he's a psychopath. They have no remorse, and they don't have the ability to learn from experience. It's impossible for this man to feel guilt or ever accept responsibility for the vile deeds he committed." She sucked in a deep breath, trying to find the strength to continue. "Ed has never shown one shred of remorse for what he's done. Not toward the families of the women he killed and not toward his own family. The family he almost destroyed."

She swallowed hard, trying to control the shakiness in her voice. "I've done a lot for the Bureau. But this?" She put her hand on Solomon's desk to steady herself. "No. You can't ask this of me. It's too much, and it would be a waste of time."

"Sit down, Kaely," Solomon said, but with a gentle tone. "Of course, you don't have to go if you don't want to. But I don't like this . . . message. Maybe it's not directed to you, but it could be. It worries me."

"But if it's a message to me from my father, why would you think he would talk to me about these killings?"

"To be honest, we think our copycat may have added the Scripture himself," Sawyer said. "Prison officials say they've never heard your father express any malice toward you or your brother."

"Serial killers rarely change their MOs, you know, although it's happened," Kaely said. "It's a pride thing."

Sawyer nodded. "And if your father isn't behind this addition to his MO, he may break away from his protégé and give us what we need. We want you to ask him about the Scripture. Coming from you, it might mean more. Get the reaction we're hoping for."

"What does Omaha think?" Kaely asked.

"They aren't sure," Solomon said. "None of us are. You're certainly not mentioned by name in those notes. Maybe our unknown subject is referring to something—or someone—that relates only to him."

"Of course, there's your brother," Sawyer said.

Kaely's body went cold again. "I didn't think. I should have—"

"Don't worry," Solomon said. "Omaha will coordinate with Colorado. They'll keep an eye on Jason."

How could she have forgotten her own brother? Could he be in danger?

As she lowered herself back into her chair, she looked at Noah. Kaely needed his strength, but she saw only compassion in his expression. For some reason it angered her. She didn't want empathy right now. She needed the power to face this. Inside, she cried out to God, praying He would strengthen her. She was a professional, but right now she wasn't acting like one. Leave it to her father to make her feel weak and frightened.

"Solomon, if I thought it would help, I would consider this no matter how hard it might be for me. But trust me, I have no influence over my father. None."

"Look," Sawyer said, "I know this isn't fair. Asking you to do this. But we're out of options. The copycat hasn't given us anything. No DNA. No fingerprints. Nothing but some tire tracks and footprints that lead us nowhere. We've reached a dead end."

"How many bodies?" Kaely asked, not really wanting to hear the answer.

Sawyer glanced at Solomon before turning back to her. "Fifteen. We believe nine of the remains were your father's old victims. You know, we always suspected there were more. We had reports of missing women that fit the general description of the victims we found, but we couldn't prove anything without bodies. Besides, the so-called Raggedy Man left his kills in plain sight as if he were proud of what he'd done. He wanted people to see his . . . work." Sawyer shook his head. "We weren't looking for bodies buried somewhere. It appears we made a grave mistake."

Kaely had a sudden urge to laugh at his inappropriate pun, but nothing about it was funny. Her nerves were knocking her a little off-balance.

"After all this time, finding DNA on or near those bodies to match your father's will be next to impossible," Solomon said. "But as Chief Sawyer says, the age of the older remains is correct for him to be the killer. Adding the fact that there was never any indication he had an accomplice, the Omaha office believes these victims are his." He drummed his fingers on his desktop, a habit when he was upset.

"What can you tell me about the newer bodies?" Kaely asked.

"Not much so far." Sawyer leaned forward. "Like I said, same MO, but this guy is being very careful. Probably wearing gloves. Everything's been sent to the lab at Quantico. The only DNA so far comes from the victims—and some incidental transfer. Nothing we can link to the UNSUB." He hesitated. "There is one more difference in your father's MO and this guy's, though."

Kaely looked at him with raised eyebrows.

"We don't think it's significant," Sawyer said, "but your father used chloroform to subdue his victims. This guy prefers a stun gun. Easier, more reliable. Less struggling."

Actually, that made sense. The method was still the same, though. Disable the victims so you can control them before you choke them to death. This was just a modern revision in the technique of robbing a human being of life. Kaely took one more deep breath and refocused her attention. "At this moment, then, you can't prove Ed has anything to do with this."

Sawyer seemed to study her for a moment. "No, right now we can't prove it, but I'm convinced the older remains belong to The Raggedy Man. And as I said, no one else could have told the copycat killer where he'd buried these bodies."

"Please don't use a stupid moniker to describe this sick killer," Kaely said, her tone sharp. "My father's name is Ed Oliphant. This guy has a name too. Don't glorify either one of them by calling them something other than what they are— brutal killers. Degenerates who prey on defenseless women. Men who not only destroy their victims' lives but also the lives of the people who loved them. The murdered women all had years and years in front of them. Marriage. Children who will never be born. Grandchildren they will never enjoy. These murderers are monsters."

Kaely fought to control her outburst, but her rant came from an emotional wound never completely healed. God had brought her this far, but somewhere deep inside, the pain caused by her father's hideous deeds still ate at her like a cancerous lesion that refused to be excised. She looked at Solomon, who studied her as if he'd never seen her before.

"I'm . . . I'm sorry, sir," she said. Then she turned to Sawyer. "I apologize. I didn't mean to—"

"That's enough, Kaely," Solomon said, again gently. "You're not a robot. You've been through an ordeal most of us could never understand."

"I appreciate that, but I'm fine." She swallowed hard, trying to regain her composure. She might not be a robot, but she was an FBI agent, and she was determined to act like one. "How long have the new bodies been there?"

Sawyer rubbed his hands on his pant legs. A pacifying action. "Buried there sometime in the last six or seven months."

"And you believe my father, after twenty-one years, has recruited someone to pick up where he left off? Why in the world did it take him so long to find this . . . apprentice?"

"I can't answer that question," Sawyer said, frowning. "But we certainly have to explore the possibility. Surely you can see that."

Kaely ran the facts through her mind, trying to separate emotion from truth. As Sawyer pointed out, if the older victims belonged to her father, he had to be involved somehow. He was the only one who could have led the copycat to the field. She clasped her hands together to stop them from trembling. She'd prayed her father would eventually just fade away. Rot away in prison, where he couldn't touch her. But here he was again, spreading his wickedness, bringing his malevolence into her life. Truth be told, she hated him for it.

"It's a lot to dismiss," Noah said, speaking for only the second time. "Sounds like Ed Oliphant's implicated somehow." He looked at Kaely. She knew he was trying to help, but she didn't need his input. She understood the ramifications of the findings in the field.

"Doesn't the prison monitor his letters and phone calls?" she asked. "Wouldn't they know if he was in contact with someone?"

"I wish they had perfect control," Sawyer said, "but some things get past the safeguards. Messages are passed along by other inmates. Maybe someone from the outside, a visitor, is communicating through another prisoner. Inmates who work in the mailroom could be passing along letters secretly. It's pretty easy to bribe prisoners with cigarettes, money in their accounts." He sighed and leaned back in his chair. "Some of the inmates are clever. Your father could certainly be corresponding with our killer somehow. We've contacted the warden and asked him to tighten Oliphant's security."

"You've checked all his visitors?" Noah said.

Sawyer snorted. "He doesn't allow visitors. And although quite a few women would like to correspond with him, he doesn't respond to them. These are foolish women who write to serial killers as if they're some kind of Hollywood stars. It's disgusting."

"You say he hasn't written to any of them?" Noah asked.

"No. Doesn't even accept their letters—unless there's money in them. That's why this caught prison officials off guard. He's one of the most isolated inmates they've ever had."

Kaely wasn't surprised. He'd kept to himself quite a bit before he was caught. Didn't like having people over to the house. He'd worked at the church but only attended required meetings. He rarely went to social events or spent personal time with the parishioners. There was no chance any of them would visit him now. Kaely and her family had been deserted by almost everyone they knew when the identity of The Raggedy Man was revealed. Even if someone requested a visit, she was certain he wouldn't agree to see them.

"So, then, the only human contact he has on a regular basis is with other prisoners and the guards?" she asked.

"As far as I'm aware." Sawyer shrugged. "The warden would know more about that than I do."

Kaely leaned forward and stared at the man. "You need to investigate everyone around him. Everyone he talks to."

"Omaha has opened a Domestic Police Cooperation case," Solomon said. "They've sent in the Evidence Response Team. And the lab will be available."

Kaely frowned. She'd assumed Des Moines would want to avail itself of the full resources of the FBI.

"So the BAU isn't coming?" she asked.

"Not at this time. That could change. For now, your insight would be welcome."

"But I can't—"

"If asked, you can offer advice," Solomon said. "You understand?"

Kaely nodded, still not sure she wanted anything to do with this. They could ask for the Behavioral Analysis Unit. Why hadn't they?

"Noah, you'll be accompanying her as lead agent," Solomon said.

Sawyer turned to Noah. "You'll be helping her prep for the interview, taking notes, reviewing visitor logs and mail, and interviewing prison personnel. We need to know if Oliphant might be conning or blackmailing someone to get messages out of the prison. You might also be talking to other prisoners, searching for some kind of connection. Someone is helping him, and we need to find out who it is. Fast."

"Ed hasn't actually said anything about the killings," Kaely said softly. She was talking to herself, but Sawyer took it as a question.

"Right. As I said, we've tried several times to get information out of him. We've even tried to bribe him. Offered to give him more freedom. More time outside. Even move him to a larger cell with a window." He sighed. "He wasn't interested. He just sat there, refusing to talk. His therapist won't reveal anything—doctor-client privilege. You're the only option left to us. You're a trained behavioral analyst, and I understand you're exceptional at what you do. I believe you can tell us more, see more about your father than anyone else."

He locked eyes with her. "Special Agent Quinn, we truly believe you may be the only person in the world who can stop these murders."

FOUR

Kaely stared at the seafood salad she'd ordered for lunch. Noah was devouring his patty melt, and the aroma of the grilled onions on his sandwich made her stomach flip. But mostly, the idea of facing her father again horrified her. She felt as if she were locked inside a nightmare and couldn't find her way out. She just couldn't do it. She had to say no. Had to get back to the life she had before walking into Solomon's office this morning.

She'd called Jason and told him what was going on. And about the Scripture. He'd dismissed her concerns. "Dad's not out to get us, Kaely. I'm sure of it." She didn't argue with him, just told him that the FBI in Colorado would be contacting him. He wasn't happy about it, but she was relieved to know they'd keep an eye on her brother.

Noah put down his sandwich and wiped his mouth. "Kaely, you don't have to face your dad. You've been through enough because of him. Let the FBI do its job. Other behavioral analysts exist, you know. Someone will get him to talk. This isn't on you. Really. Just say no."

Kaely had to smile. "Not sure repeating Nancy Reagan's antidrug motto from the eighties will help me."

"You know what I mean. Couldn't talking to him be dangerous?"

Kaely shook her head. "No, I seriously doubt it. He'll be chained. He can't hurt me."

"Maybe not physically, but I worry about what this will do to you emotionally."

Kaely picked up her fork and jabbed at a piece of crab. "But what if Chief Sawyer is right? What if Ed is willing to talk to me? How can I live knowing someone died because I couldn't face my fears? Omaha obviously didn't call in the BAU because they think I'll have more success." She sighed. "They really believe I'm the only one who can get my father to talk."

"For crying out loud, Kaely. You're not responsible for everything." He tapped his fork on the side of his plate with force. "I don't think you should be put in this position. And, frankly, I have to wonder how the Omaha office feels about you questioning your dad. Why did the request come from Chief Sawyer? Why didn't it come from them?"

"Good point," Kaely said, frowning. "Maybe they *don't* want me." A spark of hope ignited inside her. If Omaha didn't want her to confront her father, she couldn't do it. "But why would Chief Sawyer come all this way if he thought Omaha would resist bringing me in?"

Noah shrugged. "What did you pick up from him?"

"I didn't detect any dishonesty. He was nervous, though." Kaely took a deep breath. "I can read people's physical reactions, but I don't know exactly why he was uncomfortable. Was it because he knows Omaha isn't behind his request? Or was it because he didn't like having to ask me to do what he knew would be traumatic for me? I wish I knew the answer."

"I assumed you could read Sawyer and figure out what he was thinking. You seem to know every thought that pops into my head."

Kaely paused a moment. "Some of them. Not all. Ever since we came back from Nebraska, I'm almost never sure what you're thinking. I wish you'd talk to me about it."

Noah's expression immediately tightened. "We've gone over this more than once, but I'm not convinced you get it."

"You're still angry about what happened in Darkwater?"

Noah stared at her a moment before answering. "You put yourself in terrible danger, Kaely. I understand the original plan, but you pushed it way too far."

"I just wanted to make sure we brought down our perp."

Noah swore. "At what cost? Your life?" He shook his head. "And it wasn't the first time."

Kaely felt a flash of anger. "Look, nothing is more important to me than doing my job. No matter what it takes."

"I know that, believe me." He took a drink of his soda and then put the glass down. "Look, let's just leave it. We're friends. That will never change. I just . . . I just can't get too close to you. You're dangerous. I didn't think I could make it after Tracy died. If anything happened to you . . ."

Kaely searched his face. She knew what he was saying, but neither one of them had admitted to the feelings that had developed between them. It seemed that the only way Noah could cope was to keep their relationship in the friend zone. That was okay with her, but their friendship wasn't the same because of the wall he'd built around himself. She couldn't get through it no matter what she said or did. Not knowing what else to say, she picked up her fork and stared at a piece of shrimp.

"Are you going to actually eat that or just admire it?"

Kaely put her fork back in her salad. "I seem to have lost my appetite. I think I'll take this back to the office and put it in the fridge. It will make a great supper."

"Do you have any other food at your place?" Noah asked, his tone dry.

"Sure. I have plenty of food, thank you."

"I'm not talking about cat food."

Kaely frowned at him. "Okay, maybe not much human food. I'll get to the store. I've been busy."

"Busy in your *war room*? Still looking over cold cases from across the country?"

"Maybe. Talk about reading someone's mind. I think you might be better at it than I am."

Noah finished his sandwich and then stuck several fries in his mouth before washing them down with his soda. "Comes from experience," he finally said. "There's not much I don't know about you."

His statement made her feel uncomfortable. "You're delusional, you know that?" She tried to sound lighthearted.

Noah chuckled. "So you've told me more than once even though you're the one with the invisible friend."

Kaely snorted. "Wow, am I sorry for telling you about Georgie."

Kaely had invented Georgie several years ago to bounce ideas off of when she had no one else to talk to. Kaely had never seen Georgie as a negative thing, but Noah had expressed concern about her depending too much on someone who wasn't real. Kaely couldn't really understand why Georgie worried him. Kaely had never confused her with a real person. She was simply the other voice in Kaely's head, the voice that cautioned her. Encouraged her. Even warned her. Since coming back from her forced vacation, Kaely hadn't called for Georgie, and so far, her invisible friend had stayed away.

"I'm worried about that Scripture, Kaely," Noah said, changing the subject. "Why did the killer put it there? *Do* you think it's a message to you and your brother?"

"I doubt it. Could just be his signature. The reason he kills. He could be referring to himself. Some kind of family thing." But something deep inside told her the message was directed to her. Maybe she was just being paranoid. Not everything that happened in the world was about her.

"What can I do to help?" Noah asked. "How about I bring some Chinese over tonight and we'll talk this whole thing through?"

Kaely turned Noah's offer over in her mind. She felt the need to spend some time by herself. To try to figure this out. But the truth was she didn't want to be alone. The entrance of her father back into her life had affected her more than she wanted to admit. And something that happened in Nebraska kept flitting through her mind—a warning from an invisible UNSUB during one of her unique profiling sessions. "Okay," she said. "That would be great."

"About seven?"

Kaely nodded. "Sounds good. Mr. Hoover will be happy to see you."

Her cat, a Maine Coon, loved Noah. He'd head straight for Noah's lap whenever he came to visit. At first, she tried to make him get down, but Noah waved her away. "I don't mind," he said. When he started petting Mr. Hoover and smiling when the cat produced a loud purr, Kaely realized Noah wasn't being mannerly. He really liked the large feline.

"I have a new toy for him," Noah said.

Kaely sighed. "You know Mr. Hoover doesn't like toys. I've got a basket full of stuff he doesn't pay any attention to. I think you bought most of them."

Mr. Hoover was nothing if not reserved. He always stared at the toys Noah brought as if to say *I'm way too cool for this. What's wrong with you?* Then he'd stick his tail straight up in the air and walk away as if slightly offended. Kaely thought it was funny, but Noah took it as a challenge. He was determined to find something Mr. Hoover would react to. If Mr. Hoover's toy basket got much fuller, she'd need additional storage for all his rejected playthings.

"Well, he doesn't have this one. Five bucks he'll love it."

Kaely stuck out her hand, and Noah reached over the table and shook it.

"Five dollars," she said. "I hate to take your money. This is too easy."

Noah smiled. "We'll see. I'm nothing if not committed."

Kaely raised an eyebrow. "I think you mean you should *be* committed."

"Funny. You're just hysterical."

"I know." Kaely gestured to their waitress. When she came to the table, Kaely asked for the check and a to-go box.

Noah wiped his mouth and downed the rest of his soda. "What are you going to tell Solomon?"

"That I need some time to think. Maybe you and I will come up with something tonight." She was horrified when tears suddenly filled her eyes. "I . . . I don't want to see him, Noah. I really don't, but then I remember the times he acted . . . like a dad. Taking us to the state fair. Showing up at school activities for me and Jason. I've tried to forget all that, but memories pop into my head. I can't help it." She dabbed her tears with her napkin.

Noah was quiet for a moment. "Maybe that's okay. You've done this long enough to realize that a lot of these people are more than just the evil they've done."

"But my father is a psychopath. He had to have been pretending all that time. Trying to *look* like he cared about his family." She grunted. "Besides killing all those women, he cheated on my mom, you know. Doesn't sound like a loving, dedicated husband and father."

"No, it doesn't."

"The thing is, I could swear he cared about us. I fell off my bike once, and we thought my leg was broken. My father picked me up in his arms and held me while my mom drove us to the hospital. You should have seen his face. He looked terrified. Had tears in his eyes. And he used to grab my mother when certain romantic songs came on the radio. They'd dance in the living room like two kids in love. He even sang some of the songs to Jason and me." She shook her head in frustration. "Why weren't we enough?"

Noah frowned at her. "This had nothing to do with you, and you know that."

"Yeah, I do. But even though I understand the psychology behind Ed's . . . proclivities, it's like a child is still living somewhere inside me. An angry child who wants him to explain why he did those things. It doesn't make sense, but it's there. I know I'm not the only child of a serial killer to go through this. Dennis Rader's daughter, Kerri Rawson, was hit really hard when the truth about her father came out. I read her book." Kaely sighed deeply. "Boy, could I relate. But it also confused me."

"What do you mean?"

Kaely was quiet for a moment as she tried to gather her words. "Rader was so similar to my father. He was organized. Planned his kills. Had no compassion. Showed no mercy. But both of them . . ."

"Appeared to care about their families?"

She nodded slowly.

"I don't know the answer to that, Kaely. You're the expert." He shrugged. "Maybe as much as we understand, we'll never comprehend everything."

Kaely nodded again. "You're probably right."

The waitress came back to the table and gave them their bills. She handed Kaely a box to put her salad in, smiled, and walked away.

"Rader's daughter made the decision to never see her father again. But she does write to him." Kaely scooped her salad into the box. "I've never written to my dad. I believe in forgiveness, but something like this . . . The idea of forgiving him makes me feel as though I'd be accepting what's been done. That I'd be almost complicit in it."

"I don't know much about it," Noah said, "but I don't think forgiving someone means you have to tolerate their behavior. Tracy used to say forgiving means you let it go but you don't necessarily forget. You still need to protect yourself. Your heart, your emotions." He appeared to scrutinize her. "Sometimes I think you ask too much of yourself."

Kaely turned his words over in her mind. His wife had been a wise woman. Kaely wished she could have known her. "I've said the words, you know, that I've forgiven my father, but I still feel anger . . . and hurt. I'm depending on God to bring me the rest of the way. Kerri got there. If she and God can do it, maybe I can too."

Noah's eyes searched hers. "I'm really not sure you should do this, but I have to wonder if seeing him again will help you in some way."

Kaely put her money in the bill carrier, then grabbed her box of salad and stood. Could Noah be right? Was God's will for her to do the unthinkable—to look into the eyes of the man she'd despised all these years?

FIVE

He relished the written accounts of his deeds, and he watched the TV as horrified news reporters shared the findings uncovered in the ground at the deserted railroad yard. He was surprised they'd found the bodies so quickly. He'd planned to call in an anonymous tip telling police to search the yard. But before he could do it, some unsuspecting jerk had stumbled onto his latest achievement. After he thought about it, though, he realized this was better. Much better.

As he pored over every report he could find, no one suggested his work was connected to Ed Oliphant. He wasn't surprised the police were trying to keep that quiet, but he was disappointed. He'd phone the media on an old burner phone in a couple of days—anonymously, of course. The kind of phone without the GPS chip. He'd bought several, purchased before the chip was added. Whatever phone he used would be thrown away anyway—just to be completely safe. And if they didn't respond, he'd write letters. He respected the way the Zodiac had kept authorities on their toes. Maybe he'd emulate him . . . just a little. Of course, The Raggedy Man hadn't written letters. If he stayed true to Ed Oliphant's legacy, he'd have to stay silent. He'd wait to see how things progressed.

He'd heard the police had asked the FBI for help. Exactly what he'd hoped for. That didn't mean they'd request Ed's daughter to join the investigation, but that's why he'd added the Bible verse—to lure her in. If that didn't work, he had another plan. He was determined to get close to Kaely Quinn.

41

Kaely was working in her war room when she heard the doorbell ring. Mr. Hoover, who was curled up in a pet bed next to her, lifted his head and looked up as if asking her to explain the interruption.

She closed the files she had on her desk, cases from other parts of the country not assigned to her. She wasn't allowed to officially serve as a behavioral analyst since being kicked out of Quantico, but bringing killers, rapists, drug dealers, serial arsonists, and especially sex traffickers to justice was the cry of her heart. Something she couldn't turn off even if the FBI told her she wasn't allowed to pursue it—something she believed was her calling. And working on her own, she'd phoned in several anonymous tips that had led to the capture of criminals.

"It's Noah," she told Mr. Hoover, who stood and stretched his large body.

Usually, she'd get a call from the security guard before someone was allowed into her gated community. Noah was the only exception. All the guards knew him.

Kaely got up and followed Mr. Hoover, who ran down the stairs and stood at the door meowing. Kaely laughed at him. He was a smart cat who didn't like most people. He had reason to feel that way after being abused, and he especially didn't like to be around men. Except Noah. It was weird. It was like the big cat was so in tune with Kaely that he knew who was trustworthy and who wasn't.

Kaely picked up Mr. Hoover before she answered the door. He'd never tried to get out, but the possibility worried her. If he suddenly ran outside, would she lose him? It was a chance she didn't want to take.

The bell rang a second time before Kaely swung open the door. Noah was holding a large bag of food from her favorite

Chinese restaurant in one hand and another bag in the other. Two large drinks sat tucked into the crook of one arm.

"About time," he grumbled on his way into the kitchen, where he sat the food and drinks on the counter.

"Sorry," Kaely said. She closed the door and locked it. Then she put Mr. Hoover down, and he immediately ran over to Noah, who leaned down and stroked his back.

"Hey, big fella," Noah said. "How you doin'?"

"You gripe at me and then cozy up to my cat?" Kaely said with her hand on her hip. "I'm not sure what to think about that." Noah was wearing jeans and a dark blue polo shirt that brought out his gray-blue eyes. His black wavy hair was getting a little long. Not a standard cut for an FBI special agent, but she really liked it.

"Sorry I'm late," Noah said, straightening up. "When I went to pick up the food, they had the order all wrong. I had to wait while they got it right."

"And that put you in a bad mood?"

Noah sighed and crossed his arms across his chest. "Yeah, this is a defensive move. Once in a while couldn't we eat something besides Chinese food?"

"You mean there's something else? I had no idea."

"Very funny."

"We eat other things. I just like Chinese because you always buy too much. It keeps my fridge stocked for days."

Noah's eyebrows shot up. "That's . . ." He laughed. "Actually, it's pretty ingenious. You could have just told me, you know."

"Where's the fun in that?"

Noah shook his head and started taking food out of the bags.

"You're upset," Kaely said. "And not about the restaurant messing up our order."

43

Noah stopped what he was doing and stared at her. "What in the world did I do to make you think that? You know, sometimes I'm afraid to move because you'll use it to figure out what I'm thinking."

Kaely sat down on one of the stools next to her breakfast bar. "I told you, I'll try not to read you. We're friends. You're hardly a suspect, but I'm not blind. You're tense. You keep swallowing. What's the problem?"

Noah pushed Kaely's food toward her, along with the root beer she'd wanted. After getting forks and napkins, he came around and sat down next to her.

"I guess the more I think about what you're being asked to do, the angrier I get." He opened his container of food and grabbed his fork. "Let them figure this out on their own." He lowered his fork and gazed into her eyes. "I'm attempting to be objective. I'm just here so you can talk it out and make your own decision. But . . . well, you've been through so much over the past several years. Asking you to do this just doesn't seem right."

Kaely smiled. "Thanks. If the situation were reversed, I'd feel the same way." She hesitated a moment. "Look," she said, "I need you to do what you just said. Just listen to me. Let me figure this out myself. Please don't guide me toward the choice you want me to make."

"I know. I won't. I promise." He sighed. "But it's hard. I remember Tracy asking me to listen to her when she was upset, to not offer my opinion. Wish I'd tried harder to do that, but I was raised to believe men are supposed to protect women. My first reaction is to help. Fix things. You've taught me that's not always the right reaction."

"I'm sure Tracy understood. She was a smart woman."

Noah stared at his food, turning his fork around and around

as if his chow mein needed to be stirred. "She was," he said softly. "Except for you, she's the smartest woman I ever met." He looked up and smiled sadly. "You would have liked her. Have I ever told you that?"

Kaely shook her head. "I don't think so, but I've thought the same thing. I think we would have been friends, and as you know, I don't make them easily."

The expression on Noah's face pulled at Kaely's heart. What would it be like to be loved the way he loved Tracy? She couldn't imagine. She'd wondered once if someday Noah might feel that way about her, but not anymore. He'd closed that door. As she watched him eat his food, a wave of deep-seated emotion washed through her. It startled her enough that she let out a small cry.

"Are you okay?" Noah asked, his eyebrows arched in concern.

Kaely felt heat rise in her cheeks. "Yeah. Sorry. Knocked my foot against the bottom of my stool." She immediately felt guilty about lying, but no other excuse had come to mind.

"Sure you're all right?"

"Yeah, I'm positive." Kaely picked up her root beer and took a drink. She needed a moment to collect herself. When she finally put down her cup, she realized Noah was studying her.

"You must be really thirsty," he said.

"Who's reading who now?" Kaely asked, unable to keep a note of irritation from her voice.

Noah didn't say anything, just stuck another forkful of chicken in his mouth.

Maybe inviting him over tonight had been a mistake. She was still feeling the shock of being asked to confront her father. Although she'd tried to push away the fear that threatened to overtake her, it was sliding through her mind and body like a snake looking for a place to strike. She and Noah were both upset about this turn of events, but she needed him to be calm. Analytical. Usually she was the logical one, but tonight she wanted him to take that role.

She put her fork down. "Thank you," she said softly.

"For what? Making things worse?" He shook his head. "I came to help, and now I've upset you. We've been snapping at each other ever since I got here."

"You're concerned about me," Kaely said, mustering a small smile. "That doesn't upset me at all. But I need you to push that aside and be the rational one tonight. Can you do that?"

The muscles in his face seemed to tighten. "I can be whatever you need me to be. We're friends."

"I know."

He frowned at her as Mr. Hoover curled up at the bottom of his stool. "Can you actually talk about this unemotionally? Not sure I could."

Kaely didn't respond. Instead, she just stared down at the food she didn't think she could eat. She still had her salad from lunch in the fridge, and this meal was probably going to join it. Uneaten food was beginning to pile up.

She was horrified when tears filled her eyes. Twice in one day. This had to stop. "The truth is I'm terrified." Her voice trembled. "I've helped catch serial killers. I've even faced them one-on-one. But this is . . . different."

"This is your father," Noah said.

"That's just it." Kaely tried to find words to express what she was feeling, but she wasn't sure she could. "I've had awful dreams for years because of him. Horrible nightmares. Sometimes I wake in the night screaming. I'm afraid, but I'm not sure why. And . . . I've worried that something in my genes might make me like him. I'm not sure I should ever have children. What if one of them turns out to be . . . like him?"

46

"Kaely. Nothing suggests those traits are passed down."

"I realize that." She pointed at her forehead with her index finger. "I know it here. It's here where I have the problem." She jabbed at her chest.

"But . . . you're a Christian. Why doesn't your faith give you peace?"

Kaely opened her mouth to answer him, but no words came out. Noah was right. Right now, her fear felt bigger than her faith. She was no longer Ed Oliphant's daughter. God was her Father. Why couldn't she walk in that? Why was she having so much trouble grabbing her real Father's hand?

She leaned on her elbow and looked past Noah. "You're right." She took a deep, shuddering breath. "But just when I think I'm free of my father, he pops back up." A tear slid down her cheek. "What am I going to do, Noah?"

"You're going to face this like you have everything else. With courage and strength. I have faith."

She laughed lightly. "I thought you didn't believe in *faith*."

"I may not have faith in God, but I have faith in you, Kaely Quinn. Now, let's figure this out."

SIX

oah encouraged Kaely to eat at least half her food, then he packed up all the leftovers and put them in the fridge. He brewed some coffee, poured it into cups, and carried them into the living room. It was a lovely spring evening, so Kaely opened one of the windows to allow the air to drift inside. If their conversation wasn't going to include a vicious serial killer, this visit would be relaxing.

Noah reached into a plastic bag he'd tossed on the couch when he'd come into the condo and took out a long stick with a string. At the end of the string was a feather.

"That's it? This is what will enthrall Mr. Hoover?" Kaely asked with a grin.

"Sure. It's foolproof. I've never seen a cat that could resist it."

"And how many cats have you personally played with using this . . . toy?"

"My sister has four cats, and they love it," Noah huffed.

"You told me your family lives in Vermont, but I don't remember you mentioning a sister."

"Yeah, Zoe is five years younger than me. I haven't seen her for a couple of years. I need to take some vacation and catch up. We've always been close. This job tends to force everything else into the background." Noah sat down on the couch and called for Mr. Hoover. The big cat usually followed Noah around like a love-starved puppy, but now that Noah wanted him, he stayed where he was, curled up in his second pet bed positioned across the room.

48

"Come here, Hoovy," Noah said, prodding. "Here, kitty, kitty, kitty."

He heard Kaely snort and looked over to see her biting her lip to keep from laughing. He grinned and continued trying to get Mr. Hoover's attention. But the cat wasn't having it. Like most felines, he wasn't fond of following instructions. Any interest he showed had to be his idea. Finally, Noah gave up and went over to where the big cat lay, watching Noah through half-opened eyes. Noah sat down on the floor next to him and brought the toy out from behind his back. He jiggled it in front of the uninterested cat.

"Get it," Noah said, urging him. "Come on, Hoovy, get it." When Mr. Hoover still failed to respond, Noah put it in his face, tickling the cat's nose. Before Noah had time to pull it away, Mr. Hoover grabbed the feather in his teeth. Then he yanked it off the string and spit it out. Noah sat there for several seconds with the stick and string, not sure whether to be hurt or offended. Kaely burst out laughing behind him.

He smiled to himself. Hearing her laugh made him feel great. He got up and walked over to the couch, then placed the stick with the empty string on the coffee table.

"I think you owe me five dollars," Kaely choked out between giggles.

With a sigh of defeat, Noah took his wallet out of his back pocket and then handed Kaely a five-dollar bill. "I don't get it. Never seen a cat not respond to that thing."

"Oh, Mr. Hoover responded okay. I think he was telling you to get it out of his face. Either that or he was reacting to you calling him *Hoovy*."

"I just thought he needed a nickname. Mr. Hoover seems so . . . formal." He stared at Kaely and raised one eyebrow. "You're enjoying this, aren't you?"

Kaely nodded, her auburn curls bouncing. "I really am. Thanks."

"You're welcome." When Noah slumped down onto the couch, Mr. Hoover immediately ran over and jumped onto his lap. Then he turned around and flopped down.

"Are you kidding me?" Noah said. "After costing me five bucks?"

"He may have hated your toy, but he loves you." Kaely's smile slipped. "I guess even when someone you care about does something you don't like, you still . . . accept them."

Noah stroked Mr. Hoover's fur as the big cat began to purr. "I still accept you, Kaely. I'm here, aren't I?"

Kaely sat down on the other side of the couch. "Yeah, you're here. Just not all of you."

"You told me you lost your friends after your dad was arrested," Noah said, trying to change the subject. "That's one reason you created Georgie. You've shared a little about the real Georgie, but I'd like to know more."

"Yeah, why?"

"Just trying to get a better idea about your past. You know, with your dad. Maybe it will help you decide what to do. Besides, I've been curious about her."

"Okay," Kaely said with a sigh. "Georganna—Georgie— and I met in first grade. When her mother brought her into the classroom the first day of school, she was crying, afraid for her mom to leave her. For some reason I decided to help, and I stayed by her side so she wouldn't be scared. We bonded immediately. Imagine my surprise when I found out she lived three houses away from me. It was like we were meant to be together. It didn't take long for us to become best friends. I guess that's why I turned to her when I needed someone to talk to."

Kaely picked up one of the pillows on the couch and hugged it to her chest. She had taught him this was a pacifying gesture. He wondered if she realized it now. "I still see her as a teenager. The way she was the last time I saw her." Kaely paused for a moment as if trying to remember. We spent all our extra time together," Kaely continued. "Her parents were great. They had such a wonderful family. Lots of love and warmth." She looked past him. "Not like my house. It wasn't as if my parents weren't involved in our lives. It was just . . . well, there was a detachment there, you know? My father was never abusive to me or to my mother. That's rather surprising, actually. Many serial killers come from violent homes and pass their anger along."

"What do you know about your grandparents?"

"Loved my mom's parents. They lived in Arizona. I didn't get to see them a lot, but they were super. They're both gone. I never met my dad's parents. His mom died when he was a teenager. Suicide, I think. His father took off not long after that, and his sister died when she just a child."

"He had a sister?"

Kaely nodded. "He never brought her up to Jason and me. I found out about her from Mom. I asked Dad about her once, and he snapped at me. Told me she was long gone and talking about her wasn't going to bring her back. Her name was Melissa, but my dad referred to her as Missy."

"I have to wonder if his background had something to do with his . . . activities."

"I'm sure it does, but no matter what happened, it doesn't give him the right to slaughter innocent people."

"You're right. What happened to the real Georgie?"

Kaely shrugged. "I told you about this already, but if you want to hear it again . . ."

"I do."

"When my dad was arrested, the news was splashed across every TV channel and newspaper in the country. TV news vans camped outside our house, and we couldn't leave without being assailed by reporters. The second day after it happened, I snuck out my bedroom window and made my way to the back of Georgie's house. I tapped on her window, and she pulled back the curtains. I waited for her to let me in, but she just shook her head. She was crying. I think she wanted to see me, but I guess her parents told her to stay away from me. The next day my mom, my brother and I went to stay in an apartment on the other side of town, some place the U.S. Marshalls used as a safe house. We stayed there until my father was sentenced. Then we moved to Nebraska. I never saw Georgie again."

"Why Nebraska?"

"Mom grew up there. Her parents moved to Arizona after she got married and moved away. Even though she had no family or friends in the state, she felt comfortable there. She went back to her maiden name. Changed our names too."

Noah took a sip of his coffee. "I wonder if you should have talked to Georgie and her parents. I think you're reading a lot into what happened on one night."

Kaely waved her hand at him. "I don't want to talk about Georgie or what occurred years ago. I need to figure out what to do *now*."

"Sorry. I'm just trying to take you back to your childhood in a way that wouldn't be too painful. I'd hoped talking about Georgie might help give you some perspective."

"If it wasn't so hurtful, it might. I appreciate it, but maybe we should just confront the situation head-on."

Noah nodded. "Okay. What are the positive reasons for talking to your father? And what are the negative reasons?"

Kaely snorted, her face contorted in anger. "Well, one negative reason is that I hate him. I detest him for what he did to those women. And I'm angry about what he did to our family."

"I understand that. But is that a reason? Or is that just how you feel?"

Kaely jumped to her feet and started to walk away, but then she turned around and glared at him. Her expression twisted with resentment. But before she responded, her body suddenly relaxed. "Okay," she said. "You're right. It's not a good enough reason."

She returned to the couch, but this time she sat on its arm, her stockinged feet landing on the cushion. Then she put her elbows on her knees and rested her head on her hands. "We both know what I have to do, don't we?" she asked in a voice so small it reminded him of a child. "If he'll even talk to me. Not sure he will."

"Kaely, I certainly don't believe you *have* to do this. No matter what Sawyer said, they've just started interviewing him. Two weeks isn't enough time. They couldn't have tried everything. And the Bureau has agents trained to deal with people like your father. The FBI has lots of professionals who will step in to help when they're needed. And what about the BAU? Why not send them in before contacting you?"

"Because if they do, I'll never get the chance to talk to him. Sawyer seems completely convinced I'm the only one who can do this."

Noah sighed. "Look, maybe you should tell them to try again. Even if it doesn't work, it might give you a week or two to get yourself acclimated to the idea of facing your father."

Kaely's dark eyes met his. Every time she looked at him that way, he felt something like electricity course through his body. It took all his strength to ignore it.

When they'd come back from Nebraska, he'd been so angry

that staying away from her had been easy. But as his anger eased, he realized how much he missed her. He'd toyed with the idea of asking for a transfer. To get away from her for good. But he'd promised her once that he'd always be there for her, and he felt bound by that promise even though being near her caused him pain—like a wound that wouldn't heal. But until she quit putting herself in danger unnecessarily, he had to hold on to whatever self-control he could muster. He honestly believed that losing her would destroy him.

"And if someone dies while I'm trying to get myself together?" she asked. "How do I live with that?"

"It might not happen."

"But it might." Kaely clasped her hands together and stared at them. "I made a vow, Noah." She took a deep breath and said in a low voice, "I solemnly swear that I will support and defend the Constitution of the United States against all enemies, foreign and domestic; that I will bear true faith and allegiance to the same; that I take this obligation freely, without any mental reservation or purpose of evasion; and that I will well and faithfully discharge the duties of the office on which I am about to enter. So help me God."

"But you didn't say you'd go toe-to-toe with your serial-killer father," Noah said.

"How is this different? My father is a domestic enemy. I promised not to respond to any mental reservations. That I would faithfully discharge the duties of my office." She offered him a tremulous smile. "I don't really have a choice here, do I?"

Noah studied her for a moment. He knew Kaely Quinn. And he knew the answer to her question. "No, I guess you don't." He sighed again. "I'll let Solomon know I'm willing to go with you. Not sure he was actually giving me a choice, though."

Kaely pushed herself off the arm of the couch and plopped

down next to him. She leaned her head against his shoulder. "Thank you. I'm not sure I could do this without you. I'll be fine. Really."

Her assurance sounded hollow. Kaely would do whatever she had to do to prepare herself for what she would face. But could she pull it off? Noah fought against the urge to stroke her hair. If he said too much, made the wrong move, he could lose himself in her. And he couldn't take that chance. Not now. Not ever. He quelled the rush of emotions that surged through him.

"We're friends and partners," he said in carefully measured tones. "I meant it when I told you I'll always be there when you need me. Always."

SEVEN

Solomon hung up the phone after talking to the special agent in charge in Omaha, John Howard. His office oversaw Iowa, and they were working with the Des Moines PD. Everything had been arranged for Kaely and Noah to do this. A few months ago, they'd been on temporary assignment in Nebraska through the Omaha office, so they were already acquainted with Howard's agents. Although Solomon wasn't crazy about Kaely having to face her father again, he couldn't very well tell her she couldn't do it. She was a grown woman and a stellar agent.

Still, he worried about her. She'd been through a lot. A devastating betrayal last year and a tough case in Nebraska that involved her mother. Although Kaely kept saying she was okay, Solomon wasn't so sure. He'd encouraged her to talk to a therapist who sometimes worked with the Bureau in Missouri, and his report had been less than reassuring. Although Dr. Barber determined she was fit for work, he was concerned that she wasn't dealing realistically with her feelings. That she was so busy trying to live up to the image she had of a strong and capable FBI special agent that she wasn't allowing herself to be human. Kaely seemed to believe that giving in to her emotions was a sign of weakness.

"Watch out for her," Dr. Barber had warned. "She may reach a point where she'll have no choice but to face her demons. None of us can simply ignore everything that happens to us. We all have breaking points, and we can deal with only so much before we must ask for help."

"She has a strong faith," Solomon told him. "Maybe that will see her through?"

"Still, a refusal to admit she needs help could lead her to a pretty dark place," the doctor had said. He'd walked toward the door but turned back before leaving Solomon's office. "I'm sorry I can't do more for her. At this point, we're at a standstill. If something changes, let me know. I'm willing to do anything I can." He'd nodded at Solomon and left.

Solomon turned the conversation over in his mind. If Dr. Barber was right, could Kaely be teetering on the edge of an emotional cliff? What if facing her father was the final straw?

He drummed his fingers on his desk. The rhythm soothed him, helped him think. He was also worried about the Scripture found in the victims' mouths. What did it mean? Was it directed toward Kaely? It was possible it had nothing to do with her. Still, it bothered him. Dr. Barber said she was stable right now, but even so, Solomon had thought more than once about pulling the plug on this thing. Of course, if he did that, especially if Kaely decided to talk to her father, she'd be furious with him.

Solomon took a deep breath. He would have to trust Kaely's training and ability. The truth was he wanted to protect her. Be the kind of father she'd never had. But that wasn't his job. He was her boss, and he had to treat her like any other agent. Whatever she decided, he would support her, no matter how hard it was. At least Noah would be by her side. Solomon knew he cared deeply for Kaely and that he would do whatever it took to keep her from falling into the dark abyss they feared waited for her.

He glanced at the clock on the wall. She'd be here any minute. Whatever she was about to tell him, he was prepared.

At nine o'clock, Kaely arrived at Solomon's office. Grace smiled and waved her in, and when Kaely knocked on his door, his familiar deep voice told her to enter. She pushed the door open and found Solomon sitting at his desk, going through a stack of papers.

She slid into the leather chair facing him and waited until he put down his pen and looked up.

"Good morning," he said. "Coffee?"

Kaely shook her head. "No, thanks. I'm fine."

Solomon leaned back in his chair. "I assume you've made a decision."

Kaely nodded and swallowed hard at the same time. Even though she and Noah had talked into the early morning hours, she found herself wavering as she sat in front of her boss.

She took a deep breath. "I want to go," she said firmly.

Solomon's only reaction was to raise his eyebrows slightly. Kaely got the feeling he'd expected her response.

"Are you sure?"

"No. But if I don't do this, if I don't face him, every new death will be on my conscience. I'll wonder if I could have prevented it."

"He may not talk to you either," Solomon said. He pulled his chair closer to his desk and clasped his hands together. "I don't want you to be upset if he doesn't respond to you. Just do your best. That's all anyone can ask."

"Thank you, but I hope I can get something from him that will help to catch the person killing these women." She smiled at him. "I'll be fine." She met Solomon's direct gaze. "I can do this. I really can."

Solomon nodded. "I realize that, Agent Quinn." His voice had taken on an official tone she was familiar with. Even though he couldn't acknowledge his personal concern for her, somehow knowing he cared gave her strength.

"You and Noah get ready to leave. Head out tomorrow. Do you want to fly?"

Kaely shook her head. "It's only six hours away. I'd rather drive, if it's okay." She hated flying. She didn't like handing over control if she didn't have to.

"Okay. Pick up one of our vehicles in the morning. I'll tell SAC Howard to expect you sometime in the late afternoon. I believe your father is still housed in Anamosa State Penitentiary?"

Kaely nodded. Anamosa had a maximum-security section, and her father had been there ever since his sentencing.

"Then I'll have Grace make hotel reservations near the prison." Solomon paused for a moment. "Thank you for accepting this assignment. And please keep in touch. Let me know how things progress. You're assigned to Omaha for thirty days. Even if you can't get your father to respond to you, I'm sure you can find a way to help. As Sawyer said yesterday, Noah can help prep you for the interview, if you wish. He'll also review visitor logs, look at mail received and sent, interview prison personnel, see if anyone else has information that will help you find out how your father is getting information to his . . . associate."

Kaely stood. "Will they want me to provide a profile?"

Solomon hesitated before answering. "I think Sawyer knows you're an asset they need. I wouldn't be surprised if you're asked to at least give your input. But be careful. That's not why they're asking for your help. Focus on interviewing your father."

Kaely cleared her throat. "I . . . I'd like to take Mr. Hoover with me. I hate leaving him behind again."

Solomon nodded. "I'll tell Grace." He stood and extended his hand. "Good luck, Kaely. Call me when you can. Keep me in the loop."

Although it wasn't protocol for her to share information from the investigation in Omaha, Kaely understood Solomon was more interested in her well-being than in details of the case. She took his hand and shook it. "I will. Thank you, sir."

She rarely called him *sir*, but for some reason it just felt right.

Kaely left Solomon's office and went to her desk, where she sat down and pulled up everything she could find on the murders in Des Moines. As she worked, she tried to ignore the whisperings inside that wanted to fill her mind with fear.

EIGHT

He waited down the deserted street. She left for work every night at the same time, and sure enough, the front door of her house opened, and she came out, headed to her car parked by the curb. She was small, dark haired, conservatively dressed. He picked up the bags of groceries and then put the crutches under his arms. His hair was stuffed under a wig, and thick black glasses hid some of his face. He had to concentrate to stay off the leg he'd covered with a fake cast.

As he approached her car, he dropped one of the sacks. "Oh no," he said, not looking at her, not letting her know he'd even seen her. Out of the corner of his eye, he watched as she hesitated. Then, as he knew she would, she came over, putting her car keys in her pocket.

"Can I help you?" she asked.

He looked up at her, as if startled to find he wasn't alone. "I can pick it up myself," he said. "But thank you." He smiled at her. "Broke my leg playing football with my brothers after church on Sunday. Stupid. My mom tries to help me, but I hate to bother her. Her health isn't good. Thought I could at least walk to the store by myself."

"Where do you live?"

"Two blocks down."

She was kneeling, putting the groceries back in the sack, when he took out the stun gun and put it under her chin. When the jolt hit her, she fell to the ground, unconscious. He looked around to make sure no one was watching. He put the stun

61

gun in his pocket, then reached down and pulled her up, making it look as if she were simply leaning against him. Then he dragged her to his car parked not far from hers before opening the trunk and shoving her in. He removed his cast and threw it and the crutches in, too, before quickly picking up the spilled groceries.

Then he got into his car, started the engine, and took off. The woman hadn't even noticed his hands were clad in latex gloves, to make sure he didn't leave any fingerprints behind.

She would be out for a while. Twenty million volts under the chin guaranteed keeping her that way. He removed the spool of red ribbon he stored in a special box, along with one of the angels he'd fashioned from wire. The Scripture was in a baggie in his pocket. Everything had gone off without a hitch.

As he drove way, he found himself whistling a tune he'd heard on the radio. It was a country western song. *When Daddy hears about the things I've done, will he forgive the man that I've become? Will he send me on my way? Or will he plead with me to stay? Oh, Daddy, your child is on the road to home.*

He smiled as he headed to the spot he'd chosen for his new acquisition.

Kaely was quiet as they drove toward their hotel in Anamosa. Monday night she seemed to open up. She'd shared her feelings about her father. But today her professional persona was firmly in place. She was Special Agent Kaely Quinn, not Kaely, the confused woman who'd leaned her head on his shoulder. This was a familiar pattern with her. And if he tried to challenge her, she'd deny there was a problem.

Noah couldn't help but compare her to Tracy. Tracy had been an open book. Kaely was a book that slammed shut if you got too close. And then there was the fear that if you tried to pry open the cover, the book would close for good.

While Kaely hid her emotions, Tracy had been transparent about both her fears and her hopes as she battled cancer. She almost had him convinced she was going to beat the horrible disease that ate at her. But toward the end, she'd grown tired of fighting. Told him she wanted to go home. He'd insisted that home was here, with him. But she'd begged him to release her. To say good-bye. As hard as it had been, he'd done as she'd asked.

After she died, he'd gone on with life, putting one foot in front of the other. One of the walking wounded. But a place inside him screamed her name every day. He tried to tune it out, but when he did, he felt as if he were betraying her. Being paired with Kaely over the past year had helped him more than anything else. It hadn't filled the hole inside him, but Kaely gave him something else to think about. Her conflict, her brilliance, her battles had provided purpose. A reason to get up in the morning.

Before he'd met her, he'd turn off the alarm clock every morning, lie on his back, and try to find a reason—just one reason—to put his feet on the floor. For a long time, he got up, got dressed, and went to work only because he was supposed to. He saw himself as a robot—no feeling, no emotion, just following orders until the day ended and he could crawl back into bed, praying he wouldn't dream about Tracy.

"I'll give him one chance to talk," Kaely said suddenly. "If he doesn't, I'm out of there."

"We're stuck working for Des Moines for thirty days," Noah said, reminding her. This was their second assignment out of Omaha. In February they'd assisted with a drug case just so they could look into a series of arsons in the small town in

Nebraska where Kaely's mom lived. That was the first time they'd met Special Agent in Charge John Howard. He was a fair-minded man, but Noah wondered what they'd do if Kaely couldn't get her father to talk. Would Omaha assign them to a different case? He doubted it. He suspected they needed all the help they could get with this one. He was fairly sure they'd give them something to do still connected to this serial killer.

He glanced at the clock on the dashboard. A little after nine o'clock. "We're making good time. Let's grab something to eat."

They were supposed to check into their hotel in Anamosa and then drive back to the Des Moines field office, but they were ahead of schedule, and Noah was hungry. He'd only had time to scarf down a granola bar before they'd headed out.

"Sure. That sounds fine," Kaely said, sounding distracted.

"We'll have to eat in the car, though. It's too hot to leave Mr. Hoover out here without air conditioning."

Mr. Hoover was in a crate in the backseat. He seemed content to sleep and hadn't raised a fuss yet.

"We need to eat fast," Kaely said. "I want to feed him and set up his litter box before our meeting."

Noah shook his head. "A litter box? We used to let our cats outside when I was a kid. We lived out in the country, so there was very little chance they would get run over or anything."

Kaely snorted. "Oh, the hotel would love a cat running around, making a mess. Besides, your cats knew the area. Mr. Hoover will be in a brand-new place. It's not safe." She stared at Noah through narrowed eyes. "It's really not safe to let cats outside anyway, you know. Too many predators in the country. Too much traffic in the city. A lot could go wrong."

Noah shrugged as if he disagreed with her, but the truth was his family had lost a couple of cats just the way Kaely mentioned. He could still feel the pain of those losses. If he ever decided to get a cat or dog, he'd make sure it went outside only when it was leashed.

"What are you hungry for?" Noah asked, thrusting the hurtful memories away.

"Don't care. Anything's fine."

Noah had seen a sign advertising several restaurants in a small town about twenty miles this side of Des Moines. He took the exit to the town and found a place that had lots of cars out front. Kaely asked for some kind of muffin—something that wasn't too messy. Once inside, Noah sat down on a stool in front of a large counter. He'd wondered if it was a mistake to try some out-of-the-way place in a town so small that Mc-Donald's was one of their main restaurants. However, if the food matched the aroma coming from the kitchen, taking a chance could be well worth it.

A waitress came over and handed him a menu. After reading through it, Noah ordered a banana nut muffin for Kaely. He decided on the Sunrise Special—scrambled eggs, corned beef hash, and hash browns.

As he waited, he noticed a small TV mounted on the wall. Noah called the waitress back. "Would you turn that up, please? Just for that story?"

"Sure, honey." The waitress, whose name tag read *Suzie*, picked up a remote control sitting on the counter by the cash register and then pointed it at the TV.

"The body of a young woman was found in front of an abandoned gas station on the edge of town," a reporter was saying. "Police aren't confirming that it's the work of a copycat killer, but speculation seems to point that way. A source tells us the body was placed there sometime last night."

Noah noticed the crawl across the bottom of the screen

capitalized *Copycat Killer*. Kaely would hate that, but she wouldn't be surprised. Worse, the fact that this killer was copying her father was out now. Someone in the know had evidently clued in the press.

The reporter seemed to be distracted by something. Then Chief Sawyer walked past her, and she tried to get his attention, asking him for a comment. He ignored her. Noah could see agents from the Bureau in the background. That told him the body definitely had the trademarks of whoever was trying to mirror Ed Oliphant's killings.

"Thanks," Noah said to Suzie, who turned down the sound so it was loud enough to hear only if you strained your ears and wouldn't disrupt conversation in the restaurant.

"Hope they catch that creep," the waitress said. "I remember The Raggedy Man. I was a teenager when he killed all those women. Made me afraid to leave the house. Feel the same way now." She cocked her head toward the parking lot. "The cook, Richie, walks me to my car every night. Waits until I drive out of the lot before he leaves. I'll keep doin' that until it's safe again. They say this guy is tryin' to copy that Oliphant guy."

She shook her head. "It's like he's come back. I'm prayin' they catch the Copycat Killer quickly. We don't need to live through that again." She exhaled loudly. "Sorry. Hard not to talk about it." She looked back toward the kitchen. "Your food will be ready in a few minutes."

As she walked away, Noah's concern about Kaely facing her father lessened. She was right. She had to do this. Suzie had put a face on the terror Des Moines had gone through. It wasn't right to allow it to happen again. Kaely was in fighting mode. She would battle tooth and nail to find this now-named Copycat

Killer. Noah would have to hope the strength she'd summoned to face her father was enough.

When Suzie came back with a large bag that contained their food, he paid her and then headed to the car. Kaely was getting ready to confront her nightmares, and Noah hoped the cost wouldn't be too high.

NINE

Kaely and Noah had checked into their hotel and then driven back to Des Moines. Now they were waiting at the field office to speak to John Howard, special agent in charge; Tobias Bell, head of the FBI Resident Agency in Des Moines; and Chief Sawyer. Chief Sawyer had called them not long after they arrived to confirm their meeting at the Des Moines FBI office. He made it clear that Howard and Bell were both willing to let Kaely approach her father. Kaely was relieved, but she was pretty sure the powers that be at Quantico weren't too happy about it. She was certain they wanted the BAU on-site. She was also certain that if she failed, they'd be called in.

The door to the small waiting area opened, and Chief Sawyer walked in. Behind him was John Howard and another man who was probably Tobias Bell. Kaely was surprised by Bell. He was younger than most SSAs. His hair was silver, but he looked close to Kaely's age. He was tall and lanky with intense sky blue eyes that locked on her and appeared to be sizing her up. An odd thought popped into her head. If this were a movie, Bell would be perfect for his part.

When John introduced her and Noah, Bell put out his hand and shook theirs. His handshake was firm, and his smile seemed genuine.

"Let's go into my office," he said.

Noah and Kaely walked through the door he held open. It led to a spacious office with a large wooden desk. A dark brown leather couch was pushed up against one wall, and bookcases covered the other walls except for a small area with a coffee bar and a mini refrigerator. Kaely noticed that he had just two photographs. Both showed him with an older couple, probably his parents. No siblings, so Bell was probably an only child.

His office was pristine, and all the wood was polished. Bell was a man who liked order and discipline, something Kaely had seen before in only children.

Bell pulled two high-backed leather chairs from in front of his desk and positioned them next to the couch before waving his hand toward them. "Please, have a seat. Anyone thirsty? I have coffee, water, apple juice . . ." He paused for a moment. "A couple bottles of green tea. Very good."

He knew exactly what supplies he had, and Kaely would have bet her next paycheck that his small refrigerator was clean and shiny inside. No expired food. He would probably be horrified by her fridge.

They all declined his offer. After moving some neatly stacked files and papers out of the way, Bell sat down on the edge of his desk. Kaely noticed he was wearing light blue socks that matched his tie . . . and his eyes.

"We have a few questions," John said.

Kaely nodded and looked at SAC Howard expectantly. However, the first question came from Bell. "I understand you're willing to talk to your father, Special Agent Quinn."

"Yes, sir. I doubt he'll talk to me, but I'll give it a try."

"I know this must be hard for you."

"Yes, it is difficult. I haven't had contact with him since before he was convicted."

"This is a request, you know, not an order," John said.

"Thank you, sir. I understand that."

"From my research, it seems your family thought he was innocent right after his arrest?"

Kaely nodded. "That's right. You probably know it's not unusual for friends and relatives to deny the possibility someone they know, someone they trust, could be a monster."

Bell's eyebrows shot up. "You see these killers as . . . monsters? Inhuman?"

Shocked by his question, she frowned. "Of course. Don't you?"

He hesitated a moment before saying, "I think what they've done is terrible, but I believe they're sick people, usually twisted by the past. That doesn't mean they don't deserve the sentences they're given, though. They should never step outside of prison walls again."

"Then you think they can be . . . rehabilitated?" Kaely said, trying to control her irritation at his naiveté.

Bell shrugged. "With intensive therapy, I think they have a chance. Something everyone should have, don't you think?"

His condescending tone and the way he straightened his shoulders were signs that SSA Bell considered himself an expert on things he knew nothing about.

"My father feels no remorse for his actions," Kaely said. "He's proud of what he's done. Even if he admitted it was wrong, inside he wouldn't really believe it. And the gratification he got from all the attention he received from the media and even law enforcement? It stroked his ego." She glared at Bell. "Do you understand what I'm saying? He enjoyed seeing himself on TV. Reading articles about himself. He loved the attention he got for viciously slaughtering fourteen women." She swallowed. "Maybe more. If that isn't monstrous, I don't know what is."

"May I ask why we're talking about this?" Noah asked.

Kaely could hear the annoyance in his voice. He was clearly

upset because of her reaction to Bell's comments. She hadn't meant to react so strongly. Bell was allowed his opinion. Ever since she learned she was coming back to Des Moines, though, she'd felt the need to remind herself that her father was a psychopath. Was it her way of protecting herself? Not seeing her father as a human being but a textbook case?

"We just want you to be prepared, Agent Quinn," John said.

"Yes, sir," she choked out. "I'm sorry."

"It's okay. Perfectly understandable." He tossed her a small smile. "We've asked a lot of you. You're allowed to be a little upset."

Kaely wasn't sure her level of upset could be called *little*, but she appreciated his attempt to placate her. She couldn't afford to come across as unstable, or they would pull her off this case. She needed to cool it.

"Your father may try to play on your emotions," Bell said. He leaned forward and fastened his eyes on hers. "You'll need to remember why you're here. Can you do that?"

There it was. She had to keep her emotions in check. If she didn't, she'd be asked to leave. She was surprised to find herself fighting to stay.

"Trust me. That won't happen," Kaely said, calm but firm. "First, I'm a behavioral analyst. I understand the psychopathic personality." She had to bite her tongue not to add *much better than you do*. "Besides, no one knows him better than me. I spent fourteen years with him. I've heard his lies many times. Nothing he could say or do can manipulate me."

She looked at John. "I can do my job. I won't let you down."

"I hope that's true, Agent Quinn," he said. "I appreciate you answering our questions. Even though I'm in charge of this . . . operation, I wanted Tobias to meet you. Put his mind at ease. We're all going to be working together."

"What do we do now?" Kaley asked.

"We haven't told him you're coming," John said.

Kaely's mouth dropped open. "You expect me to walk in and say, 'Surprise, Pop. Guess who!'"

"Uh, actually, no," John said, his tone dry.

Kaely sighed. "You're trying to catch him unaware. You think it might cause him to open up."

"That's the hope," Bell said.

Kaely shook her head. "Won't work. Ed doesn't have the kind of reactions you're looking for. Mainly because he doesn't care."

"I thought people like that were called sociopaths," Chief Sawyer said.

"Sociopaths are similar to psychopaths, but they're volatile and disorganized," Kaely said. "Psychopaths can mimic feelings even though they don't have them. They can be charming. And they're organized. Calculating. That's my father. He won't be disturbed by my surprise entrance. Trust me. If he reacts at all, he'll see my visit only as an opportunity to get something he wants."

"Kaely, do you think your father ever loved you?" Bell asked. "Ever had feelings for you and your brother? For your mother?"

"You have to understand. My father saw us as possessions. Possessions to be protected because we belonged to him. That's why I'm not sure this is going to succeed."

The room fell silent. Kaely could almost hear the gears turning in their heads. Was this going to work? Or were they wondering if they'd made a mistake by bringing her here? She'd certainly given them a reason to worry about her ability to handle herself in the situation.

"We don't have other options," John said. "We realize we're asking a lot of you, but we've tried everything else. I don't want to sound overly dramatic, but you're our last hope."

Exactly what Sawyer had said in St. Louis.

"You know, usually psychopaths like to talk," Kaely said, frowning. "It strokes their egos. Gives them a chance to prove how clever they are. I don't understand why my father won't speak to you. Doesn't make sense."

"We're aware of that," Bell said. "We've appealed more than once to his ego. Nothing."

"That's unusual behavior." She was trying to see her father as any other psychopath. They really did love to drone on and on about themselves. She couldn't help but be somewhat intrigued. "I already told you I'd confront him," she said. "I'm not going to back out, but I have some requests."

Bell's eyes narrowed. "Like what?"

"I need to see what you have so far. Including the bodies."

"I prepared a file for you," Sawyer said. He reached into a briefcase he'd brought with him and extracted a file folder, which he handed to her.

"There's more," she said when he put down the briefcase. "I go in alone." She shot a quick glance at Noah and saw his lips thin, but she kept going. "And remove Ed's shackles."

"Absolutely not," John said. "It's too dangerous. Warden Galloway would never allow it."

"I'll be safe. Hurting me won't help him, so he won't do it."

"Is that it?" John asked, his face creased in a deep frown. It was clear he wasn't happy about her requests.

"No. He wears regular clothes. Not an orange jumpsuit."

"You're trying to make him feel at ease?" Bell asked.

"No. I need to walk in there like his daughter, not an FBI agent. If I come off as being more powerful than he is . . ."

"You don't want him to feel inferior to you," John said.

Kaely nodded slowly. If she had her way, she'd go in wearing her FBI jacket with her gun in view. She wanted this man to know he hadn't ruined her, that she was okay. That she was strong. Stronger than he was. Humbling herself in front of her father might be one of the hardest things she'd ever do, but it was the only chance they had.

"I don't know," John said, shaking his head. "It sounds too dangerous."

"I don't like it," Noah said to her. "You need to rethink this. You say your father doesn't care about you. Doesn't that mean he wouldn't hesitate to hurt you? What if the guards can't get to you fast enough? At least keep him shackled."

Kaely saw the fear in Noah's eyes. Would this push him even further away? She looked away from him. She really had no choice. Couldn't he see that?

Before she could respond to Noah, Chief Sawyer's cell phone rang. "Excuse me," he said, looking at the display on his screen. The rest of them waited while he took the call. Kaely saw his expression change. When he broke the connection, he said, "We have confirmation from the ME that the body found at the gas station was put there by our copycat." He locked his gaze on John. "Please, give her whatever she asks. We have no other choice."

John didn't reply. He just nodded.

TEN

Noah studied Kaely as she looked over the dinner menu at a restaurant she'd recommended in downtown Des Moines. They had a long drive back to Anamosa, but this seemed important to her. Tomorrow morning Bell and Sawyer planned to meet them at the prison. John Howard wasn't certain he could be there, and now the chief was a maybe because of the discovery of the body at the gas station.

Noah was still angry about Kaely's decision to meet her father alone. No matter what she said, it sounded dangerous. Ed Oliphant had strangled at least twenty-three women. What in the world would keep him from killing Kaely if he became angry? Still, John had made it clear they'd be watching Ed's every move on camera. If they thought for even a second that Kaely was in danger, the guards posted outside the door would storm into the room with stun guns and mace. Frankly, Noah would feel better if they had guns, but only the tower guards were armed at Anamosa. Even he and Kaely would have to surrender their weapons when they checked in to the prison.

"What do you recommend?" Noah asked, trying to keep his feelings in check. He was determined to keep an emotional distance between him and Kaely. If this was her decision, he had to live with it. She was a friend, yes, but it still wasn't really any of his business.

Seemingly lost in her own thoughts, Kaely looked up from her menu, staring at him as if she'd forgotten he was there.

"Uh, let me see," she said, looking down at the pages again.

She'd been staring at it so long she should have memorized it by now. "I have no idea," she finally said, lifting her face to meet his gaze, her dark eyes searching his. "I've never eaten here before. I always wanted to, but this place was way too expensive for my father. We rarely ate out, and when we did, we usually ended up at Denny's."

"We're fulfilling a childhood wish to eat at Mort's, then?" Noah asked. "I like that." He put down the menu. "Think I'm gonna try the Steak de Burgo seared with mushrooms. How about you?"

"The Bow-tie Creole sounds good."

He could tell she didn't really care what she ate. Her mind was somewhere else. She'd never planned to see her father again, but tomorrow she'd try to get him to talk to her about a copycat killer he could be controlling from prison.

Even though he'd told himself he wasn't bringing it up again, he couldn't stop the words that tumbled from his lips. "I understand why you feel it's best to go in by yourself to talk to your father, but I really wish you'd reconsider. Let me come with you."

She put the menu down and closed it. "Thanks, but I think I'm right about this. In my father's mind, you would be there as protection, which is the truth. That gives you power over him—and me. I need him to feel as if he's the most powerful person in the room. It's the only way to get him to let down his guard." She shook her head. "Even though he did a lot of *father* things when Jason and I were growing up, he always had to be in control. He gave my mother grocery money. She had to get his agreement if she wanted to buy something—even clothes. He wasn't mean about it, but you knew who was in charge. That's what I'm trying to recreate."

Kaely's reasons made perfect sense, but he still thought what she wanted to do was incredibly dangerous. He wanted to say more, but any further comments would be seen as argumentative. Why couldn't he just shut up? Leave it alone? In many ways Kaely was the strongest person he'd ever known, but in other ways she was extremely fragile. She admitted to it, so that made it easier to handle.

But he couldn't help but wonder if their relationship would ever become a two-way street. Maybe she needed to acquiesce to him once in a while. Even as the thought entered his mind, he dismissed it, feeling guilty for even thinking that way. He knew she cared about him. If he wanted to stay near her, he'd have to carry the lion's share of their friendship. At least for now. Maybe he needed to walk away after this case. Close the door for good. Protect his heart. But every time he considered this option, the idea of not having her in his life was more than he could bear.

The waitress came to take their drink orders. Kaely asked for iced tea, but Noah ordered a whiskey sour. He needed a drink tonight. Badly.

Kaely looked at him strangely. Kaely didn't drink, and that was fine, but he didn't feel the need to shun alcohol for her—or anyone else. He felt a slight flush of resentment. He spent too much time feeling as though he was somehow letting her down.

Noah told the waitress they were ready to order their meal as well. She wrote down what they wanted. "Good choices," she said, smiling.

As she walked away, Noah wondered if any waitstaff ever said *Don't order that! You'll hate it!* He chuckled to himself, and Kaely smiled.

"What's so funny?" she asked.

He told her what he'd been thinking, and she laughed. "You're right. I've never had that happen. I can certainly think of a few times it should have."

He grinned at her. The mood had lifted some, and he was grateful. "Okay, the worst meal you ever ordered in a restaurant. Name it."

She looked away for a moment, and then the sides of her mouth turned up. "A place in Virginia known for their hamburgers. I ordered a Swiss and mushroom burger." She giggled.

"They cooked it wrong?"

She shook her head. "No. I mean, I don't know."

He frowned at her. "What do you mean you don't know?"

"The mushrooms and cheese looked great. Unfortunately, they forgot the hamburger."

Noah laughed as the waitress brought their drinks. When she left, he took a swig of his whiskey sour. He felt the warmth of the alcohol rush through his body. It helped him relax.

"Your worst meal?" Kaely asked.

"Easy. A little restaurant in Iraq when I was in the army."

"Not used to foreign foods?"

He smiled. "No, it wasn't that. I just wasn't used to finding a dead mouse in my soup."

Kaely's eyes widened, and her mouth formed an almost perfect O. "Seriously?"

He nodded. "But he didn't drink much."

"Very funny. What did you do?"

"My buddy and I politely paid for the meal, left, and never went back."

"You paid? Even though they served you a dead mouse?"

He nodded again. "We were very careful to treat the locals with respect. Didn't want to project a bad image."

"It must have been tough. Serving overseas."

Noah took another swig of his drink. It had been tougher

than she could ever imagine, and he had no intention of talking about it. "It wasn't too bad. I was glad to get home, though. No dead mice in my soup."

Kaely smiled and then stared at her iced tea. "I keep going over and over what to say tomorrow. To Ed, I mean."

Noah took a deep breath. "Well, you're going in as his daughter. I guess you have to carry that through, right?"

"Yes, but I'm not completely sure how to do that. Remember, we didn't talk much." She picked up the wrapped straw the waitress had brought and drew invisible circles on the table.

"Except at dinner, I remember." An idea flitted through his brain. Should he bring it up? Or was it stupid? He decided to take a chance. "What if you did this over food?"

Kaely chuckled and shook her head. She picked up her glass and had it halfway to her mouth when she stopped and put it down. She stared at him, her eyes wide again. "You might be the smartest person I've ever known."

Noah wasn't quite sure what he'd done to deserve her compliment. "What are you talking about? The idea about food? I just . . . I mean, if you always talked over supper . . ."

"Exactly. But we'll have to do it in a way that won't make him suspicious. That doesn't come off like we planned it." Kaely pulled her phone out of her pocket. Then she got a card out of her purse. After she punched in a number, Noah listened as she talked. It was clear she was speaking to Chief Sawyer. He'd given her his private cell phone number.

When she smiled and hung up, Noah asked, "You think that will work? Your father won't think it's a setup?"

"Not if they do it the way I just asked them to."

"Someone will bring you lunch while you're talking to your father, then."

Kaely nodded. "I'll go in around lunchtime. When they bring

it in, I'll get upset and tell them to leave it outside until I'm through. Hopefully, my father will tell me to go ahead and eat."

"But how can you count on that?"

Kaely shrugged. "I can't. But instinct tells me he will."

"Then what?"

"Then I offer him part of it. You heard me ask them to bring a large Italian sandwich. He used to love them. I'll tell him it's too big for me and offer him half. Once we both have food, I'm hoping it will put him back in the mind-set he had when we talked at the dinner table."

"Ingenious," Noah said. He downed the rest of his drink and motioned to the waitress for another.

Kaely was quiet for a moment. "Please don't worry. I know you're concerned, but everything will be all right. Trust me . . . just a little, okay?"

Noah sighed. "I'm trying, Kaely, but it's not just your interview tomorrow that bothers me. No matter what you say, that Scripture is disturbing. What if this killer does have you in mind? You know, you talk a lot about gut feelings. Well, it's my turn."

Kaely shook her head. "Look, we have connecting doors between our rooms at the hotel. We'll leave them unlocked. If I need help, you can be there in seconds. And you'll be with me—or at least nearby—every minute we're at the prison."

She reached over and touched his hand. His immediate response was to pull it away, but he didn't.

"Let's find our UNSUB and then go home safe and sound, okay?" she said. "You have my promise. I won't put myself in any situation you feel is dangerous again. But first I have to do this. I just have to."

He nodded, but he couldn't shake a sense of dread so strong that it made his stomach hurt.

ELEVEN

After dinner, Kaely and Noah drove back to their extended-stay suites in Anamosa, then parted in the hallway before going inside for the night. Mr. Hoover seemed to have made himself at home in Kaely's rooms. He was curled up on the couch as she went to her kitchen and grabbed a bottle of water. Then she sat down next to the sleeping cat. He raised his head and opened his eyes, looking her over, then fell back into his relaxed catnap. Kaely wished she could unwind as easily.

"Need to talk this out?"

Kaely looked up to see her old friend Georgie sitting in the chair across from her. Did she really want her here? Had she subconsciously summoned her? "I . . . I don't know," Kaely said. "I'm trying not to rely on you. Noah thinks it's a bad idea."

Georgie frowned. "And what do you think?"

Kaely sighed and chugged some water. Then she said, "The therapist in St. Louis says talking to you is . . . counterproductive. That I need to learn how to solve my problems on my own."

Georgie studied Kaely for a moment. "You are on your own. I'm you. Besides, I wouldn't be here if you didn't want me."

Kaely blinked back tears. "I know. But I can't tell anyone I'm talking to you again."

"Well, I certainly won't share our secret." A smile lit up Georgie's delicate face, and her brown eyes twinkled.

In spite of herself, Kaely laughed. She'd missed her friend so much. She glanced at the door to Noah's room. "We need to keep it down," she said. "Noah might hear."

"And think you're bonkers?"

"Pretty much." She nodded toward Georgie. "Maybe I am."

"Do you really believe that?"

"I don't know anymore. I really don't." She took a deep breath and pushed it out with force. "I'm a Christian, and I need to rely on God alone. Not . . . not someone I made up."

"But I'm not *someone*. I'm you."

"I know." She should probably tell Georgie to go, but she just couldn't. The past few years had been tough. And Noah pulling away from her had shaken her—deeply. Now she had to face her father. She'd tried hard to make Noah believe she wasn't afraid, now that she was completely in control. But it wasn't true. She really needed someone to talk to, and since she couldn't be completely honest with Noah, maybe talking to Georgie one more time would be okay.

She was about to face a past she'd been running from for years.

She glanced at the door between her room and Noah's again. Frankly, she was sorry she'd told him about Georgie, thinking it might ease the tension between them. Because it hadn't. It had made it worse.

"You're concerned about the way Noah treats you now," Georgie said suddenly.

Kaely leaned back on the couch. "He says I take too many chances. That he needs to protect himself from me."

"Yet he's here," Georgie said, her tone gentle.

"Yet he's here," Kaely repeated.

"You've been thinking about the Scripture found in the dead women's mouths."

Kaely nodded. "I know I'm loved by God. Accepted by Him. It isn't that I think God will visit some kind of Old Testament beatdown on me to punish me for my father's sins. It's just . . ."

"You still worry that because your father is mentally ill, you are too."

Kaely leaned forward and grabbed her water bottle. "Of course I do. I'm talking to someone who isn't here. What do you think?"

"But there's something else."

Kaely rubbed her temples. "What happened in Darkwater."

"You mean what your UNSUB said?"

"Yeah."

"It got out of control, didn't it?"

Kaely ran her finger up and down the side of the plastic bottle in her hands. The UNSUBs were taking over her process. Inserting comments that seemed to come from their own minds. But that was impossible. How could that happen?

"It's proof you're losing your mind," Georgie said.

Kaely gasped, and a sob forced its way out of her throat. "Yes. Yes." She stared at Georgie through tears. "I'm going crazy. You're not real. The UNSUBs aren't real. Yet I see them. I see you. It was okay at first. But now . . ."

"What the UNSUB in Darkwater said worries you."

"Yes."

"It should." Georgie frowned at her. "You need to say it."

"He . . . he quoted Shakespeare. 'By the pricking of my thumbs, something wicked this way comes. Open, locks, whoever knocks.'"

"And then what?"

"He said, 'You're going to die. It will not happen here, in Darkwater, but it will happen. And soon.'" Kaley put down her water bottle and wrapped her arms around herself. "It's like . . .

like I feel it. That it's going to happen." She locked eyes with Georgie. "I've felt since I was a teenager that I was going to die young. Then when I found God, I put it out of my mind."

"But it's back."

Kaely wiped the tears from her face.

"You're not facing the truth," Georgie said.

"What do you mean?"

Her friend sighed. "You know what's really happening. Invisible UNSUBs can't threaten you. Can't speak outside of what you allow."

Kaely was quiet. She knew exactly what Georgie was saying, but this was something she didn't want to think about. Something that frightened her.

"Why are you afraid?" Georgie asked.

Kaely ignored the question and shrugged. "I can profile another way. That's not the only way to do it."

Georgie was talking about Kaely's method of profiling unknown subjects. As she was training as a behavioral analyst for the FBI, she couldn't help but wonder if her father had exhibited signs that would have pointed to his psychological inclinations. What had she missed? Had there been something she should have seen? Could she have stopped his deadly killing spree? Since the only time she really talked to him was at supper, something he insisted his children do every night, she sat down at a table and pretended to interview him. That morphed into a technique she used many times when trying to understand unknown subjects for the FBI. After asking a few questions, an image would begin to form in the chair across from her. Quite a few dangerous criminals were now in prison because of her unique way of profiling.

"And the warning that you're going to die? Do you think a different method of profiling will make that go away?"

"I . . . I don't know." Kaely stared at Georgie. "What are you saying?"

"Do you mean what are *you* saying?"

Kaely nodded.

"'For we do not wrestle against flesh and blood, but against principalities, against powers, against the rulers of the darkness of this age, against spiritual hosts of wickedness in the heavenly places.'"

"You're talking about spiritual warfare."

"Yes. But why are you afraid? You fight living, breathing monsters all the time. Do you think invisible evil spirits are any different? You've encountered them before. Some of the worst of the worst."

"I know that."

"Then act like it."

Kaely looked at Georgie in wide-eyed surprise. Was her imaginary friend reprimanding her?

"Don't be shocked," Georgie huffed. "You're only chastising yourself. You know you have to face this."

Kaely sighed. "Okay, okay. You're right. But not right now. I have too much going on."

"Sure. Let it sit for a while. I'm sure the devil will take a break too."

"Okay," Kaely said, feeling cross. "Knock it off. I get it. You need to go."

Instead of disappearing, Georgie said, "Kaely, this is serious. He's trying to kill you. This isn't a game. Can you understand that?"

"I . . . I guess."

Georgie was quiet for a moment. "If you die, I die, too, you know."

"Don't be ridiculous."

"You're weak. You haven't prayed much lately. Why?"

Kaely stared at her. That was a good question. Why had her prayer life dwindled? And she used to read the Bible every day, but lately she'd let it slide. It wasn't that she had changed her mind about God. She hadn't. Life just got in the way.

"I need to pray," she said. "I need God to strengthen me. To teach me how to battle the invisible as well as the visible."

"The rest of that Scripture is 'Therefore take up the whole armor of God, that you may be able to withstand in the evil day, and having done all, to stand.' Your armor has slipped, Kaely. You've got to prepare for battle, not only against the words you heard in Darkwater. You're about to face your past head-on. You've come so far with God, but this is different. It will be hard. Maybe harder than you realize." Georgie's eyes locked on hers. 'Blessed be the Lord my Rock, who trains my hands for war.' Time to go to war."

With that, Georgie disappeared.

Kaely tucked her legs under her and cried out to God.

Noah felt guilty pressing his ear against the door that separated him from Kaely, but he was worried about her. Kaley was strong. She'd made it through more than most people could ever face. But facing her father was different, and her assurances that she could handle this situation sounded hollow. He wanted to drop his defenses and go all in to help her, but he was afraid of losing himself completely.

He couldn't make out everything Kaely was saying, and of course he couldn't hear Georgie, but he knew that was who Kaely was talking to. When Kaely grew silent, Noah walked away. He sat down on the edge of his bed, wondering what to do. Should he contact Solomon? Tell him he didn't think Kaely was . . . what? Capable of handling this assignment? That she was too fragile? Maybe mentally unstable? It felt disloyal. As if he were turning his back on her. The truth was he wanted to trust Kaely Quinn as an agent, but he feared he was watching his friend disintegrate right before his eyes.

TWELVE

Kaely had asked Noah to drive them to the prison so she could look over the file Sawyer gave her. As she read through it, she shared its contents with Noah, but there wasn't much to talk about. Information about the last murder wasn't in the file. They had been told, however, that forensics hadn't found any useable DNA or fingerprints, nothing left behind from the UNSUB that could point to him. Yet the MO was still similar to her father's original killings.

"Why were so many of the bodies found at the train yard buried?" Noah asked.

Kaely was silent for a moment. "I really don't know. Serial killers have been known to change their MO, but it's usually because they're afraid of getting caught. From the age of the original bodies, they were killed long before—"

Noah was used to Kaely halting in the middle of a sentence. It meant she'd realized something. He used to tease her. Tell her she reminded him of Agatha Christie's character, Hercule Poirot. Poirot would refer to his "little gray cells," meaning he had to think. And his thinking led to the truth—and an arrest. Noah was quiet, allowing her to process her thoughts without interruption.

Finally, she said, "I believe the women in the field were killed before my father made himself known."

Noah's mouth dropped open. "What are you saying? That they were . . . practice?"

Kaely looked at him and nodded. With all the evil she'd seen, she still had the ability to look horrified by the terrible things people were capable of.

"When he was ready, when he felt capable of getting away with his crimes, he began to leave the bodies on display."

What she was saying began to filter through his mind. "You're saying the reason our copycat killer left this new body in public is that he's through practicing—just like your father was. He's moved on?"

Kaely nodded again. "No one but my father knew about this killing field, Noah. He had to tell his apprentice about it. He probably instructed him to follow his own pattern. It's terrible, but it makes a sick kind of sense."

"I still find it hard to believe someone just stumbled over the last body buried there."

Kaely snorted. "Trust me. Our UNSUB had a plan to reveal his work. That wasn't it."

"Why do you say that?"

"First of all, he's proud of what he's done. Second, it proves he knows things about my father no one else does. And the last victim in the field, Rebecca Jergens, was buried in a very shallow grave. Not like the others. He wanted her to be found. I'm certain if someone hadn't accidentally discovered her, the UNSUB would have alerted the authorities some other way."

"I didn't realize Rebecca Jergens was buried differently than the others."

Kaely went back to looking through the information the chief provided. "It's going to be hard to identify the older bodies. I suspect they're prostitutes."

"Women already missing or hiding from their families."

"Yes, but regardless, I'm sure the families of some of these women have been looking for them. The others, though . . ."

She shook her head. "So sad. Tossed away like trash so my father could hone his skills. They deserved better."

"They may have lived lives that put them in danger, Kaely."

"That's true, but many times prostitutes have been sexually exploited as children. Or they're addicted to drugs." When she turned to look at him, he could see the compassion in her face. It touched him.

"Maybe they'll be identified," he said. "It's not impossible."

"I hope so. I would hate to see these women buried in unmarked graves without anyone there to mourn them."

Noah shifted his gaze back to the highway. "This guy. The Copycat Killer. Is he exactly like your father? I mean, other than the Scripture and using a stun gun?"

"No. My father didn't need to pattern himself after anyone. And their signatures are different. My father killed out of deep-seated anger. This guy has a plan. He wants something, but I'm not sure what it is." She took a deep breath. "Did you know there are different kinds of psychopaths?"

Noah grunted. "No. What kind is your dad?"

"He's a tyrannical psychopath. Obsessed with control. But he also has some traits of a malevolent psychopath. The worst kind."

Noah raised his eyebrows. "And the copycat?"

"I don't know yet. The explosive psychopath can't control his rage. The new deaths seem like controlled kills, so I would probably rule that out. And the abrasive psychopath is defiant. He has his own views and isn't easily led. If this guy has that quality, then eventually his relationship with my father will splinter. That will help us catch him. If at any point my father feels slighted, he may tell us who he is."

"Wow. Different kinds of psychopaths. That makes it even harder to understand them."

"Sounds like it, but they all have one thing in common. They're inspired by evil." She sighed again, this time more deeply. "I've realized that Satan is the king of psychopaths."

"I don't understand. Blame it on my lack of religious education."

Kaely laughed lightly even though the subject wasn't humorous. "Psychopaths don't have the ability to love. To care for others." She paused for a moment, then said, "Think about it. The devil knows he's destined for destruction. That in the end God will throw him into eternal fire."

"If you believe in that sort of thing."

"Yes, if you believe in that sort of thing," Kaely repeated, her voice growing soft. "Why doesn't he fall on his knees before God? Beg for forgiveness? God is merciful. Maybe He would pardon him."

Confused, Noah just shrugged. Where was this going?"

Kaely turned her head and stared out the car window, watching the scenery go by. Noah didn't say anything, just waited.

Finally, Kaely looked at him. "Satan is the king of the psychopaths because his spirit is dead and because he has no access to God. There's no compassion in him. No conviction. He has no ability to accept forgiveness and no ability to change. He can appear as an angel of light, but it's a learned behavior. A trick to deceive. And Satan is a liar. He doesn't care about the truth."

"Are you saying psychopaths like your father are really . . . possessed by the devil?"

Kaely hesitated before saying, "Some of them. Or at least influenced by him."

"But people aren't the devil, Kaely. At least that's what Tracy believed. She said no one was beyond the love of God. No one."

Kaely frowned at him. "You're not arguing with me. You're letting Tracy argue with me."

Noah felt a quick flash of resentment at her comment, but then he realized she was right and laughed. "So how did she do?"

"Pretty well. And she's right."

"So maybe there's hope for your father?"

Kaely shrugged. "I can't go into this interview thinking about that. I have to view him logically. We'll be playing a game, and for me to win, I can't let him manipulate me."

Noah didn't respond. What was there to say?

"I . . . I've let the job get in the way lately," Kaely said. "I haven't spent the time with God I should have. I'm trying to fix that." She shook her head and turned back toward the window. "I tend to get a little focused on solving cases. The past few months it's almost all I've done. At work. At home. It's affected me. Made me weaker. Like I said, I'm working to change that. Hopefully, I'll be up to this today." She flipped through the file again before saying, "I wonder if we're going to hear from this UNSUB."

"Your dad never communicated with the police, did he?"

"No. But this guy has already added a new component. He's proud of what he's doing. I think he'll feel compelled to let the police know he's smarter than they are. That he's better than my father."

"Why do you think your father never communicated with the authorities?"

"His kills were left out in public. That was his way of making a statement. He didn't need to tell authorities he was responsible. His ego was satisfied. The police knew who he was."

"With the red ribbon and the wire angel?"

"Yeah."

"Why did he use those things?"

She shrugged. "I have no idea. He never told anyone."

"You're a profiler. Sorry, a behavioral analyst. Don't you have any ideas about it?"

Kaely grabbed the container in the cup holder in front of her and took a long drink of coffee. When she put it back, she said, "I haven't really profiled my father, Noah. Not completely, anyway. It's too . . . too painful. I've spent twenty years trying to forget about him."

Noah felt guilty. "I'm sorry. I didn't think."

"You're not the first one to ask that. After all these years I should be able to answer your question." She rubbed her hands together as if she were cold. "My guess is that the red ribbon signifies his disdain for his victims. Red . . . like red light districts. And the angel? Maybe he was referencing the devil. The fallen angel. Maybe that's how he sees women in general. Fallen."

"But the women he killed weren't prostitutes, at least not the ones he displayed."

"Frankly, I think he sees all women as cheap and worthless. He was a serial adulterer. He pretended to love my mother, but he didn't have the capacity. He certainly didn't value her."

"I wonder if he loved his family in some other way. I mean, not the right way but—"

"You're the profiler now?" Kaely's remark was sharp. Edged with annoyance.

"Sorry. You're right. I think I need to shut up. You need time to prepare, not listen to me blither on and on."

Kaely reached over and touched his arm. "No, I'm sorry. And you're wrong. Your blithering is keeping me sane." She smiled. "Blither on. But maybe after I finish reading this file?"

Noah nodded. As Kaely concentrated on the coroner's report on the bodies they'd removed from the old rail yard, he had to fight a strong urge to turn the car around and head back to St. Louis. Why couldn't he shake this feeling of disaster that kept his body constantly tense?

THIRTEEN

Kaely and Noah checked in at the prison, turning in their weapons, which was standard procedure. Kaely tried to shake off a feeling of vulnerability as Georgie kept trying to talk to her, whispering in her ear. But Kaely wouldn't listen. She couldn't allow her here. Not now. Instead, she was determined to hold on to God with everything she had. He was the only one who could get her through this. She wasn't sure how He would do it, but she was convinced He wouldn't abandon her. The only reason she was here was to save lives—if she could.

Noah didn't say anything as they passed through the various doors, getting closer and closer to the room where she would meet with her father. Kaely's heart beat so loudly she could hear it in her ears. She kept gulping breaths, fighting to keep away the terror that sought to overpower her.

She whispered a Scripture as they approached the final door. "'For the weapons of our warfare are not carnal but mighty in God for pulling down strongholds.'" She knew Noah heard her, but he still didn't say anything. A tall, thin, dour-faced guard unlocked the door that took them to a hallway just outside the room where her father no doubt waited. The guard told them to stay where they were until someone came to assist them. Kaely thanked him for his help. When he walked back through the solid metal door and pulled it shut, the clang made Kaely jump.

She wore black slacks and a soft blue blouse with darker lace on the bodice, but as they waited outside the room, she changed her mind about her hair. She pulled out the tie that held it back and let it fall around her shoulders. Then she ran her fingers through the curls, trying to shape her hair into place. She needed her father to see something of the child she used to be, although, again, right now making herself more vulnerable was the last thing she desired. She'd rather her father realized that she was okay, that she'd recovered from him, even though she didn't feel that way at the moment.

"When I was a kid, I never tied my hair back," she said to Noah when she noticed he was staring at her. She was surprised at how small her voice sounded. Would her father see her as a frightened child?

Noah suddenly grabbed one of her hands. "That's not what I'm concerned about," he said. "You're shaking like a leaf in a strong wind. We can walk away, Kaely. Seriously. Let's just go."

She looked up into his stormy blue eyes. "I can't. I have to do this. If I don't . . . I'm afraid I'll lose myself. I'm putting myself in God's hands. I have to believe He'll see me through."

He took her other hand. "Look, I know this will sound strange coming from me, but Tracy used to pray something . . . Maybe it will help you." Noah closed his eyes. "Thank you, God, that you have not given Kaely a spirit of fear . . ." He halted a moment, obviously trying to remember the rest.

"But of power and of love and of a sound mind," Kaely finished for him. She took a deep breath and let the words flow through her body, then felt it relax.

"I . . . I pray this in the name of Jesus," Noah said. "Amen."

Kaely opened her eyes and met his gaze. "I can't believe you just prayed for me," she whispered. "Why?"

He released her hands. "Look, I'm still not completely sure about God, but I am certain of one thing. You. You make me do things I never thought I could do. Believe it or not, I've prayed for you before." He stared down at the floor. "Let's just say that God and I are talking again. That's all I can say for now, but we've started having regular conversations for the first time since Tracy died. And it's because of you."

Kaely glanced around to see if they were still alone. "But I'm such a bad example, Noah. You know that." •

He let loose a long, soft sigh. "But you fight, Kaely. I've never known anyone who fights so hard to find her way. When you fall down, you get up and try again. It isn't your success as a Christian that's touched me. It's your struggle. If your relationship with God is that important to you . . . Well, maybe a relationship with Him should be important to me too."

From somewhere deep inside, she *knew* God was affirming Noah's words. That God loved her willingness to seek after Him no matter how many times she messed up. And that He treasured her. It was at that moment she truly knew she could face her earthly father because she was secure in her heavenly Father's love and approval. Even with all her weaknesses, He accepted her. And she could stand secure on His word because it was spoken out of His love. He had made her strong. He had indeed prepared her hands for war. And she was going to win.

She smiled at Noah. "I will never be able to thank you enough for what you just said. And for your friendship." She wrapped her arms around him. At first, she felt resistance, but then he relaxed and returned her hug. It felt so reassuring that she could have spent all day in his arms. But it was time to do what she'd come to do. She gently pulled away just as the door at the end of the hallway slid open.

John Howard, Bell, and Chief Sawyer walked in together. Another man joined them, and Bell gestured toward him. "Special Agents Quinn and Hunter, this is Warden Galloway."

"Nice to meet you, agents," he said in a perfunctory tone. His tall, slender frame made him seem rather frail, but Kaely saw steel in his eyes. He was a man in charge. A man to be reckoned with. She noticed a slight twang. Texas? Kaely could tell he wasn't thrilled with what was going on but felt he had no choice.

"Nice to meet you, too, sir," Noah said. He turned to look at John. "I thought you weren't going to be here today."

"I decided this was more important than what I had on my schedule. I'm here to support Agent Quinn." He searched her face. "I can only guess how difficult this is for you."

"Thank you," Kaely said. "I'm glad you're here." She really was. John Howard was a calming influence. Smart. Professional. Yet compassionate. The kind of agent she longed to be.

He smiled at her. "Are you ready?"

"Yes, sir."

"We have your food coming," Sawyer said. "It will be here in the next few minutes. Why don't you use a code word or phrase to let us know when you're ready for it?"

Kaely nodded. "How about when I mention my brother? I don't believe he knows Jason is married. I could bring that up."

All three men fell silent, and Sawyer looked at Warden Galloway.

"What is it?" Kaely asked. "Tell me now before I go in there. I don't want any surprises."

"Your brother's been here to see your father twice," Galloway said.

"I'm sorry," John said. "We just found out. Arrangements were made through your father's therapist."

"But *you* knew," Kaely said to Sawyer. "You told me no one visited him."

Sawyer looked guilty. "I'm sorry. Your brother didn't want anyone to know. Especially you."

"Especially me?"

"For crying out loud," Noah said. "Didn't it occur to any of you that she would need this information before she faced her father?"

"I should have told you yesterday," Sawyer said. "Hitting you with it at the last minute was a mistake."

Kaely wanted to rip into the police chief, but there wasn't time. Jason had mentioned wanting to witness to their father. She'd tried to tell him it wouldn't do any good, but obviously he hadn't listened. Clearly, he hadn't told her about the visits because he knew she'd be upset.

Kaely took a deep, steadying breath. "Okay. When I ask him if he needs anything, bring the food in." She glared at Sawyer. "Anything else you're keeping from me before I go in there?"

"Because we've questioned him, he knows about the killings, of course," Sawyer said, "but we haven't told him about the Scripture. If he's working with someone, though, he already knows about it."

"News from the outside does get in here," Galloway added. "We have a TV in the community room, but your father never goes there. Doesn't watch TV. He would rather read. Reads voraciously."

"We haven't released anything about the Scripture, though," John said. "The media doesn't know about it." He pointed to a door down the hall from where they stood. "We'll be in that room, watching the camera feed from the interview room. We'll be able to see and hear everything that's happening. If anything goes wrong, we'll have guards with mace and stun guns inside the room within seconds. They're standing by, waiting for our signal."

Kaely walked over to the door but held up her hand as a sign to wait. She breathed deeply in and out, setting her mind on

God, silently putting herself in His hands. The Scripture Noah mentioned ran through her head again. *God has not given me a spirit of fear.* Kaely realized that Georgie's urgings were gone. The only voice she could hear was her own. She was ready. Slowly, she put her arm down and nodded. She was going to do something she'd promised herself she'd never do.

Galloway knocked on the door, and it opened. A guard stood on the other side. He held the door wide so Kaely could walk through, and once she was inside, he closed it.

She was in a rather large room. In the middle was a table with two chairs. A man sat there, his back to her. Although she couldn't see his face, she recognized her father. His once-black hair, which he used to be so proud of, was streaked with gray.

Kaely turned to the guard. She was surprised to see he was rather short. But then she noticed his muscular build. Hopefully, he could manage Ed if he got out of control. She had to trust that Warden Galloway had chosen this guard because he knew he could depend on him.

The guard's expression made it clear that he wasn't completely comfortable with the orders he'd been given. He shook his head as he walked over to the table and told her father to hold out his hands. Then he unlocked the cuffs that held the chain around his wrists before coming around the table. Ed turned to the side, and the guard leaned down and unlocked the cuffs around his ankles. He pulled away the shackles and carried them to a nearby hook on the wall, then attached them to the hook and walked back to Kaely. "Are you sure—"

Kaely shook her head and raised her finger to her lips. "I'll be fine," she said quietly. She appreciated his obvious concern and glanced at his badge. Kenneth Beck. "Thank you for your help, Kenneth."

Kenneth nodded, then walked slowly toward the door in the back of the room. He looked back before opening it.

Kaely smiled, trying to reassure him. He shrugged and then finally walked out. The door banged shut, and a wave of something like claustrophobia hit Kaely. It didn't make sense. The room wasn't small. Of course, the lack of windows didn't help. She looked up at one of the cameras mounted on the ceiling. She felt reassured to know that Noah was watching. Kaely glanced around the room and counted at least four other cameras.

The Scriptures she'd heard played over and over in her mind as she walked toward the table where her father waited.

FOURTEEN

Kaely didn't say a word as she approached the table. She stepped around the side and pulled out the chair across from her father, then steeled herself to look at him. When she did, a shock ran through her body. She'd spent so many years pushing him out of her mind that she'd actually forgotten what he looked like. Seeing his face again brought it all back in a rush of images. Her childhood. The times she'd spent with him. Even though she'd always felt rather distanced from him emotionally, he'd played the role of father to the hilt. For the first time in twenty odd years, she remembered that she'd once loved him. That she'd looked up to him.

She felt frozen. Couldn't speak. *For the weapons of our warfare are not carnal but mighty in God for pulling down strongholds . . . God has not given us a spirit of fear, but of power . . .* Kaely pictured the photos of the women her father had slaughtered, reminding herself why she was here. The man sitting across from her wasn't her father. He was a psychopath. He was a forgery dreamt up by a sick mind. The father she'd loved didn't exist. Never had.

Slowly, Special Agent Kaely Quinn filled her, driving out the scared child who'd forgotten for a moment who she was. She was here because she had been trained to understand someone like Ed Oliphant on a psychological level. And even more important, she was a child of God, and she had the upper hand.

"Hello, Dad," she said. Although she spoke softly, her voice stayed steady.

101

At first Kaely wasn't sure he was going to acknowledge her. Would he follow the same routine he'd presented to other law enforcement officers? Total silence? Refusing to respond? After several seconds, he met her eyes. "Hello, Jessie," he said in his familiar, gravelly voice.

"It's been a long time."

"I know how long it's been. Time goes by slowly here."

"Do you know why I'm here?" There was no reason to try tricking him. He knew the FBI had asked her to talk to him. They might as well tackle the elephant in the room first. Get it out in the open.

"They think you can make me crack. Tell them about these killings."

"Will it work?"

His eyes narrowed. "You're with the FBI now?" he said, side-stepping her question. "You hunt down people like me?"

Kaely shook her head. "I don't hunt anyone. I just help law enforcement narrow down the possibilities."

"Like the guy who helped the police find me."

"Yes. Just like that."

He leaned forward in his chair and put his elbows on the table. Kaely could smell sweat and cigarettes. She'd forgotten that her father smoked. The aroma made her stomach churn. She hated the smell of cigarette smoke. Now she remembered why.

"You look the same," he said, a hint of surprise in his voice. "How old are you now? Thirty-five? Thirty-six?"

"I'll be thirty-five at the end of the month."

He nodded. "August thirtieth."

"Right."

"Yet you still look fourteen," he said. "How can that be?"

Kaely managed a smile. "You're seeing what you want to see, Dad."

"Maybe." He shifted in his chair. "So what information are you supposed to get out of me, Jessie? I really don't know anything about these . . . what are they calling them? Copycat killings?" He shrugged. "Obviously, someone is trying to emulate me, but I don't know who it is. He's not connected to me in any way. Look around you. How could I possibly be in contact with anyone on the outside?"

Kaely studied her father closely. She hadn't noticed any signs of deception, but as she looked at him, he suddenly blinked several times. Did that mean he was lying? She couldn't be sure. The air from a nearby vent could be drying out his eyes. She considered her next move. She had to be careful. If she pushed too hard, he might clam up.

"Do you need anything, Dad? Maybe some money in your account?"

"I wouldn't turn it down. Helps to pay for cigarettes. Candy. Toiletries."

"Okay. I'll take care of it before I leave." She frowned at him. "How do you usually get money?"

For the first time he grinned. "Women. Women send money."

"What women, Dad?" Kaely had decided to call him Dad to remind him of the man he'd pretended to be. If she could get him to slip into that role, it would help her. Most psychopaths had more than one persona. They tended to cling to their other, better personality in an attempt to convince themselves they weren't the monsters they actually were.

Ted Bundy had worked on a suicide hotline, helping people battling with depression. Ann Rule, who ended up writing about her time with Ted, was convinced he'd saved many lives. Even faced with solid evidence, it took her a long time to accept that the Ted Bundy she knew was a twisted, perverted serial killer. Even after he was convicted, Ted continued to slip into the personality he'd created—the good guy who cared about people.

If Kaely could get her father to do the same thing, maybe his father persona would tell her what she needed to know.

"These are crazy women, Jessie. Women who think they know me. Want to be close to me." He chuckled. "I don't mind taking their money. I don't write them back, though. They're nuts." He held up his hands. "It happened a lot when I first got here, but people forget. I don't hear from them as much as I used to. That's why I could use some help."

Kaely couldn't stop staring at his large hands. Hands that had stroked her hair when she cried. Hands that helped Jason put together model cars. Hands that held hers when there was ice on the sidewalk. Hands that had strangled fourteen women. Correction. If investigators were right, closer to twenty-three. A chill ran through her, and she couldn't control the shiver that took over her body. Her father noticed.

"Are you cold? I can ask the guard to turn up the heat."

His comment made her feel sick. Pretending to care for her. "Thanks, Dad. I'm fine. Should have brought a jacket, I guess."

Before he could respond, a knock came at the door. The young-faced guard who'd left earlier came in, carrying a bag. She tried to remember his name, something that shouldn't be so difficult. But her mind felt almost overwhelmed with the knowledge that she was just inches away from her father. With effort, she pulled up his name. Kenneth.

"Sorry to interrupt," he said, "but your lunch order arrived. Do you want it here? Or would you rather wait?"

He was playing his part perfectly. "Are you serious?" she asked, frowning. "I don't want it now. I'm talking to my father."

"I . . . I'm sorry. I'll take it out."

"No, go ahead, Jessie," her father said. "It doesn't bother me."

Kaely hesitated. "Eat. But I didn't come here to eat, Dad. I came here to talk to you."

He smiled at her. "When you were a kid you could eat and talk at the same time. Has that changed?"

Kaely returned his smile, trying to push back the nausea she felt. "No, it hasn't changed. I guess if you really don't mind. I didn't have breakfast. I'm hungry."

"I insist. Eat."

Kenneth brought the food over and put it on the table. "Do you want something to drink?" he asked. "There's a pop machine in the hall. Or we have a pot of coffee in the community room."

"Any bottled water?" Kaely asked.

Kenneth nodded. Then he turned to his prisoner. "Anything for you, Ed?"

Her father looked a little surprised, but he nodded. "Cola?"

"I can do that."

Kaely reached into her pocket for money, but Kenneth waved her hand away. "Don't worry about it." He winked. "I've got the key to the machine. Won't cost me anything."

"Thanks, Kenneth," Kaely said.

The guard smiled shyly. "Call me Kenny. Everyone else does."

"Then thank you, Kenny."

Kenny left the room, and Kaely opened the bag. A large sandwich was wrapped with yellow paper, and a bag of chips was in the bag as well. Kaely pulled them both out and slowly unwrapped the pungent Italian sandwich. She could almost see her father salivating.

A sandwich shop had been near their home when Kaely was a kid. Her father loved it. Would never order anything except the Italian Hero. She and Jason used to tease him about it. The memory made her sad for a moment, but she quickly gathered herself.

When she finally exposed the sub, she shook her head. "I asked them to order me the six inch. I can't possibly eat all this." She looked at her father. "You've probably already eaten."

"No, lunch isn't served until twelve thirty. I'll probably miss it since I agreed to talk to you."

"Do you want part of this?"

He grinned. "That would be great, thanks. The food here is barely edible."

Kaely pulled the sandwich apart. Thankfully, it was already sliced in the middle. She took a napkin out of the bag and sat half of the sandwich on it. She was just pushing it toward Ed when the door opened again, and Kenny came in. He held a bottle of water in one hand and a bottle of cola in the other.

"Is it okay if I share this sandwich with my dad?" Kaely asked as he came toward them.

"Doesn't bother me," he said. "Go for it." He put the bottles down and started back toward the door.

"Thanks, Kenny," her father said. "I won't forget this. You know that, right?"

Although it sounded like a compliment, Kaely noticed a strange look on Kenny's face. Almost as if the comment had frightened him. Kaely wouldn't be surprised if all the guards were a little afraid of this man. He was manipulative and dangerous.

"Sure, Ed," Kenny said. He quickly opened the door and left.

Kaely started to take a bite of her sandwich when her father's voice stopped her.

"What are you doing?" he asked, indignation in his voice. "I taught you to pray before eating."

It was true. He'd always insisted his family pray before every meal. Another pretense, just like his involvement in church. It meant nothing to him. Why did he care to carry on the charade now?

Kaely swallowed the acrid bile that rose in her throat. "Sorry, Dad. I do pray. Just wasn't sure you still did."

"Of course I do, Jessie." He almost sounded offended. Kaely suddenly realized he was playing her. She'd come here to influence him, but he'd taken her plan and turned it back on her. He was on the offense, and she was now playing defense. Although she'd wanted him to feel as if he had some power in this situation, she'd needed him to somehow acknowledge her FBI persona too. But he'd deftly forced her into the role of a disobedient child who'd let down her father. Now all she could do was go along with it. There was still a chance he'd tell her something without intending to.

Kaely lowered her head and repeated the prayer they'd been forced to pray as kids. "God bless this food we are about to receive. Give bread to those who are hungry and mercy and justice to those of us who have food. Amen." She stumbled over the words *mercy* and *justice*. Her father hadn't given either one to the women he'd killed.

When she looked up, she couldn't read the look on his face. If she didn't know better, she'd say he'd been moved emotionally by hearing her pray. But she wasn't buying it. Everything he did was false. Calculating.

Without saying anything else, he picked up his half of the sandwich and began to eat. His reaction certainly wasn't a compliment to the prison food. It was as if he'd never tasted anything so delicious. Kaely had barely made a dent in her sandwich before he'd devoured his.

She pushed the bag of chips toward him. "I don't want these," she said truthfully. Getting even a bite down was almost impossible as she sat just inches away from the man who had destroyed her family along with her trust in humanity.

As she chewed on a bite of her sandwich, she tried to figure out how she could still learn something to help the investigation if Ed refused to be honest with her. If he had no respect for her. She had to fight not to stare at the camera above them. She wished she could talk to Noah. Ask his advice. But she couldn't. She was on her own. She had to figure this out. And fast.

FIFTEEN

Noah watched Kaely and her father from the security room. At first it was hard not to stare at Ed Oliphant. Being so close to an infamous serial killer was unnerving. Ed was large. Tall and muscular. Although Noah had seen pictures and videos of The Raggedy Man, they hadn't done him justice. How could he have had such a petite daughter? Frankly, he looked as if he could snap Kaely in two without any effort at all.

Noah had to battle his reaction to Ed and focus on Kaely. At first, she seemed in control. Things were going her way. But then he noticed her eyes widen. Although Kaely was good at reading other people, she had a tell, and that was it. She'd realized something important. Was it about the case or something else? Noah couldn't help but worry. Had she lost Ed? Suddenly an idea popped into his head. He remembered what Kaely said about her father needing to be in control. What if someone tried to take that away from him . . . and Kaely? Would it make him defensive? Or possibly become protective of his daughter? Noah wiped the perspiration from his forehead as he formulated a plan. He quickly explained it to the men assembled in the room with him.

"It might work," Bell said, "but shouldn't I be the one to do it? Or John? You don't have the authority to issue that kind of demand."

"But if you go in there, Kaely might think you're being serious. If I show up, she'll know something's up. She's really smart. She'll understand what I'm trying to do."

"I don't know," Bell said slowly. "She hasn't been in there long. I think we need to give her more time."

"I know her," Noah said, insisting. "Something's wrong. I think she's lost him. We need to get him back."

"You think trying to shut it down will make him less suspicious?"

Noah shrugged. "I think it might make him mad. He doesn't like to be told what to do. Maybe he feels the same way about his daughter."

No one said a word. Finally, Noah said, "Do you have any better ideas?"

The men just stared at him before John said, "Do it. Let's just hope this doesn't blow up in our faces."

"Does he know who you are?" Noah asked him.

"It's possible. I worked on a TV special a few years ago about The Raggedy Man. If he saw it . . ."

"What about you?" Noah asked Bell.

"No. Never met him. Haven't been on television."

Noah took his wallet out of his back pocket and handed it to Tobias. "I need yours."

Tobias gave Noah his wallet, which he slid into his pocket.

"Do you know what to say?" Sawyer asked.

"I have a good idea." He blew out a breath. "Cross your fingers."

He left the small room, walked down the hall, and put his hand on the doorknob to the room where Kaely and her father sat. He paused to calm himself, then opened the door. Ed turned around to stare at him. It actually shook Noah to be sized up by The Raggedy Man.

"I'm sorry to interrupt you, Special Agent Quinn," he said quickly, walking closer to the table. "We haven't met. I was out of town when this was set up. I'm Assistant Special Agent in

Charge of the Des Moines office, Tobias Bell. This interview wasn't approved by my office, and I'm shutting it down."

Kaely, who'd frowned at him when he first walked into the room, immediately fell into her role. "This was cleared by the Omaha SAC," she said, her tone sharp. "I believe you report to Omaha?"

Noah forced himself to look angry. "I believe you're actually assigned to St. Louis, isn't that right? That gives you absolutely no authority here. I'm asking you to vacate this room. Now."

"I was asked by Omaha to be here, sir. I need you to leave. You're interfering with this interview."

"I don't think you understood me, Special Agent Quinn," Noah said, taking a step closer to Kaely. "I don't need someone who got booted out of Quantico interfering with our case."

Suddenly, Ed rose to his feet. The look on his face was menacing, and Noah had to fight the fear that made his heart thud in his chest. This man, this killer, wanted to hurt him. Then the door opened behind him and two guards rushed in, along with John Howard.

"Agent Bell, I want you out of here. Now." Howard was playing it for all he was worth. The rage in his expression was so realistic Noah had to remind himself this was an act.

The guards stood next to Ed. The one called Kenny quietly ordered him to sit down or be removed from the room and taken back to his cell. For a moment, Noah wondered if Ed would obey. But then he plopped down into his chair.

"Let's go," John said to Noah.

"This isn't the last you're going to hear about this," Noah said, a note of hysteria in his voice. He glared at Kaely and then headed out the door. Then he hurried back to the viewing room to see what happened next.

He watched as John thanked the guards and dismissed them. Then he addressed Kaely. "I'm sorry about this, Agent Quinn. If you want to end this interview, I would understand. I doubt we're going to get what we need from this prisoner. Why don't you come with me?"

"No," Ed said suddenly. "Leave her alone. I . . . I want to talk to my daughter."

John stood there for a moment, just staring at him. Finally, he said, "All right." He pointed at Kaely. "Thirty minutes and this is over. Understand?"

Kaely nodded. John turned on his heel and left.

Noah held his breath, hoping the ruse had helped. The idea was to make Ed feel as if he and his daughter were on the same side. Being oppressed by those in authority. Had it worked? As they watched the feed, he prayed he hadn't made Kaely's situation worse.

"They really think I know something about this copycat killer, right?" her father asked. His face was flushed. He didn't like being told what to do. Never had.

Kaely nodded. "But if you don't, there's nothing you can do. Forget about it." She pushed the remainder of her sandwich his way. "Do you want the rest of this? It's a little too spicy for me. Not like the sandwiches we used to get at the little shop near the house." She smiled. "They were great."

"Yeah, they were," he said. Kaely heard a hint of sadness in his voice. It almost sounded real.

Her father stared at her sandwich for a moment. Then he reached over and took it. After a couple of bites, he put it down.

"Why do they think this guy has anything to do with me?" he asked as he chewed. Kaely suddenly remembered her mother chiding him about talking with his mouth full. What an odd thing to think about now.

"Bodies found in a field. The older bodies look like . . . yours. The new bodies follow your pattern. Tied with red ribbon. And something the killer shouldn't have known about. Wire angels in their right hands."

Kaely watched her father but saw no surprise on his face. He already knew. Since no details had been released, the copycat could have gotten that information only one way—from Ed. Although she'd become certain he was involved somehow, this confirmation of her suspicions caused rage to rise within her like a tsunami. Hadn't Ed Oliphant caused enough destruction? She glanced quickly at a camera, trying to make it look as if she was just trying to work the kinks out of her neck. She needed to feel as if she could still connect to Noah. It helped her calm down. She took a deep breath and reminded herself that she was an FBI agent and needed to act like one.

"You know we're going to be here for a while," she said. "Looking through things. Letters, communications. We'll be talking to other prisoners. Guards."

"Yeah, I know. But you won't find anything."

"Maybe not, but I know you're connected to this, Dad. I wish you'd just tell me the truth. For once in my life."

Her father didn't respond. He just stared down at the table.

Kaely took a drink of her water. "Do you hate me?" she asked when she put the bottle down.

That question seemed to surprise him, and he looked up. "Why would you ask me that?"

"The Scripture found in the victims' mouths."

His eyes widened, and his jaw went slack. He didn't know about the Scripture.

"What are you talking about?"

Now Kaely had his total attention. "Written on a piece of paper and jammed into the mouths of the new victims. It read, 'I, the Lord your God, am a jealous God, punishing the children for the sin of the parents to the third and fourth generation of those who hate me.' Maybe it isn't directed toward me, but you can see why it concerns me."

Before Kaely had any chance of stopping him, her father stood, his face a study in fury. In one fell swoop he lifted the metal table and upended it. Kaely managed to scoot her chair back to avoid being hurt. Then she jumped up and moved away from him. The door swung open, and guards flooded the room, grabbing her father and wrestling him to the floor.

Noah and Chief Sawyer were right behind them. Noah ran to her and grabbed her hands.

"Are you all right?" he asked.

Kaely nodded.

She'd discovered something important. Whoever the Copycat Killer was, he'd colored outside the lines.

SIXTEEN

Kaely sat at the head of a long table inside some kind of conference room. Noah was next to her, and Sawyer, Bell, and John sat on the other side. Warden Galloway had just left after telling them her father was in solitary confinement.

"Did we do any good here?" Bell asked.

It was clear to Kaely that he wasn't happy with the results. Her father hadn't confessed or given away the name of his apprentice.

"I think we accomplished quite a bit," she said.

"You want to explain that?" Chief Sawyer asked.

Noah cleared his throat. It was obvious he was nervous. Probably felt guilty about his plan to loosen Ed's tongue, but it had been a good one. It had caught her father off guard. Without that, he might have been able to control his temper when he heard about the Scripture. And that reaction told her something they all needed to know.

"As you said, my father knew about the Copycat Killer. He wasn't surprised when I mentioned the red ribbons and the wire angels."

"He *is* working with someone, then," John said.

Kaely nodded. "Yes, I'm convinced he is."

"Is that it?" Sawyer asked, sounding irritated. "Because we already knew that."

"No, that's not it. He really lost it when I told him about the piece of paper with the Scripture written on it."

"Obviously, but why would that set him off?"

"The pupil disobeyed the teacher." Kaely smiled at the puzzled

115

faces looking at her. "The Scripture wasn't my father's idea. He's angry because our UNSUB inserted himself into my father's modus operandi."

"Will that help us?" John asked.

Kaely nodded again. "Any fissure caused by disagreements will help us gain some ground. If he decides to punish his pro-tégé, he can do it by giving him up."

"I get that, but in the meantime we need to figure out how Ed is communicating with this killer." He turned to Noah. "Why don't you start going through records, his mail, talking to guards. They may have noticed something that will help us. Talk to other inmates he might be communicating with."

"I really don't think you'll find anything there," the chief said. "According to Warden Galloway, he has very little contact with other prisoners. Certainly not enough to plan something like this."

"Okay," John said. "But we have to cover every possibility. Start with his mail. Then talk to the guards before interviewing other inmates."

"All right," Noah said.

"My father told me we won't find anything this way," Kaely said, "but of course, he could be lying. Trying to steer us away from discovering something he doesn't want us to find. I'd like to help Noah, if it's okay. I'm sure there's a lot of information to pore through. We need to search for evidence that he's conned, bribed, or blackmailed any staff members. That includes guards, infirmary staff, social workers . . . anyone who might be smuggling communications in or out." She frowned at Noah. "We also need to identify anyone who might idolize him. Someone who's willing to do his bidding."

"Sounds good," John said. "I'd like to have your input. Just in case you see something the rest of us have missed."

"It will probably take some time to gather everything we need to look through," Kaely said. "Why don't we attack that in the morning?"

Sawyer nodded. "Anything else today?"

"I'd like to visit with Warden Galloway. And then I want to meet with the chief medical examiner." She frowned at him. "Have all the bodies been released?"

Sawyer shook his head. "All the newer bodies except the most recent one. She's still there. Some of the older bodies have been identified, their families notified. A few were released. Four are still unidentified. We've gone through missing persons reports from around the time these women were killed. That's how we identified the others, but we haven't found anything yet. It's possible we never will."

"Seems like someone should have reported them missing," Noah said.

"It doesn't happen as often as it should," Kaely said, saddened by the thought. "I'd like to see those bodies, along with the most recent one," she said to Sawyer.

He stood. "I'll make that happen. Stay here. And I'll ask Galloway to sit down with you." He looked back and forth between Noah and Kaely. "Need anything to drink?"

Kaely grinned. "Might be nice. I lost my water when the table flipped over."

"I wouldn't mind something," Noah said.

"What do you want?" Sawyer asked.

Kaely requested another water. Noah opted for a cola.

After Sawyer left, Kaely leaned closer to Noah. "I hope you don't feel like I'm trying to take over. You're lead agent, and you're in charge of talking to staff and going through the records."

Noah chuckled. "I'm not that insecure. I'm glad we're doing

this together." His smile faded. "How are you? You confronted Ed, and you're still standing."

"Yeah, I am." Kaely was relieved it was over, but to be honest, she wasn't as distressed as she thought she'd be. God had given her strength and peace. And in the end, she'd walked out with the upper hand. That felt pretty good.

"You're really okay?"

She smiled at him. "I am. Your prayer helped me so much. Thank you, Noah. Now I just want to figure out what's going on." Kaely stretched her body and shifted in her chair. She felt tired, wrung out. Probably because she'd expended so much energy preparing to talk to her father.

Sawyer walked into the room and handed them their beverages. Kaely took the cap off the bottle of water and took a long drink. She was thirstier than she'd realized. She looked up to see Sawyer staring at her, concern in his expression. Although he treated her with respect, sometimes when he looked at her, she was pretty sure he saw a fourteen-year-old girl whose world had imploded.

"I've got something else to attend to," he said. "The chief medical examiner in Des Moines will see you at four thirty. Here's the address." Kaely took the card from Sawyer just as the door opened again and Warden Galloway walked in.

Sawyer nodded at him, then said to Kaely, "We'd like you to try talking to your father again."

"Not tomorrow. Give him a day or two to think. In fact, it would be better if he'd ask to speak to me. Can you give it a little time?"

Sawyer shrugged. "I have no idea. I'm not sure when our copycat killer will strike again. The woman found yesterday at the service station had been dead less than twenty-four hours. The one in the railway yard was there four or five days before she was found. He's not taking long between kills."

"I understand. I assume you want a profile, but I'm not ready yet."

"We're not asking for a profile. You're not responsible for that. Just share whatever you can with us."

Kaely nodded. Of course, he wanted a profile, but since she wasn't with Quantico, they had to call it something else. Cloak it in terms that wouldn't cause problems.

Sawyer turned and walked out the door as Warden Galloway slipped into a chair across from her and Noah.

Kaely looked at Noah, not wanting to usurp his authority again.

"We need copies of all correspondence sent to Ed Oliphant," he said.

The warden nodded. "Okay. But Ed was only interested in letters from his family. And any mail that included money from sick fans."

"Were there ever letters from family?" Kaely asked.

"Your brother has written several times."

"What about the people Ed sees?" Kaely asked. "Who does he have contact with?"

"Look, I know you're trying to find out if anyone in the prison is involved with this copycat killer. But it just isn't possible. Ed has very little to do with other prisoners. We've tried to assimilate him, but for the most part, he won't have it. To be honest, the other prisoners are afraid of him. A couple of inmates speak to him, but he doesn't respond well to them. Just ignores them."

"That could be an act," Kaely said. "We need the names of those prisoners." She glanced at Noah to see if he was offended by her suggestion. He didn't seem bothered. He nodded in agreement.

"What about staff?" Noah asked.

Galloway's face darkened. "My staff is above reproach."

"I believe you," Kaely said, trying to mollify him. "But they might have seen something. Might be able to get us on the right track."

The warden took a quick breath, and his expression softened. "Sorry. I'm very protective of our staff. They go through a lot working here. The other day a violent prisoner headbutted one of our guards. Put him in the hospital. My people take abuse but keep doing their jobs. They're heroes in my book."

"Absolutely," Noah said. "We'll treat them with the utmost respect. You have our word."

Galloway nodded. "Thank you. What else can I do to help you?"

"Can you can think of anyone else Ed sees?" Noah asked. "I know it seems as if we're asking the same question over and over, but we need you to tell us everything you can think of."

The warden thought for a moment. "Well, yes. I assumed you knew he sees a therapist. He visits her once a month."

"Yes, we were informed about her. Can you give us her contact information? And I'll need a list of all the guards who've had anything to do with Ed."

Galloway's expression tightened again. "All right."

"Thank you," Kaely said. "But if anyone can help us with this investigation, your guards can. It's obvious they're well trained and observant."

Thankfully, Galloway took a deep breath and appeared to relax. They needed his cooperation to do their job. Kaely hadn't lied. So far, she'd been impressed with the guards they'd met.

"When can we start talking to them?" Noah asked.

"It will take me a few days to revamp schedules and set this up. I'll let you know as soon as it's done."

"Warden Galloway, we may not have a few days. We need to talk to them as quickly as possible."

"Tomorrow is Friday, and then we hit the weekend," Galloway said with a sharpness to his voice. "Different guards. Different schedules. Even though I don't think Ed's spent significant time with any of them, if you really want to talk to every guard he's had contact with, the list is long." He ran his hand through his hair. He was noticeably irritated. "I'll do my best to put this together quickly, but I can't promise anything. You don't want them all at the same time, do you?"

"Not together," Noah said. "Individually, if you can arrange it."

"Good. I can't pull too many guards off duty at once. Too dangerous."

"And the therapist?" Kaely asked. "What's her name?"

"Dr. Melanie Engle. A good person. She's done a lot for the prisoners who will talk to her."

"Frankly, I'm surprised my father agreed to therapy."

Galloway shrugged. "I guess everyone needs someone to talk to."

Kaely frowned at him. "Do you know anything about their conversations?"

"Sorry. Can't help you there."

Kaely was pretty certain that would be his response, but she had to try. She wondered if Dr. Engle would be forthcoming. People were dying. Kaely didn't want to hear about *privileged communication*. She just wanted to stop her father's terrible legacy from destroying more lives.

SEVENTEEN

Everything was going according to plan. He smiled to himself. Kaely Quinn was walking right into his trap. Frankly, he was a little disappointed at how easy this was. He thought she'd be a much tougher opponent. Of course, it was still early. There was plenty of time for him to test her. Push her. She would know who he was at some point. He couldn't wait to see the look on her face.

He was alone in the house, so he could look at his treasures. He kept them in a secret place. Not behind a wall like Ed Oliphant had kept his. Under the floor where no one would ever find them. He didn't need expensive things like that one woman's diamond engagement ring. He just wanted something that reminded him of his success.

He fingered photos of Kaely Quinn and her brother, Jason. Then he picked up a red marker and laughed as he drew a circle with a line through it on their faces. They would pay the price. The ultimate price. And it would be soon.

Kaely and Noah arrived at the medical examiner's office around four fifteen. After announcing their arrival, the chief ME's assistant asked them to wait, so they sat down in chairs lined up against one wall. An elderly woman sat near them, her face a mask of grief. Kaely assumed she was here to identify a body. Dealing with the families of victims was one of the toughest jobs an ME had.

A young woman in scrubs opened a door and called the older woman's name. She got up slowly and started toward the door but suddenly swayed. Noah jumped up and took her arm, steadying her. The woman looked up into his face and then patted his arm. He helped her over to where the ME assistant waited. She put her arm around the woman and nodded at Noah, who let her go. Kaely watched with tears in her eyes. Through the entire incident, no one had said a word. It wasn't necessary. Nothing they could say would change anything.

Noah stood looking at the closed door a few seconds before turning around. She knew he'd been attempting to compose himself. He was much more sensitive than he let on, which was one of the . . . Kaely almost gasped. If she hadn't reined it in, her finished thought would have been *reasons I love him so much.*

As Noah came back to sit down, Kaely looked away from him. Did she truly love him? *It's not possible.* She didn't want to love anyone. She wasn't ready. God was still healing areas of her life. She knew she was getting better, but she had a long way to go. Sure, she wanted love, marriage—even children despite her qualms about what they might inherit from her father. But not yet. Perhaps she needed to quit working with Noah. He had already stepped back from her. Was that for the best?

Maybe when they were finished here, she should go to Solomon and ask for a transfer. She was hoping to return to Quantico. It had been three years since she was asked to leave—the length of time that had to pass before an agent could be considered eligible to return. It would still take a small miracle, but she had to try. It was her dream. The one person who would fight to keep her out had been transferred to a different part of the BAU. That meant she had a better shot at being accepted now. She glanced at Noah. And it would solve other problems too. Even though it seemed like an acceptable way out, Kaely's chest suddenly constricted, and she took several quick breaths.

"Are you all right?" Noah asked.

Kaely nodded, not trusting herself to speak. Thankfully, the door opened again, and they were called in to speak to the ME.

Noah and Kaely followed a young man, also wearing scrubs, down a long hall to an office door. A sign on the door read *Dr. Charles Redgrave, Chief Medical Examiner*. The man knocked on the door and opened it when a deep voice called "Come in."

Kaely stepped inside and found Dr. Redgrave sitting at his desk, a stack of files in front of him. He was a heavyset, balding man with large black glasses balanced on a rather bulbous nose. His pockmarked face showed past evidence of acne. Kaely noticed that although he appeared to be busy, his body was relaxed. When he looked up, she was struck by what she saw in his eyes. They had seen too much. How could a human being face the dark shadows of death every day and not be changed? She immediately felt compassion for him.

Noah and Kaely introduced themselves and showed the doctor their credentials. Dr. Redgrave waved his hand toward the utilitarian chairs in front of his desk. Kaely took the seat closest to her. It was hard and uncomfortable. She wondered if the doctor had chosen them so visitors wouldn't stay too long. Noah sat down next to her.

"I understand you're here about the bodies found in the old train yard," Redgrave said, staring over the top of his lenses.

"Yes, sir," Kaely said. "We'd like to see your files, if you don't mind. We understand you have several of the older bodies as well as the most recent ones. Do you believe they're all connected?"

The doctor stared at them. He seemed to be sizing them up. Finally, he said, "I'll have one of my assistants copy my autopsy notes for you. If you'd like to view the bodies, I can have some-one take you back."

"Can you tell us cause of death?" Noah asked.

"It's my opinion that all of them were strangled. The hyoid bone is broken in every case. The older ones and the newer ones."

"Their hands and feet were bound with red ribbons?" Kaely asked.

"It's obvious in the newer cases. Some signs with the older bodies. Remnants that may have been red ribbons. As you can understand, there's a lot of disintegration. They all had a metal object in their hands . . . or at least near the skeletons in the older cases."

Kaely took a deep breath. "But the recent kills. They had something in their mouths. A piece of paper?"

The doctor nodded. "In a sandwich bag. Said 'Deuteronomy 5:9: I, the Lord your God, am a jealous God, punishing the children for the sin of the parents to the third and fourth gen-eration of those who hate me.'" He paused a moment before saying, "Do you know what this means?" His razor-like focus locked on Kaely.

This man had the ability to shake her façade of self-assurance. She'd never met anyone quite like him. "I'm not sure," she said.

Redgrave's expression didn't change. He wasn't buying it.

Kaely tried to match his piercing stare. Two could play this game. "Look, I'm not sure we need to know what it means. Even if we knew for certain, it wouldn't change anything."

"You're right," he said finally. "But it might help me to un-derstand why these people died. That's my job."

"With respect," Noah said, "your job is to tell us *how* they died. Not *why*."

"You're wrong. Many times, motive gives us clues. Shows us where to look and what to look for. But let's leave it there."

Redgrave reached over and picked up a phone. "Jerry will show you to the morgue." He made a quick call and then put the phone down.

"The most recent victim, Wendy Mayhew, will be released in the morning. You'll find that her death was a little different from the others."

"What do you mean?" Kaely asked.

"She fought pretty hard. It's possible your killer was injured."

"Any skin under her fingernails?"

"No, sorry. And no blood on the victim. But she has bruises that the other women didn't have. And one leg is broken."

"Could she have been bruised prior to her abduction?" Kaely asked.

"Possibly, but I don't think so. They're fresh, and their location makes me believe she got them from her attacker." He leaned back in his chair. His eyes narrowed as he stared at Kaely. "You're aware he uses a stun gun to subdue these women?"

She nodded.

"Well, my guess is either he didn't make contact the first time he tried it or for some reason she wasn't knocked out completely. He may have even put her in his car thinking she was unconscious. She came to either in the car or when he tried to remove her." He sighed. "Whatever happened, she resisted as hard as she could. This woman wanted to live." He leaned forward and put his hands on his desk. "Your killer didn't leave behind any evidence, I'm afraid."

"Every contact leaves a trace," Kaely said softly.

"I'm aware of Locard's exchange principle," the doctor said brusquely. "Of course, we found fibers, but we have nothing to match them to. Most are probably incidental. We'll keep them, of course. When you have a suspect, we'll see if we can give you the evidence you need to lock up this animal forever."

Every medical examiner knew about Dr. Edmond Locard. He was a pioneer in the field of forensic science. He was called the French Sherlock Holmes. Thanks to him, the field of forensics had grown and developed, helping law enforcement catch and convict thousands of criminals who might have otherwise gotten off scot-free. Locard was one of Kaely's heroes.

The door opened, and a young man stepped inside. Must be Jerry. He smiled at her and Noah. "Would you come with me, please?"

Kaely stood. "Thank you, doctor," she said. "I appreciate your time."

"I hope you find him," Redgrave said. "I really do."

"We're doing our best," Noah said. "If you think of anything else that might help us, please give us a call." He put one of his cards on the doctor's desk, and Kaely added hers.

Dr. Redgrave didn't respond, just lowered his head and went back to work on the files in front of him.

Kaely was impressed with him. Maybe he was a little gruff, but he obviously cared and wanted to stop this UNSUB as much as they did.

Jerry led them to the morgue, where another ME took over. Unfortunately, their visit to the morgue's cooler didn't provide many clues. As Dr. Redgrave had said, Wendy Mayhew sported several suspicious bruises, as if she were held down with force. The bruises on her neck were expected, as were the burn marks under her chin from a stun gun. But the bruises on her arms didn't line up with the killer's MO. The medical examiner pointed out additional bruises on the victim's legs.

"Her leg is broken here," he said, as he pointed out the black-and-blue areas on her knees. "I think the killer sat on her to hold her down."

"Did you find that on any of the other victims?" Noah asked.

"No."

Kaely tried not to look at Wendy's face. Sometimes it helped her to think of the victim as a body, not a person. But it was difficult not to stare at the other bodies lying on carts in the room. There were several, all covered in body bags.

The ME, Alvin according to his ID badge, zipped up Wendy's bag.

"She'd been dead only a few hours before she was found, then?" Kaely asked.

"Right. Less than twenty-four."

"Rebecca Jergens was found about three weeks ago, right?"

Alvin nodded. "She'd been dead around four days."

When would he kill again? Had he already located his next victim?

Alvin led them out of the refrigerated room. "We have the older remains in the back."

Noah and Kaely followed him to a large door in the rear of the building. Kaely had a weird image in her head of Alvin the Chipmunk. Their Alvin had a round face like the famous rodent. She realized she was trying to quell the increasing tightness in her gut. All she could think about was that she was getting ready to see firsthand the result of her father's reign of terror. Kaely had never faced his victims in person. Even though these poor women were nothing more than bones, it was still unnerving. They were once people. Women with futures. Women with dreams.

While Alvin unlocked the door, Kaely swallowed the bile that bubbled up from her stomach. She steeled herself to do this, trying to ignore the dread that seemed to wrap itself around her like the body bags wrapped around the dead. The dead like Wendy Mayhew. Kaely began to gulp air, feeling as if she couldn't get enough.

"You can do this," a voice said. "This is a clinical analysis. Nothing more."

Kaely turned toward Noah, but to her dismay she saw Georgie standing next to him. Who had spoken to her? She couldn't remember if the voice was male or female. She tried to say something, but she couldn't get out any words. She couldn't even breathe.

Kaely tried to grab Noah's arm as she slid to the floor.

EIGHTEEN

When Kaely's eyes fluttered open, she realized she was lying on an autopsy cart. Noah leaned over her, looking concerned.

"Are you okay?" he asked.

"Thankfully, I am." She patted the sides of the cart. "Were you planning for a different outcome?"

"Funny. This was all that was available. Alvin went to get Dr. Redgrave."

"No. Please. I'm fine." Kaely sat up, but the quick motion caused a wave of dizziness. Noah let her lean into him.

"I should have realized how hard this was going to be for you," he said. "I'm an idiot."

"Don't be silly. I haven't been eating enough. You know how I get sometimes. We need to focus on the case. That's why we're here."

Noah scowled at her. "Don't lie to me, Kaely, please. This had nothing to do with food. You were terrified to go in there and see those bodies, knowing they're your father's victims."

"I'm not terrified."

"Okay, how about a little discombobulated?"

Even though she didn't feel like it, Kaley laughed. "Discombobulated? Where did that word come from?"

Noah sighed loudly. "I knew my mother's phrases would come out someday. And here they are."

"You've never said a negative word about your mother."

"She's a very nice woman and a great mother, but I don't want to repeat everything she ever said. If I did, before long I'd be calling you a sweet little sugar pie."

"Wow," Kaely said, sniggering. "Is she from the South?"

"Yes, my mother was a Southern belle. Still is in many ways. What of it?"

Kaely straightened up and slid her legs over the side of the table. "I thought you said your family was Italian."

"I did. And she is. By marriage. I tease her that she's Southern Italian."

"When she speaks, then, she says, 'Leave the gun, take the cannoli, y'all?'" Now she was grinning.

"You're hysterical."

"I know."

Teasing Noah helped Kaely dispel her embarrassment. She had to get herself together. She hated looking weak.

When Noah helped her down to the floor, Kaely straightened, trying to ignore the pain in her neck and head. Although she usually avoided medicine, an aspirin might be welcome. Her headache was obviously stressed-induced, but it hurt like crazy. "Really, I'm okay. Please don't make a big deal about this. You'll embarrass me."

Noah grunted. "That's the most important thing, isn't it? Making sure the great Kaely Quinn never actually appears to be human like the rest of us."

Kaely put her hand on the side of the cart. "That's not fair. I've been . . . human. I've opened up to you more than I have with anyone else."

"Okay, but even if that's true, it took you forever to tell me about Georgie. And I know something happened in Darkwater. During one of your . . . *procedures*."

"My procedures? You mean my way of profiling?"

"You know exactly what I mean. Something happened to upset you, but you won't tell me what it was."

"This isn't the time or place to talk about this, Noah." The words of the UNSUB she'd tried to profile in Darkwater swept into her thoughts even though she didn't want to think about it. *"You're going to die. It will not happen here, in Darkwater, but it will happen. And soon."*

"All right, but you need to tell me, Kaely. And soon."

When Noah repeated the same words as the UNSUB—*and soon*—Kaely's stomach flip-flopped. She remembered Georgie's admonition about fighting this battle with spiritual weapons. She had since prayed about that, but she still felt unprepared. Fainthearted. Why?

The door to the room opened, and Dr. Redgrave walked in, Alvin trailing behind him. "I hear you fainted," the doctor said.

"I'm fine," Kaely said, her tone firm. "Really."

Redgrave walked up next to her. He placed the ear tips of the stethoscope that hung around his neck into his ears and placed the diaphragm on her chest. Kaely started to pull back. She didn't appreciate medical exams without her permission. Then a question popped into her mind that made her bite her lip to keep from laughing. Why would an ME have a stethoscope? If his patients had a heartbeat, something was terribly wrong.

The doctor took her wrist and held it for a moment before letting go. "You seem fine now. You know, a lot of people are squeamish around bodies. Even FBI agents."

"That's not it—" Noah got out before Kaely turned to glare at him, slightly shaking her head. Noah scowled at her.

"You're right, doctor," Kaely said. "Sorry to cause you a problem."

"Do you still want to view the remains of the older victims?" Redgrave asked.

Kaely nodded. "Yes, thank you."

He stared at her for a moment, then addressed Alvin. "You get back to work on those reports. I'll take care of this."

A look of surprise flashed across Alvin's face, but he turned and left. The doctor nodded at Noah and Kaely, and they followed him into the adjoining room. These bodies weren't covered, since only bones were left. The remains were laid out on different carts.

"Not a lot to learn from these bodies. They're female, and like I said, they most likely died of strangulation."

"Most likely?" Noah asked.

Kaely was glad he'd asked the question. She was trying hard to maintain a pretense of calm professionalism, but inside she was in shreds. These bones were once living, breathing people. Now they lay on a cold metal table, their dignity stripped away.

"Their hyoid bones are broken just like with the more recent victims. That would certainly cause death. But without skin and blood, we can't tell for certain if it happened perimortem or postmortem." He sighed. "My guess would be perimortem. My research into The Raggedy Man serial killer tells me he strangled them, but he never sexually assaulted them. Not the usual modus operandi for a serial killer. Same thing applies to our copycat. Taking their lives is the only thing he wants, but I can't tell you why."

"You researched The Raggedy Man?" Kaely asked.

The doctor frowned at her. "Of course. We wanted to make sure these deaths belonged to him. I wasn't here during the time he was active, so I had to do some homework."

"And you're certain they do?"

"As certain as I can be at this point. All these women were killed in the same manner. We also found this in their hands." He picked up a plastic bag near the skeleton's feet and held it up in front of Kaely. Inside was a piece of metal. Someone had twisted a wire into a figure eight and then looped wire on each side, fashioning wings. "As I'm sure you know, the angel was never made public. Unless someone connected to the case suddenly decided to kill these women in the same manner as The Raggedy Man, which would take a huge stretch of the imagination, these bodies are his."

Kaely reached for the bag, and Dr. Redgrave allowed her to take it. She stared at it. Her father had made these. Why? In all the years she'd lived in his house, she'd never seen anything like them. It didn't make sense.

"You've got to identify these victims," Kaely said. Her tone was sharper than she'd meant it to be, but she desperately wanted to bring some kind of justice to the human beings denied life by her father.

Dr. Redgrave studied her a moment before saying, "We're doing our best, but even with everything we can do, we need someone else to look for these women. The police have searched every female missing persons report from the time they were killed. Nothing panned out."

"Can you get DNA from bodies this old?" Noah asked.

"It's possible, but if the victims aren't in the system or no one claims them, it wouldn't help."

A sob erupted from Kaely. She'd tried to hold it back, but she just couldn't. She turned to flee the room, but Dr. Redgrave gently grabbed her arm and kept her from leaving.

"We're going to identify these women," he said. "But surely you realize you're not responsible for this. Your father is to blame here. No one else."

Kaely turned quickly to meet his gaze. "How did you find out?" she asked, anger seething through her. Someone had told him. Who? Noah?

"I told you I did some research on Ed Oliphant. I saw pictures of his young daughter. Remember, I look at bodies all the time. No matter what you change on the outside, your bone structure stays the same. And ears never change. Yours are small—just like the girl in the photos. Your hair is also distinctive. Put that together with your reaction to these bodies . . . Well, it didn't take much skill to figure it out."

"It's no one's business," Kaely said, wiping away tears that sprang from resentment. "I don't want anyone else to know."

The doctor let go of her arm. "It won't come from me, I promise." He gently took the bag with the angel in it from her grasp.

"I wasn't going to take it," she said.

"I know that." The doctor leaned against the cart. "I've been in this job a long time, Special Agent Quinn. And I've seen a few things. Mothers who blame themselves after their child dies from an overdose. Parents who wonder if they should have seen the symptoms sooner after their child dies from an illness. And then the suicides. Plenty of blame to go around with that kind of death. The list goes on and on."

"I assume you have a point?" Kaely asked. Her voice quavered, and it upset her.

"When things hurt us, our instinct is to find someone to blame. Even ourselves." He took a deep breath. "My point is that a lot of situations are out of our control. Some people are so broken we can't fix them. Like your father. He decided to take the path he walked. It had nothing to do with you. I believe you know this down deep inside. You're a profiler, right?"

Kaely nodded.

"Then you're aware of how this works. Probably more than I am. Your father betrayed you. Betrayed the life you thought you had. Betrayed your mother, your brother. Made you think he was one kind of person but turned out to be someone completely different. That kind of betrayal is devastating." He looked at her over his glasses. "You know you have PTSD, right?"

Kaely shook her head. "No . . . I . . . I don't know. I'm getting better. I really am."

"Maybe you are, but it's clear you've got a long way to go." Dr. Redgrave took her hands in his. "Please, Agent Quinn. Get help. And quit blaming yourself. It will only cause you more grief, and you've had enough, haven't you?"

Kaely pulled her hands from his and stormed out of the room. As she jogged toward the front of the building, she heard Noah's voice behind her, calling her name. She ignored him and ran outside to their car, but she realized at the last moment that Noah had the keys. She slumped down to the ground and leaned against the car door as she sobbed, her body trembling.

NINETEEN

Noah helped Kaely into the car, not sure what to do or what to say. He'd realized she was in trouble, but it was getting worse. She'd never fully dealt with her father and his crimes. And now all the emotions she'd refused to face were forcing their way out.

A few minutes into their drive, she stopped crying. Then she stared out the window, not saying a word. Noah almost passed a Chinese restaurant but pulled in at the last moment.

"I'm going in for some food. We'll take it back to the hotel." He didn't ask. He just told her. She didn't argue, so he assumed he was doing the right thing. He got out of the car and went inside, where there was a buffet. The woman at the front counter told him he could load his own to-go containers. He carried one box through the line, scooping Kaely's favorite dishes into it. He carried it back to the counter and then went back for his own food. When he was finished, he paid for everything, and the lady he'd talked to earlier put the containers in a large plastic bag, adding plastic utensils, napkins, sauces, and fortune cookies. He thanked her and left.

They were just around the corner from the hotel. When they arrived, Noah asked Kaely if she needed help getting inside.

"Of course not," she snapped. She sighed and turned to look at him. "I'm . . . I'm sorry, Noah. I really appreciate everything you're doing. I'm sorry about . . . well, about acting like this. It's embarrassing."

"There's nothing to apologize for. Let's get you inside and get some food in you."

She nodded toward the bag he'd placed on the backseat. "Did you remember my crab Rangoon?"

He slapped his head. "Oh no." Then he laughed. "Of course I got it. I'd be afraid not to."

She smiled for the first time since they'd left the ME's office. "Thanks."

"You're welcome."

Just as they were getting out of the car, it started to rain. They ran through the hotel's large glass front doors and into the lobby. Then they took the elevator to the second floor.

On the way to their rooms, Noah said, "Let's eat at my place. That way you won't have to deal with the mess."

Another smile. "I like that idea."

While Kaely checked on Mr. Hoover, Noah put the food on the counter in the kitchen. When she returned, he nodded toward the breakfast bar and then the coffee table in his small living room. "Where do you want to eat?"

"The living room, if it's all right." She walked to the fireplace and picked up a log wrapped in paper. "Do you mind if I light a fire?"

Noah shrugged. It was August. Not cold outside, but he assumed that wasn't the reason she wanted to sit by a fire. "Sure, go ahead. I'll get the food ready."

Kaely unwrapped the log, placed it on the grate, and took a match from the container on the fireplace's mantel. She struck the match and touched it to the log, which was actually made out of compressed paper. It immediately ignited.

Noah moved to the thermostat and turned down the temperature a couple of degrees so the room wouldn't get too warm.

As he took the food out of the bags and got plates from

a cabinet, he watched Kaely throw away the match and then open the drapes that covered the floor-to-ceiling windows and sliding glass doors that led to a small balcony. The rain and the fire gave the room a cozy feeling, obviously what Kaely was going for. Then she sat down on the small couch several feet from the fireplace. As Noah placed the food on their plates, he began to smell smoke. He stopped what he was doing and hurried over to the fireplace, quickly opening the flue so the smoke could escape.

"I'm sorry," Kaely said. "I forgot."

He smiled at her. "It's okay."

He grabbed the plates, along with some napkins and utensils, and carried them to the coffee table. Kaely thanked him, picked up her fork, and speared a shrimp. She dunked it in the sweet and sour sauce and put it in her mouth. "Yum. This is good. Thanks for picking it up. I don't feel much like going out tonight."

"Me either." Noah took a few bites of his beef and broccoli and then put his fork down. If he wasn't so worried about Kaely, he would have called the ambiance perfect. He still wasn't sure what to do, but he felt like he had to say something. "Don't be mad at me," he said, as gently as he could, "but I think we need to go home. Asking you to do this is . . . well, it's wrong. It's expecting too much of you."

Kaely chewed slowly and then swallowed. "Are you saying you don't think I can do my job?"

"No, but I think you need . . ."

"Help?"

Noah leaned back on the couch. "Yes, Kaely. I believe you need help. I'm not a psychiatrist, but I had an uncle who came back from Vietnam with PTSD. He didn't deal with it, and it tore him up inside. Eventually, he took his own life."

Kaely snorted. "Don't be ridiculous. I have no intention of killing myself."

"I believe you. But I think you may be suffering from the same thing. So did Dr. Redgrave. It's not your fault. It's something that happened *to* you, not something you're responsible for."

"I'm a Christian. God takes care of me. I don't need therapy."

"Oh, Kaely. Even Christians need help sometimes. You're still human." He noticed she kept looking at the chair next to her. What was that about? Surely Georgie wasn't there now.

"My God will supply my every need, Noah," she said. "I don't believe in psychiatrists."

"Well, if He supplies everything, why do you go to the doctor for your physical ailments? Maybe you shouldn't do that."

"I wish I had that kind of faith, but I don't yet. Maybe someday I will."

"But what's the difference? If you need help for your body, why can't you seek help for your mind?"

Once again, Kaely looked toward the chair. Then she laughed. She turned to stare at Noah for a moment before saying, "Look, you're right. But you need to let me decide if I want to seek that kind of help. And if I do, when and how I get it. It's true that this situation has knocked me for a loop. I've pushed back memories of my father for a long time, ignored the truth, and now it's all coming back. It's a lot to handle, but I really am okay. If I feel I'm losing control, I'll get in touch with someone right away, okay?"

She reached over and touched his arm. "I really appreciate your concern. And, frankly, your analogy about medical doctors hits home. I hadn't thought about it quite that way." She gave him a big smile. "Let's table this for now, okay? I'm feeling much better. Let's talk about the case instead."

Although Noah thought she was trying to change the subject, he wasn't going to fight her. At least she'd promised to seek guidance if she thought she needed it. Maybe that was the best he could hope for now.

When Kaely got back to her room, she found Mr. Hoover sleeping on the floor near her own fireplace. She flopped down on the couch. Her room was a carbon copy of Noah's, but the colors were different. His were greens and oranges. Hers were russet and blues. She liked her colors better. She slipped off her shoes and sighed.

"You should listen to Noah, you know," Georgie said as she sat down next to her on the couch.

"And you shouldn't show up when I'm talking to him." Kaely glared at her. "I mean it. Don't do that. If Noah had suspected you were there, he would have really thought I was nuts."

"You think you are."

"Why do you keep repeating that?" Kaely snapped. She wrapped her arms around herself. Georgie was right. She was beginning to doubt her sanity. She looked up toward the ceiling. "God, I need Your help here. You've brought me through so much, and I really thought I was getting better. I did pretty well at the prison. So why is this happening?"

Although she heard no audible answer, she felt a peace that not only surrounded her but flowed through her. God hadn't abandoned her. He was here. He wouldn't let her fall so far down the abyss that she couldn't find her way back.

"You've been afraid to deal with this for a long time," Georgie said. "You told yourself you were handling everything, but it doesn't work that way. You have to deal honestly with God—and yourself—before you can really be healed."

Kaely straightened up and stared at her. "How can *you* tell me something like that?"

Georgie smiled at her. "It's because you already know it. You've known it for a long time. You just refused to pay attention."

Of course, Georgie was right. This wasn't the first time Kaely had faced this kind of situation. When she first became a Christian, all kinds of memories had flooded her mind. Circumstances she'd ignored, thinking it was the best way to manage past hurtful situations. God allowed them to surface so He could help her face them and find freedom. Noah was right. Dealing with her father's crimes felt too big. Too painful. She really did need help. But she couldn't let them out now. If she did, she was afraid she'd break into a million pieces.

"That's what's happening, you know," Georgie said. "You can't suppress the past anymore."

"But I can't. I just can't . . ." Kaely tried to stop the tears flowing down her cheeks, but she couldn't. "I won't survive. I really won't."

Georgie shook her head. "You have to, Kaely. You don't have a choice. It's time. God wants to walk you through it. You think seeking help from a person means you're not trusting Him. That just isn't true. Ask Him to lead you to the right person. He will."

Kaely stood, sobbing. "Not now. Not here." She ran into the bedroom and fell on top of the bed, praying, bargaining with God for more time. "Later, God. I'll deal with it later, I promise. Women are dying. I can't face this now and help them at the same time. It's too much. Please, wait until I get home, then I'll do whatever You ask of me."

When she finally stopped crying, she made a call, then took a quick shower. She thought about reading for a while, but exhaustion overtook her, and she fell into bed. She still felt God's presence, but as she drifted toward sleep, a small voice from somewhere inside reminded her that God always knew what was best for her.

But this time Kaely wasn't so sure. She felt like she was coming apart.

TWENTY

Friday morning, Noah got up early, and after making a pot of coffee, he knocked on the door separating his room from Kaely's. No response.

Last night he'd heard her talking, probably to Georgie again. He'd never seen Kaely like this. Last night he'd felt guilty for pulling back from her. For creating a distance between them. Had his actions made Kaely worse? His goal had been to protect his own heart before her recklessness cost her life, but he didn't want to hurt her.

Last night he'd finally been honest with himself. It was already too late. His connection to Kaely was too powerful. He'd lost the ability to walk away. He was hopelessly in love with her. But how could he love someone who could be mentally unhinged? Who saw people who weren't there? Whose father was a serial killer?

And then there was the whole God thing. Although he was talking to God again—praying, pleading for Kaely—he still had questions. Noah had fallen asleep praying. He couldn't quite remember what he'd said, but when he woke up, he felt better. Stronger, somehow. However, his concern for Kaely was still intense.

He knocked on the door again, this time louder. He finally heard Kaely's voice say, "I'm coming."

The door swung open, and she stood there in sweats and a T-shirt. "Do you know what time it is?" she asked, blinking.

Her curly hair was going every which way. Noah had never seen her without makeup. Frankly, she looked even more beau-

144

tiful. Seeing her this way almost took away his breath. It felt so personal.

"Coffee?" he asked, holding out a cup, hoping she wouldn't notice how much she'd affected him.

"You're definitely the best person in the whole wide world," she said with a smile. She took the cup and opened the door all the way. "Wanna come in?"

"Let me get my own cup, and I'll join you."

He got coffee for himself, and when he entered Kaely's suite, he found her sitting on the couch, her feet tucked under her. Mr. Hoover was curled up beside her, licking his paws. The aroma of pungent cat food made his stomach turn over. It was too early to deal with those kinds of stinky smells.

"This is surprisingly good," Kaely said, taking another sip of coffee.

"Yeah, it is. But I'm hungry. Why don't I go down downstairs and get us something to eat?" The hotel served breakfast for its customers in a small room next to the hotel lobby.

"I think they expect you to eat where they serve the food."

Noah winked at her. "I bet I can coax them to give me a couple of to-go boxes. What are you hungry for? And don't tell me you're not hungry. You're going to eat. Can't have you passing out again today."

A shadow flickered across her face. Noah knew she was embarrassed by what happened, but he didn't care. She had to take care of herself.

"Okay. I hear you." She was quiet for a moment and then said, "How about scrambled eggs, bacon, and toast?"

"Will you actually eat all that?"

She grinned. "Not sure, but I'll give it my best effort."

He put down his cup and stood. "That's all I can ask for, I guess. Be right back."

When he went downstairs, the women running the kitchen weren't the least bit surprised that he wanted breakfast to-go. "A lot of people pick up food and eat it in their rooms," a grandmotherly woman told him with a smile. "We don't mind."

She handed him two to-go boxes, and when he'd filled them, she put them in a bag. He added a couple of containers of orange juice and some additional packets of coffee. The food smelled great, and by the time he knocked on Kaely's door, his stomach was growling. When she let him in, she was dressed and ready to go. She wore dark blue slacks and a tucked-in, cream-colored blouse, with a lilac jacket that was the perfect choice for her outfit. She'd pulled her hair back into a ponytail. She looked great. The consummate FBI agent. No one would know that a storm that brewed behind her dark eyes . . . except him.

Noah came close to pointing out that his blue slacks and cream-colored shirt almost made them twins, but he kept quiet. Kaely would probably change clothes if he mentioned it. She didn't like to draw attention to herself. Besides, his jacket was dark blue and matched his slacks, so there was a notable difference.

He set the bag on the table, where Kaely had set out two plates, utensils, and two coffee cups with fresh coffee.

Before long, they were eating, and Noah was grateful to see Kaely actually enjoying her food.

"Talked to my brother last night," she said.

"About his visits?"

She nodded. "He'd told me a few months ago that he was thinking about going, but he never mentioned that he'd followed up on it."

Noah swallowed a forkful of scrambled eggs. Pretty good. "Are you angry with him because he visited your father?"

She shook her head. "Jason thinks Ed can find Jesus."

146

"You don't?"

Kaely didn't answer for a moment. Finally, she met his gaze. "My heart says yes. My head says no. It's my training. Psychopaths don't see the need for salvation. They have no remorse. They worship only themselves." She shrugged and went back to her eggs. "Jason is welcome to try."

"At some point we'll be interviewing staff and prisoners," Noah said, changing the subject. He didn't know what to say about Ed Oliphant's need for Jesus. Was it possible? He wanted to believe it, but like Kaely, he had his doubts. "Are you up for it?"

Kaely put down her fork and frowned at him. "What do you mean?"

Uh oh. Tread lightly here. "You weren't feeling well yesterday. Just wanted to make sure you're okay."

Kaely lowered her head and stared at her plate. Noah wasn't trying to upset her. Why couldn't she see he just wanted to help? Sometimes her pride kept her from being honest—a trait he didn't admire.

"I'm fine, Noah. Thanks for asking." When she looked up, he could see sincerity in her expression. "I really believe God will get me through this. I'm trying to be . . . more transparent." She sighed. "I don't like feeling out of control—or weak. In fact, I hate it. I think it's because of my dad. When he was arrested, I felt I had no power over my own life. I get a little testy when I think someone is trying to manipulate me."

"I'm not trying to manipulate you. I thought you knew me better than that."

"I do." She tossed him a smile that made his heart beat faster. "I'm sorry to put you through this. I realize I have a tendency to bury hurt. I'm not completely unaware of it. But this . . . this is the big one. The thing I haven't been brave enough to completely face. My father . . . " She sighed again. "I've worked through a lot of it, but it seems the hurt is still there. I tried to convince myself I'd dealt with everything. I really thought I had. Except there's always been a loop in my mind."

"A loop?"

She nodded. "When my dad was brought to court the first time, he pleaded guilty. Mom asked him to. She didn't want the process to drag on and on. The media was all over us. That's why we were moved to a safe house for a while. After they found my dad's stash, Jason and I didn't want to live in our house anyway. It's like he took our home away, along with everything else."

"But what's this loop you mentioned?"

Again, Kaely stared at her plate for a moment. When she finally spoke, her voice was so low he could barely hear her. "When he was brought into court, he had to admit to everything he'd done. I turned on the TV that day to find it being televised. Mom was out, and I watched even though I knew she'd never want me to." She took a deep, trembling breath. "It was horrible. How could this man be my father? Although he had his faults and could be controlling, he had taken care of us. He told us not to be afraid of thunder, and he took us on vacations. He showed up at our school functions."

She looked up at Noah, and he could see the bewilderment in her expression. Even after all these years of studying the motives of serial killers, she still couldn't understand her father's actions.

"That's what runs on a loop through my brain. When I joined the Bureau, I looked up my father's case. The things I saw, the things he did . . ." She shook her head slowly. "They're in my mind. They play over and over. I try to stop them, but I can't always do it."

Noah cleared his throat and looked at her, his gaze locked on hers. "I'll be here for you, Kaely. Whatever it takes. However long it takes. You'll make it through this, and you won't be alone."

She blinked several times, and her eyes grew shiny. "You said you didn't trust me. Couldn't be close to me."

"I know, and I meant it. Problem is, I can't . . ." He looked away for a moment. Her dark eyes had the power to pull him in, make him forget everything. "Just please promise me you won't take crazy chances anymore. I can't deal with it."

"I'll try, Noah. I really will. For you."

Even as she said it, in his heart Noah knew her promise could be easily broken.

TWENTY-ONE

When they arrived at the prison a few hours later, they were led to the room where Kaely had talked to Ed. The same guard opened the door and let them inside. "Thanks, Kenny," Kaely said, smiling.

"I was told you've requested phone records and any mail sent to Ed," he said. "Also copies of any letters he mailed out. Not sure you'll find anything to help you. Ed doesn't communicate much with anyone, but I wanted you to know we're gettin' all that together for you."

"Thanks," Noah said. "What about the prisoners and guards?"

Kenny was quiet as Noah and Kaely sat down at the same table. It made her feel a little unsettled, but thankfully, she wasn't seeing her father today.

Finally, Kenny said, "He does talk to some prisoners from time to time. He's allowed out in the yard for an hour a day. That would be the only time he could make any connections, but if he'd developed any real relationships, we'd know about it. There's nothin' like that. He isn't friendly with any of the guards, including me." He glanced back at the door as if wanting to make sure it was closed, then looked at Kaely. "He's had a few run-ins, but nothin' serious. We all get along pretty well with those who've been here a long time. Except for your dad. Basically, he doesn't want much to do with any of us."

"Kenny, can you think of anyone else he might talk to?" Kaely asked. "It's really important that we know."

Kenny shuffled his feet a couple of times, looking extremely

uncomfortable. "Look, I have to be careful. Some inmates and
. . . others don't like anyone talkin' to law enforcement. Their
motto is 'Snitches get stitches.'"

"But who would care if you talk to us about my father?"
Kaely asked. "If none of them are close to him . . ."

Kenny took a step closer and lowered his voice. "There was
an incident once. Another inmate took Ed's cigarettes, a member of a violent gang. We have several of them here, and they
stick together. Your dad didn't say anything, but two days later
the gang member was found dead in his cell. The medical examiner said it was natural causes, but I don't buy it."

"But how could Ed kill someone if he spends so much time
in isolation?" Noah asked with a frown.

"I have no idea, but it happened. The warden didn't follow
up on it for the reason you just mentioned. And because there
wasn't any proof. But it certainly made some of us nervous."
Kenny rubbed the back of his neck, obviously trying to soothe
himself.

It was clear to Kaely that Kenny was afraid of her father.
Still, she couldn't see how Ed could have possibly caused the
gang member's death. It seemed like a stretch.

"How could you get in trouble for talking to us?" she asked.
"It's just us in here, and we have no intention of saying anything."

Kenny shrugged. "If someone told Ed I was in here longer
than I should be or if the wrong person saw something on the
cameras . . ."

"Okay, Kenny," Noah said. "Don't let us keep you any longer.
I'm sure everything will be all right."

Even though he'd been given permission to leave, Kenny
didn't move. Noah and Kaely stayed quiet, waiting for him to
either walk out the door or share whatever else was on his mind.

"My wife, Marie, tells me I need to be braver. Say what I think. Sometimes I . . . well, I'm a little insecure, I guess."

"How long have you been married?" Kaely asked, trying to relax the uptight guard.

He smiled. "Two years. She's wonderful. Saved my life in a way. Love can do that."

"Yes, it can," Noah said. She noticed he said that slowly. Was he thinking about Tracy?

"Look," Kenny said, his voice almost a whisper. "I think you need to talk to his therapist, Dr. Engle."

The door to the room suddenly opened, and a large man wearing a guard's uniform walked in.

"The records these people asked for are ready," he said in a loud voice. "What's takin' so long?"

Kenny's eyes widened, and he stepped back from the table as he turned to face the other guard. "Just tryin' to find out what they need today. I'll fetch the records." He fastened frightened eyes on Kaely. "Would either of you like some coffee?"

"That would be great. Thank you," Kaely said. "And thanks for filling us in on some of the history of this prison. We appreciate it."

Kenny obviously realized what Kaely was trying to do and nodded. "You're welcome," he said, looking a little more relaxed. "I'll be back as soon as I can with the records and your coffee."

He turned around and hurried past the huge guard, who glared at him as he walked past. Kaely glanced at his badge. Raymond Cooper.

"Thank you for helping with the records," Kaely said. "We appreciate your time."

He frowned at her. "I didn't get 'em. I don't work with records. They just told me they were ready."

Kaely smiled at him. "Oh. Well, then, thanks for letting us know."

Cooper shrugged. "Whatever." He scowled at them and walked out, pulling the door shut behind him.

"Wow. Not everyone's glad we're here," Noah said.

"Obviously. I want to know more about this Dr. Engle." She chewed her bottom lip for a few moments before saying, "Who would know more about my father than his therapist? Of course, we probably won't get much out of her."

"Unless she's heard something that could put someone in danger."

Kaely nodded. "Right."

"I hope we didn't get Kenny in trouble."

"He'll be okay. I don't think anyone would hurt him with us here. Especially that guard. We'd be all over him. It would be too obvious."

"Yeah, maybe." He sighed. "This place. It makes me nervous. I mean, so many criminals in one place."

"Yeah, prisons are like that."

Noah laughed. "Okay. But you know what I mean."

"I do, but we need to focus on our work. Before another woman dies."

Someone knocked lightly on the door, and then a guard entered with two cups of coffee and a bag. "Kenny asked me to bring this to you," she said. "He's getting the records you asked for." She was young and pretty, and she reminded Kaely of the kind of women her father had chosen to kill. Most of them had dark hair, although in a pinch, her father would go with a blonde. Dark blond, though. Never anyone with red hair. Kaely had always wondered why. Was it because his daughter had auburn hair? Even thinking about it made her feel sick.

"Thank you," Kaely said.

The guard put the cups on the table and handed the bag to Kaely. "I didn't know how you take your coffee, so here are some packets of sugar and artificial sweetener. I also got cream and spoons."

Noah grinned at her. "Wow. Thanks. This makes you my favorite person today."

The girl, whose name tag read *Megan*, smiled nervously. Kaely was amused to notice she was a little tense around Noah. She was used to seeing women react to him. His wavy black hair framed his handsome face and his gray-blue eyes seemed to see right into a person's heart. Kaely swung her gaze from Noah to the young guard, noticing Megan's red cheeks as she fled the room.

"I think you have an admirer," Kaely said.

"Well, it's easy to understand. I mean, I wore my dark blue suit today. What do you expect?"

"Oh brother." Kaely laughed and took the plastic lid off her coffee cup. She'd had two cups at the hotel, but she usually drank at least three a day. The smell of the rich coffee relaxed her. She took a sip. Good and hot, just the way she liked it.

A few minutes later, Kenny walked in with a cardboard box that he sat on the table in front of them. "There's a lot of information in there," he said. "The names of prisoners and guards who may have had contact with Ed in the last year. My name is in there too." He wiped his upper lip with his hand. Kaely noticed he was sweating. Why?

"Is everything okay, Kenny?" she asked.

He nodded. "If you could maybe interview the other guards first, I'd appreciate it."

"Has someone threatened you?" Noah asked.

He shook his head. "No. I'd better get back to work. Here's

my cell phone number if you need anything else." He handed Noah a piece of paper and then quickly left the room.

"He certainly seemed nervous. I hope everything's okay," Kaely said.

Noah put his finger to his lips and scooted the piece of paper toward her. He'd turned it over. Someone had written *Stay away from the FBI unless you want to die* on the back.

TWENTY-TWO

Kaely carefully slid the note into her inside jacket pocket. They would have to secure it once they left the prison. For now, they couldn't act suspiciously. They had no way to know who was watching. Noah nodded slightly to let her know he understood that talking about it now might do more harm than good.

Then they spent several hours going through records of visits, mail received, and a list of guards and inmates. What they found was interesting. The entire time he'd been in prison, Ed had written only one letter—sent to Kaely via the Des Moines PD right after his incarceration. They—maybe just Chief Sawyer—were the only ones who knew where she was. Although someone had made a copy, she had no intention of reading it.

"I threw it away right after it arrived," she said. I didn't care what he had to say then, and I don't care now." She hoped Noah wouldn't make a big deal out of it.

He shrugged. "I can't imagine it has anything to do with what's going on now. It's your choice."

Looking through the letters sent to her father from sick women and sycophants made Kaely feel ill. She'd run across this behavior before, but she still had a hard time believing anyone could romanticize her father and what he'd done. She read marriage proposals, twisted expressions of love, and attempts to witness to him complete with promises to pray for him. But her father had never read any of these letters unless, as she'd been told, the writer included money. Besides the letters, he'd told prison officials he wanted letters from his family or one friend, a man who used to be close to their family. He'd written twice after her father was incarcerated. Kaely scanned those letters briefly, but since the man couldn't possibly be the copycat, she ignored them.

A couple of odd letters praised his killings. One man even wanted to be just like him. But her father had never read these letters either. Regardless, Kaely wrote down their names and addresses since it wouldn't hurt to check them out.

A little after noon, they decided to take a lunch break at a diner a few blocks from the prison. They notified the warden they were leaving and checked out. Kaely took a deep breath of fresh air as they walked to the parking lot. Being inside the gray, gothic-style building made her feel claustrophobic. Architecturally, it was impressive, and under different circumstances, Kaely would have found it compelling. But its beauty had been stained by the depravity housed inside.

When they got to the car, Kaely popped the trunk and opened her Go Bag. She carefully removed the note from Kenny and slid it into a plastic evidence bag. Then she put the bag in her pocket. "We need to get this to Sawyer," she told Noah.

"Let's get lunch, and then we'll call him. I'm starving."

"All right."

When they got into the car, Kaely sighed and leaned back into the seat, her head against the soft leather.

"What are you thinking?" Noah asked.

"About how awful it would be to be incarcerated."

Noah nodded. "I forgot you're claustrophobic."

"It's not just that. What if you had no control over your life? You couldn't jump into your car and drive wherever you wanted. You couldn't go to lunch with a friend. Or take a walk. Go to the park. Watch a movie. Spend Christmas with your family. It . . . I don't know. It frightens me."

"Because you don't like being out of control, Kaely."

She considered his words. He was right. "Yeah, but still. What an awful way to live."

"Criminals shouldn't be kept in luxurious surroundings."

"I know. I agree." She sighed deeply and closed her eyes for a moment. "I guess I'm feeling grateful for freedom."

Noah laughed. "Well, let's use our freedom for an unhealthy lunch, okay?"

Kaely opened her eyes and chuckled. "Sounds great."

The food at the diner turned out to be pretty good. Still in a breakfast mood, Kaely asked for a Belgian waffle with pecans. Noah ordered chicken fried steak. Kaely got tickled when the waitress brought his meal. The steak was almost bigger than his plate and covered with gravy. She couldn't figure out how he could eat the way he did and stay trim.

"So have we learned anything today?" he asked as he eyed his food. He was probably trying to determine how to cut into the steak without dripping gravy on the vinyl tablecloth.

"The most interesting thing is the note we got from Kenny. What should we do? If we try to talk to him about it, someone might see us. It could be dangerous for him."

Noah nodded. "I agree. Let's hold off for now. Find out what Sawyer wants us to do. Hard to know if it's a personal threat to Kenny or an attempt to hinder the investigation."

"Warden Galloway needs to be alerted. We'll ask Sawyer if he wants to handle it, but maybe he'd like us to take a copy of the note to the warden after the police have examined it."

"Okay. Anything else from what we've looked at so far?"

"That my father's only visitor is my brother." She gazed at Noah. "Jason wants to . . . save him. Did I tell you that?"

"Yeah, you did."

"Oh, sorry."

"That's okay." Noah took another bite of his huge steak. After he swallowed it, he said, "I thought nothing is impossible with God."

Kaely stared at him for a moment. "For someone who's not sure about God, you sure know how to throw Scripture in my face."

Noah just shrugged and took another bite. Probably a defensive move.

"Look, to be honest, I don't know. I *do* believe God can do anything, but how do you save someone who doesn't think they've done anything wrong?" She sighed. "Look, I . . . I don't want to talk about this right now. Sorry I keep bringing it up. It's been on my mind a lot, I guess. Let's stay focused on what we're doing."

Noah's eyes searched her face for several seconds, making her feel self-conscious. "Okay. What now?" he finally said.

"If it's okay with you, I'd like to visit with this therapist he's been seeing. I also want to follow up on the guy who wrote saying he wanted to emulate my father. He's probably just some nut, but we need to make sure we don't miss anything. I hope Warden Galloway moves faster on those interviews with the guards."

"If we rush him—"

"It might take even longer."

"Yeah. Sounds like your father hasn't had any significant contact with other inmates, but I'll be double-checking on that. We've been looking at the records of some of the men he might talk to, but we haven't found anything so far. I think it's a dead end, but I want to be sure." Noah took a drink and then put down his glass. "Do you really think the therapist could be involved somehow?"

Kaely shrugged. "If my father unburdened himself to any-one, it could be to this woman. Remember, psychopaths love to talk. To brag about what they've done. Maybe he didn't talk to the police or the FBI because he's using her to satisfy that urge."

"But you don't think she could be the so-called Copycat Killer?"

"Seriously, let's quit calling him that."

"I know, I know," Noah said, nodding. "You've only told me—"

"Yeah, many times." Kaely sighed. "Sorry. It's a thing with me."

"I've noticed."

"I doubt Dr. Engle's our UNSUB. Wrong profile. But maybe she's working with him. It's possible."

Noah leaned back in his chair and stared at her. "You doing okay?"

"I guess so. Putting one foot in front of the other. Hanging on to God. Trying to concentrate on finding our UNSUB." She shook her head and stabbed her waffle with force. "You know, I've spent years trying to push my father out of my life, but he just won't go away. It makes me a little angry."

As she chewed on her food, she prayed silently. Ed Oliphant's wickedness had pursued her to this time and place. She was determined to leave him behind forever when she left here. It was time to end his influence in her life for good.

TWENTY-THREE

Before Noah and Kaely left the restaurant, Noah called Chief Sawyer and told him about the note given to Kenny. Sawyer said he'd send someone out to the prison to pick it up but also suggested they show a photo of it to Warden Galloway.

"While you're on your way, I'll let him know about the note and ask him to provide Kenny with some protection," he said. "It's probably nothing. I've seen situations like this before. Prisoners don't like anyone talking to law enforcement—for any reason. This might not have anything to do with our investigation, but for Kenny's sake, let's err on the side of caution."

Once in the car, Kaely took out her phone and snapped a photo of the note.

They had just checked back into the prison when they were called to Warden Galloway's office. When they arrived at the entrance to that area, they found a large security door with a call button and a keypad on one side. Noah pressed the button, and a woman came to let them in. They followed her to the warden's office, passing several other office doors before reaching his. She let them into a large, attractively decorated room.

An oversized, dark wood desk faced the door, and Warden Galloway sat behind it, talking on his phone. Walnut bookshelves lined the walls. On one side of the room were a small couch and a coffee table, and a round table with four chairs sat in the corner. The warden motioned for them to take a seat in the high-back leather chairs in front of his desk.

He finished his phone conversation, then hung up, focusing his attention on Kaely and Noah. "Thanks for coming," he said when they sat down. "I'd like to know how things are going. Do you have everything you need?"

"We do, thank you," Noah said.

"We need you to see this though," Kaely said. She showed him the photo of the note on her phone. "Sawyer is sending someone to pick up the original I've bagged, but he thought you should read it."

Warden Galloway looked at it and sighed. "Yeah, he called me about it. Unfortunately, our staff receives messages like this all the time. They almost never amount to anything. They're usually attempts to frighten or control us."

"You may be right," Kaely said, "but can you please keep an eye on Kenny? I'd hate for something to happen to him because of us."

Galloway nodded. "Chief Sawyer requested the same thing. We'll keep a close eye on Kenny. Don't worry. Can I do anything else for you?"

"We'd like to talk to the therapist who meets with Ed—Dr. Engle. Can you arrange that for today?"

The warden didn't answer her, just picked up the phone. After speaking to someone Noah assumed was the doctor's assistant, he ended the call.

"She has an opening at three. Her office is just down the hall from here. Anything else?"

"We would like to work here tomorrow and possibly Sunday," Noah said. "Is that possible? We realize it's the weekend, but we feel the need to move quickly before someone else dies."

Once again Galloway picked up his phone. This time he asked

someone to come to his office. When he hung up, he said, "The deputy warden will be here over the weekend. His name is Parry Clark. Good man. He'll do everything he can to help you. I'll make sure the weekend guards at the front desk know you're coming."

"Thank you," Noah said. He frowned. "We may want to interview some of the prisoners. How do we do that?"

"Tell me who you want to talk to. I'll have guards bring them to the same room where you talked to Ed. They'll stay this time, though," he said with a stern tone. "Any further visits with Ed Oliphant will include guards as well. Seeing him alone was a mistake." He frowned at Kaely. "You could have been badly hurt. Even killed."

Noah glanced at Kaely, but she didn't seem offended.

"I'm sorry for the trouble he caused," Kaely said. "I wanted him to let down his guard. I think it would have worked, but when he learned he'd lost control over his protégé, things went sideways."

"Actually, I think the psychology behind it was spot on," Galloway said, "but some of these prisoners are temperamental, violent. I shouldn't have allowed it with Ed, but to be honest, it's the first time in all these years I've seen him lose his temper. He's usually very placid. Unemotional. Something about you, Agent Quinn, seems to affect him. I think you can use your family connection, but I'm not sure how. Maybe Dr. Engle can be of assistance."

Noah caught the quick look of disdain that crossed Kaely's face. She believed she understood men like her father better than any therapist. He looked at the warden, who didn't seem to notice her reaction.

"You should know that Dr. Engle is a Christian therapist," Galloway continued.

"That surprises me," Kaely said, her eyes widening.

The man nodded. "She's part of our Religion Center. We offer services, programs, and studies from quite a few faith groups. Christian, Buddhist, Muslim. Even Satanist and Wiccan groups. We try to cater to everyone."

"Did my father request her services?"

"Yes. I wasn't that surprised. He used to be involved in a Christian church before coming here, isn't that right?"

Kaely nodded. "Yes, but it was a sham. A way to mask his true identity. He didn't care anything about church. I'm rather startled that he asked to see anyone, especially a Christian therapist."

Galloway shrugged. "Many of our prisoners gravitate toward things or people who feel familiar. Might be what happened with your father."

A knock on the door stopped their conversation. "Come in," Galloway called out.

A short man with graying hair and kind but intelligent eyes walked in and scanned the room quickly. His gaze settled on Kaely.

"Special Agents Hunter and Quinn, this is our deputy warden, Parry Clark," Galloway said.

"Good to meet you, agents," Clark said with a smile.

The warden gestured toward the table. Clark grabbed one of the chairs and pulled it up next to Noah. He sat down and gazed at the warden expectantly.

"Parry, you know they're here to interview Ed Oliphant to see if they can find a connection between him and the . . . Copycat Killer?" Galloway said.

"Yes, sir. I'm also aware of Special Agent Quinn's reputation as an exceptional behavioral analyst."

"I'm not working as one now," Kaely said.

"I'm aware of that as well. An absolute shame. The BAU needs you."

"Thank you," Kaely said. Noah sensed he was being honest with her. He wasn't just trying to stroke her ego.

"They need to work over the weekend," Galloway said, "so they'll be interacting with you. I'm sure you'll help them any way you can. Right now, I think they have all the documents and information they need?"

He'd formed this as a question, and Kaely nodded. "We're still going through everything, looking for some kind of connection between my father and someone inside the prison. We're trying to determine how my father's getting messages to this . . . killer."

"And you're convinced your father is behind this?" Clark asked with a frown. Noah could see the skepticism in his expression.

"Yes. The killer has access to certain facts that only my father should know."

"Sounds pretty conclusive. I hear you've tried talking to Ed?"

Kaely nodded. "I plan to confront him again. I still hope I can get him to open up to me."

"I understand. I'll be available to help in any way I can."

"I knew you would," Galloway said. "Thanks." He turned his attention to Noah and Kaely. "I'm a little concerned about the information we've released to you. Rather than keeping it in our interview room, I think it would be more secure to move you into this wing. Down the hall is an empty office. Our activities consultant for the Recreation Department has left us, and we're interviewing to fill his spot. Why don't you use his office as your base while you're here?"

He reached for a packet on his desk and handed it to them. "Two keys. Please lock the office when you're here. There's a special code for the main entrance to this area inside this envelope. It changes frequently, but you'll be notified when that happens. Inmates are never allowed back here, but neither are guards. Prisoners know the guards aren't given the code, which means they have no reason to take a guard hostage to get to me or Clark or anyone else on staff." He shrugged. "It's not perfect, but we think it's a positive step and helps to protect us as much as possible."

"Your system makes sense to me," Kaely said. "I'd like to see other prisons adopt this concept."

"I would too. Anything we can do to keep prison workers safe is a step in the right direction."

Noah reached out for the packet. "Thanks for the office. We'll get everything moved right away."

"Do you need anything else from me, sir?" Clark asked Galloway.

"No, that will do for now. Would you mind showing them where their office is?"

Clark stood. "Follow me. I'll help you get set up."

Kaely and Noah thanked Warden Galloway and followed Clark into the hall. On the way they passed Dr. Engle's office. The door was closed. At the end of the hallway, Clark stopped and gestured to the last door. The office was small, but it had a desk with a laptop and monitor and a landline phone. An office chair and a couple of metal folding chairs were propped up against the wall. A large filing cabinet stood on one side. No windows.

Noah looked at Kaely. Her mouth was set in a thin line, and she was breathing more rapidly than normal. He wondered if they should ask for another place to work, but before he could say anything, she spoke up.

"This will be fine," she told Clark. "Thank you."

Clark walked over to the phone and picked up a notepad lying next to it. "This is my extension. I have an office in this section and another in an area closer to where the prisoners are housed. But if you need me, I can be with you in a couple of minutes. If I'm not in my office, your call will be forwarded to my cell phone. I'll give you that number too. I carry my phone with me at all times. I'm also writing down the password for this computer. You won't be able to access any prison files unless they're sent to you. If you want something like that, let me know, and I'll make sure you get what you need."

He handed Noah the sheet of paper with his contact information. "Glad you're here, agents. Hope we can help you stop this killer."

Noah thanked him, and Clark left. After Noah closed the door, he said, "Nice guy," then looked closely at Kaely. "Are you okay?"

"Do you mean is my claustrophobia screaming at me?" She laughed. "Yeah, but I'll be all right. I can deal with it."

"Okay. But if it gets bad, let me know. I'll see what I can do." When she didn't respond, he decided to move on. "Why don't I fetch the boxes with the records? You stay here and make this . . . workable."

"Why? Because I'm the woman, I need to make our home livable?"

Noah shrugged. "No, you can lug the boxes back here, if you want."

"Never mind," Kaely said, smiling.

Noah laughed as he walked out the door, pulling it closed behind him. But when he got into the hallway, the smile left his face. Was she telling him the truth? He was already concerned about her. Was confining her to that cramped, airless space too much?

He couldn't interfere. Kaely had to tell him if she needed help. She wouldn't let him in unless it was her idea. He was convinced that what would break Kaely Quinn was her own stubbornness, her need for control. And he had no idea how to help her.

TWENTY-FOUR

After Noah left, Kaely gazed around the room to see what she needed to do. She grabbed one of the folding chairs, opened it, and pulled it up to the other side of the desk. This way they could work together if they needed to. She unfolded the other chair but left it near the wall. Then she opened the drawers to the filing cabinet and found them empty. After sitting down at the desk, she opened the laptop computer and turned it on. As it came to life, words in red filled the screen. They looked like they were written in blood, the letters dripping in crimson. *I, the Lord your God, am a jealous God, punishing the children for the sin of the parents to the third and fourth generation of those who hate me.*

He prepared carefully for his next move. This time he would strike closer to home, and, again, everything was going according to plan—a plan that was perfect. He laughed quietly. Then he pulled on his clear latex gloves, powder free. He could wear them in public without drawing attention to himself.

He was content with the way his plan had gone so far, but he hadn't been prepared for how hard his last conquest fought. He'd have to make an adjustment, purchasing a stun gun with more power. From now on his victims wouldn't be able to cause him trouble like that. He couldn't allow them to scratch him or compromise him by leaving something behind that would reveal his identity. If he was careful, the authorities would never find him.

He also had several surprises in store for Special Agent Kaely Quinn. One had been delivered. Now to prepare the next one. He laughed again. She would never see this one coming.

———

Warden Galloway stared down at the computer screen. "I don't understand. How could someone have done this?"

"Have you kept this office locked?" Noah asked.

Galloway shook his head. "No. I mean, it's empty. No reason to. But it could only be accessed by the staff allowed in this section, and none of us would do such a thing."

"Do you have cameras in this area?" Kaely asked.

"At the entrance. We're installing a couple in the hallways, but they're not active yet. None in the individual offices. Probably won't."

"It's possible the message was sent from somewhere else, warden," Noah said. "But whoever did it would have to know about this computer—and be convinced that Kaely would see it. That's taking a lot of chances."

Galloway shrugged. "I'm not so sure. It's the only available office we have right now. Although it would be a risk, I guess it's not a stretch to assume this is where you would work."

Kaely took a deep breath. "We need to have an expert go over this laptop. Maybe this is the way we catch him."

"I'll take it to the Command Post," Noah said. "If no one there can help, they'll send it to Quantico."

"Command Post?" Galloway said.

Noah nodded. "Local law enforcement, the FBI, and other agencies are all working this case. We're not really part of that, but we turn in everything we learn to the agency in charge."

He quietly studied Kaely. She seemed calm, but seeing that Scripture must have shaken her. *Was* the killer calling her out? It was starting to look that way.

"What can I do to help?" Galloway said.

"I need a plastic bag large enough to cover the laptop," Noah said. "They'll want to check it for fingerprints as well as to see if they can trace the source of the message."

"I'll take care of it right away. Anything else?"

"Yes," Kaely said. "Please keep this to yourself. We don't want anyone else to know about it."

"Not a problem."

After Galloway left the office, Noah sat down in the chair across from Kaely. "Are you okay?"

"You keep asking me that."

"I know. Now answer my question."

"Yes. But I'm still not sure what this means." She met his gaze. "The message may not be for me. Let's not jump to conclusions. Maybe this guy is just really angry at his parents."

"Then why send this here, Kaely? To this computer?"

"Maybe it's not the only one."

"I think we would have heard something by now if everyone's computer had been taken over by a crazed serial killer."

She gave him a wry smile. "You might be right." Then she sighed deeply. "I have a question."

He waited for her to continue.

"If this message *is* for me, how did the killer know I'd come to Iowa? My father didn't ask for me." Her dark eyes locked on his. "It doesn't make sense. Could someone inside the investigation be working with the UNSUB?"

Noah just stared at her. His mind searched for a response, but he couldn't find one. She was right. It didn't make any sense. Unless, as Kaely suggested, the UNSUB had inside information.

Before he had the chance to respond, someone knocked on the door. Noah went over and opened it. Warden Galloway stood there, an odd look on his face.

"I thought you should see this right away. A Des Moines paper put out a special edition about the case." He handed the paper to Noah, who carried it to the desk and unfolded it. The headline read *Daughter of Infamous Serial Killer Investigates Murders*.

Kaely grabbed the paper and began to scan the article. After a few seconds, she said, "Not again." She gave the paper back to Noah, who finished reading through it. The information was incorrect, not anything unexpected from the media, but this was especially egregious. Supposedly the FBI, unable to find the Copycat Killer, had called in the famous profiler, Kaely Quinn, to help them. Noah was pretty sure law enforcement officers and FBI agents alike were sticking pins in their Kaely Quinn dolls right about now.

"This isn't going to make our colleagues happy," he said, putting the paper back down on the desk.

"You said, 'not again.' What did you mean?" Galloway asked.

"Let's just say that the press and I don't have a good working relationship," Kaely said.

Galloway frowned. "I understand what you're saying, but I know a reporter from this paper you can rely on. If you need to talk to him . . ."

"At this point, I think staying away from the press is my best bet. But thanks. If that changes, I will certainly ask you for his contact information."

"Sure. You can trust him." The warden smiled. "He's my son-in-law, so if he gets out of line, I can get my daughter to make his life unbearable."

"Sounds good," Kaely said. "And thanks for getting this to us so quickly."

"You bet. I'll get that plastic bag you asked for."

Once the door closed behind him, Noah leaned against it. "Are you thinking what I'm thinking?"

"If you're thinking the story came from the warden's son-in-law, yeah. Galloway goes home, talks about what's going on here, and it reaches the ears of his son-in-law. He obviously didn't write the story, but he was probably the source." She looked at Noah. "So now what?"

Noah glanced at his watch. "I'll wait here for the warden. Then I'll pack up the computer and wait for the guy Sawyer is sending for the note. I got an okay for him to take the laptop too. After that we'll take our lumps and see where we stand. You go meet with Dr. Engle. I'll see you back here when you're finished, okay?"

"Sure." Kaely stood and took the evidence bag with the note from her pocket. After handing it to him, she walked over to the door. "See you soon."

When she left, Noah stared at the door. This was the last thing they needed. The agents working this case knew they were here, but their only job was to interview Ed, try to find out how the Copycat Killer got knowledge he shouldn't have, and then leave the heavy lifting to them. This blasted newspaper made it sound as if law enforcement assigned to the case were bumbling fools who couldn't stop the killer without the great Kaely Quinn. This was additional pressure on Kaely, not something she needed right now.

He rubbed his temples, trying to chase away the beginnings of a tension headache. Kaely's question about the UNSUB knowing she would come to Iowa had rocked him. How was it possible?

TWENTY-FIVE

D r. Melanie Engle wasn't what Kaely expected. From past experience, she'd envisioned a much older woman with large glasses and hair that probably didn't get much attention. Instead, Dr. Engle was around forty, and she wore her years well. Dark hair in a cute pixie cut. Large blue eyes. Makeup just right. Smoky eye shadow applied perfectly. Not overdone.

After introductions, she led Kaely into her office, then closed the door and gestured toward two high-backed leather chairs in front of a large window. The room was painted cornflower blue, obviously intended to relax nervous clients. She offered Kaely a cup of coffee. Kaely started to say no, but then she realized she could use a pick-me-up.

"Thank you," she said. "That would be nice." She sat down in one of the chairs as Dr. Engle walked over to a small coffee bar next to the wall.

"Sugar? Sweetener? Cream?" the doctor asked.

"Just black, thank you."

Doctor Engle handed Kaely a large china mug with flowers painted on it. Beautiful. Everything about the doctor spoke of refinement. Perfection. Her reactions were relaxed. Confident. No signs that she was hiding anything. No hint of nervousness. Of course, with her training, she would know how to control her physical responses.

"I'm a little confused, Dr. Engle," Kaely said. "These chairs. They seem designed for you and a client. If you don't see any of the prisoners in this office, why are they positioned like this?"

The doctor smiled as she took the seat across from Kaely, a cup of coffee already made and waiting for her on a small glass table that sat between them. "Prisoners and guards aren't the only people I talk to. We have a rather large staff."

"The warden told us guards aren't allowed back here either."

She nodded. "He was concerned that prisoners might take a guard hostage and force them to unlock this area. Some inmates have the idea that taking the warden of a prison hostage will buy them freedom. That's a possibility we don't want to test." She shrugged. "This is a new concept. The state incorporated it after several instances of prison staff being killed by inmates. Hopefully, all prisons will incorporate it at some point."

"But aren't the guards still at risk?"

"Not as much as you might think. If there's a riot, an alert sounds. All guards are ordered to proceed to the closest secure room, where they're to lock themselves in. That has always been our procedure. But now, any guards near this area will be told to come here, where they'll be brought inside. There's no perfect system, but, frankly, I think we've reduced the danger a great deal. "

She smiled at Kaely. "I understand you're interviewing everyone who's had contact with Ed Oliphant?"

"Yes. We're looking for information, hoping someone will have an idea how my . . . at how Ed is getting messages out of the facility."

"You started to say *my father*, didn't you?"

Kaely placed her cup on the coffee table. "Yes. I've been asked to use our relationship in an attempt to get him to talk. So far, it hasn't worked."

"Why do you think that is?"

Kaely gave the doctor a slow smile. "I'm here to ask you questions, doctor. Not the other way around."

Dr. Engle's perfectly shaped eyebrows arched. "I'm sorry, but I'm sure you understand that I can't share anything your father has told me. But if you'll allow me, I might be able to help you in a different way."

Kaely frowned. "A different way? What do you mean?"

Dr. Engle crossed her hands in her lap and leaned forward. "I'd like to help you understand your father. I think it might help you in what you're trying to do."

"Dr. Engle, I was trained as a behavioral analyst at Quantico. And I lived with the man for fourteen years. If anyone *under stands* my father, it's me. I seriously doubt you can teach me anything about Ed Oliphant." She took a deep breath, trying to control her irritation. "He has an antisocial personality. Lacks empathy. He's egotistical. Narcissistic. Can be glib. Loves to talk about himself. Opinionated. He can be charming if he wants to be. He demands instant gratification. He is violent. Aggressive. Manipulative. Displays predatory behavior. Has no remorse for anything he's done." She glared at the therapist. "Do I need to continue?"

Dr. Engle was quiet for a moment. "I take it you know what the PCL-R is?"

"Of course. It's a psychological tool used to assess the presence of psychopathy. But you have to be qualified to administer it, and it's only to be used under controlled conditions."

"I'm aware of that," Dr. Engle said, her voice smooth and composed compared to Kaely's. Kaely had allowed her anger to invade her response, and she struggled to restrain herself. It really wasn't the doctor's fault. Kaely's nerves were already on edge before she saw the newspaper article. Why did reporters find her so fascinating? Would she always be known as the daughter of a serial killer?

"I have my own version of the PCL-R," the doctor continued.

"Maybe it's not as accurate as the official Psychopathy Check-list, but it's worked pretty well for me." She smoothed her dark gray skirt before speaking. It was clear she was evaluating her next move. Kaely felt guilty. The woman was only trying to help.

"I'm sorry," Kaely said lightly. "I really do want to hear what you have to say. This is the first time I've seen my father in twenty years." She was relieved to see the doctor's shoulders relax.

Dr. Engle smiled. "That's all right. I'm sure it's difficult."

Kaely gazed around the room. For the first time, she noticed the framed Scriptures on the wall. The Bible on the desk. Usually Kaely scanned a room as soon as she entered it. She was clearly too distracted. "Warden Galloway told us about the Religion Center at Anamosa."

"Yes. We have over sixty volunteers."

"You're a volunteer?"

She nodded. "But I'm a trained Christian therapist." She cocked her head toward a framed document on the wall, where Kaely saw a license from a school she'd heard of.

"Why do you do this?" she asked.

Without missing a beat, the doctor asked, "Why do you do what you do?"

Kaely grudgingly gave the therapist that point. "What do you want to tell me?"

The doctor stood to her feet, then got the coffeepot and warmed up their coffee. "Your father scores low on my test."

"How low?"

She sat down again and locked eyes with Kaely. "Fifteen."

"That's impossible. My father isn't a fifteen, Dr. Engle. His score is off the charts." Kaely sat back in her chair and studied her. "What are you trying to accomplish here?"

"Your father tells me you're a Christian."

Kaely's eyebrows shot up. "How does he—" She sighed. "My brother, Jason." She frowned at the doctor. "Have you met him, Dr. Engle?"

"Melanie, please. Yes. Great young man."

Her comment elicited a smile. "Yes, he is. I wasn't thrilled with his decision to visit our father, but I understand it, even though I think his hope that he can change him is misplaced."

"You don't believe in forgiveness?"

Kaely stared at the doctor with her mouth open. "Maybe some things can't be forgiven. I mean, God forgives, of course, but it seems that sometimes people can't. I've tried. I really have. But my father not only destroyed the lives of all those innocent women, he shattered our family."

She looked down at the floor. She was losing control in front of this woman, and she didn't like it. "Look, I've given this to God. I'm willing to forgive, but I can't do it on my own. God will have to do it through me . . . somehow." She looked up at Melanie. "Do you mind if we get back to why I wanted to talk to you?"

The doctor nodded. "Of course. What do you want to know?"

"Has my father said or done anything that leads you to believe he's orchestrating these . . . copycat killings? Iowa has a law that makes it mandatory for mental health professionals to report it when they believe patients may pose a danger to themselves or to others. You know that, right?"

"Yes, Agent Quinn, I'm aware of the law. If I believed that was the case, I would immediately contact the authorities. But I can assure you I don't feel the situation necessitates it."

Kaely studied her for a moment. "Somehow, details of my father's killings kept from the public have gotten out. Someone is helping him. Is it you, Melanie?"

Kaely watched the doctor's reaction. She was looking for

deception. A physical clue that would tell her the good doctor
was hiding something. Melanie's eyes widened in surprise, but
she never broke eye contact.

"No, it isn't me," she said, her voice steady. "Look, your dad
and I talk about his history. The way he was raised. We try to
find reasons for his past actions. We've made some progress,
but we have a long way to go."

"What do you mean . . . the way he was raised?" As she told
Noah, Kaely didn't know much about her father's upbringing.
His sister died when she was a child. His mother died, and his
father abandoned the family. He was raised by his grandparents.
He never talked about them.

"Now we're headed in a direction I can't go." Melanie scooted
forward in her chair, so she was closer to Kaely. "I would help
you if I could. I'm sorry."

"You can tell me nothing that will help us stop these murders?"

Melanie hesitated a moment. "No, not really. Have you interviewed the inmates and guards who have contact with Ed?
That would be my recommendation. Maybe he's talking to one
of them. But that's just a guess."

Kaely shook her head. "That's next."

"Look, Kaely, you have my word. If at any time I have reason to believe he's training someone to follow in his footsteps,
I'll contact law enforcement immediately. But *if* your father is
sharing details of his crimes, it isn't with me."

Kaely was about to stand when the doctor reached over and
put her hand on Kaely's arm.

"What you've been through, having your life ravaged by
finding out who your dad really was, had to be devastating.
Children who suddenly discover one of their parents isn't the
person they thought they were, that they're capable of great evil
. . . well, it can cause a child to fracture. To create unhealthy

ways to protect themselves. They can withdraw from people. Become afraid everyone is lying to them."

She glanced down at the small silver cross Kaely wore on a chain. "They may even turn to God. But the truth is they could end up holding back part of themselves even from Him. Anger and trauma can cause people to struggle in heartbreaking ways." She removed her hand and sat back in her chair. "Without help, these children may live emotionally stunted their entire lives." She smiled. "If you'd like someone to talk to—"

Kaely stood. "Thank you, Melanie, but I don't need your help. I'm here about my father. Not me."

"Kaely, many times these children enter law enforcement as a way to try to understand what happened. How the parent they loved and trusted could do such terrible things. But no one can find deliverance through studying the psychological makeup of serial killers. There's a spiritual aspect as well. If you don't understand that, you'll never find the answers you're looking for."

"Thank you, doctor. I think we're done here."

Kaely walked toward the door but paused with her hand on the doorknob. Before she turned it, she faced Melanie and said, "You're exactly the type of woman my dad hunted, you know. Think about that during your next session with him."

TWENTY-SIX

As Kaely closed the door behind her, she wondered why she'd said that. Why she'd become so angry with the doctor. But something about the woman bothered her. Something that felt . . . off. She couldn't put her finger on it. Kaely started toward the office she and Noah had taken over when she saw him leaning against the wall, obviously waiting for her.

After making sure no one was around, he said, "So. What do you think of your father's therapist?"

Kaely sighed. "I'm not sure. To be honest, I don't trust her completely. Let's get some supper and go back to the hotel. We have a lot to do tomorrow."

"Are you going to talk to your father again?"

"Yeah. It's the reason we're here. We've got to find out how he's getting information to our UNSUB. If we don't figure it out soon, John will pull us out and request the BAU. Remember, I'm here only because they think I can get information they can't. If I don't produce . . ."

"We go home."

She nodded.

He was preparing for his next move. Within hours, Kaely Quinn would understand what he'd done. That he was close and getting closer. Soon, he would take her. But before she joined his other victims, he would make sure she knew why she had to die.

Excitement rose inside him. It was almost overpowering. He couldn't wait to kill again. Except for his hatred for Kaely Quinn, killing was the only thing that gave him pleasure. And now, for the first time in his life, he was in control. He was calling the shots. No one would ever hurt him again.

Kaely and Noah went to a chain restaurant next to the hotel. He could tell how tired she was. "Well, it's been an interesting day," he said once they had ordered. He quickly downed his rum hurricane. On sale for happy hour, the drinks were pretty small. He gestured to their waiter for another. For some reason, he felt tense, as if he needed to be prepared for something. Unfortunately, he had no idea what it was, and that made him irritable.

"You might want to go easy on those drinks," Kaely said. "You're too big for me to carry into your hotel room."

Even though he wasn't in the best of moods, he couldn't help but laugh at the picture her remark put in his head. "You might have to drag me."

"Yeah, I think you're right."

As he waited for his next drink, he realized Kaely seemed uncomfortable. Was he sending some kind of negative vibe? "What's on your mind?" he asked.

Kaely took a deep breath. "It's something that . . . that an UNSUB said in Nebraska."

Noah frowned. "Kaely, when invisible people start saying things you have no control over, I think that's a cause for concern." He looked at her closely. "Don't you?"

He was disturbed to see tears fill her eyes.

"You need to talk to me," he said. "Honestly. Surely by now you trust me."

She nodded. "I do. I trust you."

She picked up the glass of iced tea she'd ordered and took a sip. Noah saw her hand tremble. He waited, staying silent. What more could he say?

"In Darkwater, the UNSUB told me I was going to die. That it wouldn't happen there but it would happen soon."

The shock that went through Noah seemed to settle in his feet. He shuffled them under the table. "And do you think you're going to die, Kaely?"

She picked up her glass again. Noah was pretty sure she wasn't that thirsty. When she put it down, she lifted her napkin and wiped her eyes. "When I was a teenager, I became convinced I would die young. I don't know where I got that idea, but it's followed me ever since."

Noah's throat constricted. He didn't want to be angry with her. Not now. But he was. He managed to say, "Does this tie into why you take so many chances? Why you're so careless? Are you convinced you're going to die anyway so you might as well not hold back?"

She shook her head, and her mouth tightened again. Obviously, he'd upset her, but he didn't care. He wanted her to be more careful. He *needed* her to be more careful.

Finally, she said, "I don't think I'm being reckless. I just care about the job. I truly believe this is what I'm called to do. If I stop the monsters, people will live. Families won't have to go through the kind of pain that lasts a lifetime." She met his gaze. "It's worth the risk."

"But that's not what I asked you. I asked if you take risks because you believe you're going to die anyway."

Once again, she wiped away tears. "I don't know. I . . . don't think so. Once I found God, I realized He was in control of my life and that He had a good plan for me. I didn't need to worry about dying young anymore." She sighed. "I thought I believed that, but now I realize I might be carrying that fear in the back of my mind somewhere. Maybe that's why I'm trying so hard to do everything I can . . . while I can." She stared at him, and her dark eyes captured him the way they always did. He found himself taking a quick breath and hoping she hadn't noticed.

"Just when did you decide you would die young, Kaely? Before or after your father was arrested?"

Her forehead wrinkled, and she looked away from him. "After. What does that matter?"

"Is it possible that since your father killed so many women, you decided you had no right to live a full life?"

"I . . . I don't know." She looked surprised. "Maybe you're right. I should have thought of that. I mean, it makes sense." She looked past him, and Noah could almost hear the wheels turning in her head.

"Why didn't I see that before?" she said.

"Maybe it's because you're so busy trying to understand everyone else that you haven't taken time to understand yourself. Maybe you should profile Kaely Quinn sometime."

Noah started to say something else, but just then the waiter brought their food. Noah had ordered a steak with garlic mashed potatoes. Kaely had asked for a shrimp salad. He had to admit that it looked good. Maybe he needed to eat healthier. He'd never really thought about it until he met Kaely. He looked at her and realized he wanted to live longer because he didn't want to miss a moment of his time with her. He now belonged completely to a woman who just might be slightly insane.

But there wasn't any cure for it. He was too far gone, and he knew it. Hopefully, the day would come when they could be more than friends. But right now, all he could do was try to protect her. Help her through the tough times. Facing her father was certainly one of the hardest things she'd ever done.

Even though he was afraid for her, he was grateful to be by her side.

Kaely waited until the waiter left. "Thanks for what you said. You might be right. I'll think about it later. But for now, we need to focus on the case."

Once again, she'd pushed her vulnerability aside. She was in FBI mode, and she expected Noah to follow her example. And he would because it was what she needed.

"Do you think he's using your father's method of getting victims?" Noah asked. "Dressing like a homeless person? Or a cop?"

Kaely crossed her arms over her chest before replying. "Believe me, the folks at the Command Post are looking at that carefully. Frankly, I doubt our guy is copying that aspect of my father's MO. He's smart. He knows the authorities are looking for someone following Ed Oliphant's MO to the letter. But remember, our UNSUB has already made a change with that Scripture reference. It was pretty obvious my father didn't know about that. His signature is different from my father's. He isn't out to just kill. There's something else behind these murders. A different motivation drives him."

"But what is it?"

Kaely shrugged. "I don't know. He's trying to prove something, but I haven't been able to get a handle on it. Copying my father isn't it. Something more is going on. I really need to understand that before I can profile him correctly."

"You're not officially here for that, you know."

"Yes, but you know as well as I do that it's one of the reasons I'm here."

"Maybe, but please don't use your special method to profile him. I don't think it's safe."

Kaely didn't say anything, just looked away from him. Her reaction upset him.

"I'll be careful," she said finally.

"I know that's what you've said, but if you do this, Kaely, I want to be there. I mean it."

Her eyes sought his, and his heart fluttered. "I don't think that would work. But I'll tell you before I use it. You have my word."

Noah wasn't satisfied with her answer, but he couldn't do much about it. He would have to take her at her word.

He cut his steak and took a bite. He was aware that it was good, but he'd lost interest in it. All he could think about was how to keep Kaely from losing herself in this case. From disappearing into her father's dark and shadowy persona.

When they'd finished their meal, they went to their hotel, Kaely driving. Noah was tired, frustrated, and slightly drunk. He crashed on the couch as soon as he got inside his room. He woke up when the phone rang, and he checked the time. It was a little past midnight. He grabbed the phone. Chief Sawyer. He answered and listened to what the chief said. After ending the call, he dialed Kaely's phone.

"Hello?" she answered, her voice thick with sleep.

"They've found another body. Her name is Marie Beck."

"That name sounds familiar," she said after a long pause.

"It should. She was married to Kenneth Beck. Kenny. The guard at the prison who tried to help us."

TWENTY-SEVEN

At Chief Sawyer's request, Noah and Kaely showed up at the Command Post Saturday morning. On the way over, she'd asked Noah if he thought they were going to be pulled off the case and the BAU brought in. Although he said he wasn't sure, she could see he was worried about that too. Would Marie Beck's death be seen as their failure to find the UNSUB? For not getting the information they needed from her father?

Even though she hadn't originally wanted to come to Iowa, Kaely was now fully invested in the investigation. She wanted to break her father, to learn how he was coordinating events with the UNSUB. The idea of turning the case over to the BAU chapped her hide. She was capable of finding the truth if they'd just give her the chance.

This murder had made one thing clear. They could now narrow the possibilities to those connected to Anamosa, so they'd concentrate solely on people associated with her father. A quick check of the letter sent to him from the man who wanted to follow in his footsteps had ruled him out. He'd been dead for three years. The other man who'd praised him in a letter was in prison in Kansas.

Tobias Bell saw them come in and motioned them over to where he stood talking to one of the techs working on a computer. The CP was housed inside an abandoned factory, where the windows were covered with brown paper to keep prying eyes from seeing inside. Especially journalists. If they were careful, the media wouldn't find them.

Kaely glanced at the large white boards covered with notes, along with a huge corkboard with photographs. The room was abuzz with activity. Computers and stations filled the space with analysts typing away, looking for something, anything to help them find their UNSUB. Kaely spotted a tall woman with dark hair who seemed to be in charge. She was probably Howard's Assistant Special Agent in Charge. Usually the SAC didn't come to the Command Post.

Kaely also knew Crisis Management agents were there as well as local law enforcement representatives. The police sent detectives to assist the FBI. And somewhere in the room was a local attorney. At least one had to be available for subpoenas, search warrants—whatever law enforcement needed to help them, when requested legal documents had to be issued quickly. Usually, at least two attorneys were on call at all times.

As they headed toward Bell, Kaely saw Chief Sawyer sitting at a table off to the side, going through files.

Bell shook their hands and then led to the table where Sawyer waited. They sat down next to him.

"Thanks for calling us about Marie Beck," Noah said.

Bell sat down on the other side of the table—covered with files and papers, evidence of a team hard at work—distancing himself from them. A power move. He wanted to make them feel isolated. Defensive.

"We should have moved faster to protect Kenneth Beck and his family," Sawyer said, looking up from the file in front of him. "I didn't take that note as seriously as I should have. I made a mistake."

"No, it's not your fault," Kaely said. "You had only a few hours to respond. Besides, Warden Galloway said they'd watch out for Kenny. No one considered Marie a target."

"Well, she should have been protected," Bell said, clearly perturbed. "Kenneth Beck and his wife."

"Of course, you're right," Sawyer said. "As I told you earlier, I take full responsibility." Kaely could tell he was trying to calm the situation. "The agents followed protocol to the letter. It wasn't their fault."

Bell sighed. "These agents should have brought the note directly to us."

"Wait a minute," Kaely said. "We're not part of this team. We were asked by Chief Sawyer to come here specifically to interview my father and try to find anyone he might be using at the prison to orchestrate these killings. If we'd taken the note to you, we wouldn't have been following procedure. The police are still in charge of this investigation. You're here at their request, as are we."

"That's enough, agent," Bell said. "You're skating on thin ice."

"No, that's enough from *you*," Sawyer said, his expression hardening. "Agent Quinn is right. We're not going to sit here and throw mud at each other. We're going to get back to work so we can stop this madman."

"Do you have the note to Kenny here now?" Noah asked, obviously trying to follow the chief's lead.

Sawyer nodded. "Yes. And the FBI Evidence Response Team will send it to the lab at Quantico."

"The notes with the Scripture found in the victims' mouths were analyzed," Bell said. "They were typed, and on paper that can be found anywhere. No fingerprints. And that prison laptop with the same Bible verse is here. We have an analyst working on it. He's one of our best. If anyone can figure out where that communication came from, he can."

Kaely gazed around the room, trying to find the man working on the laptop. She finally spotted him at a desk next to the far wall. She didn't have a good feeling about the results of his search. Their UNSUB was smart. He wouldn't leave a trace of himself on the computer or fingerprints on the notes. She was certain all roads would lead to . . . nothing.

The woman with the dark hair Kaely had assumed was the ASAC walked over to them. She noticed Bell scoot back in his chair, the corners of his mouth turned down and his jaw tight. It was clear to Kaely that he resented her.

"Special Agents Hunter and Quinn, this is the Assistant Special Agent in Charge, Pauline Harper," he said.

She sat down near them. "I'm sorry to be late. I needed to take care of something."

"Glad to meet you, ASAC Harper," Noah said. "We're distressed about our UNSUB killing Marie Beck. But as awful as it is, this confirms the person we're looking for is probably inside the prison."

"It certainly looks that way," she said. "But let's not shut the door on other possibilities just yet."

Kaely understood Harper's concern, but her gut told her they were looking for someone working at Anamosa. Someone who wanted to send Kenneth Beck a message.

"Are you looking into Kenneth Beck, Chief Sawyer?" Harper asked. "In cases like this, the spouse has to be our first suspect."

"Yes. Beck claims Marie went to the store last night but never returned. We're investigating his story, but so far everything checks out. The ME is working on time of death, and we'll know more after the postmortem." Sawyer shook his head. "I truly believe this murder was retribution for Beck's interaction with these agents."

"I feel the same way," Harper said, "but we need to be sure."

Sawyer nodded. "We'll continue to investigate that angle."

"Chief, I'm sure you're feeling some anxiety about the threat-

NANCY MEHL

ening note sent to Mr. Beck," Harper said, running her hand through her dark hair. "Don't. Everyone followed procedure. Putting a watch on Beck's house would have been premature. First you should have confirmed it was a serious threat, and there just wasn't time." She offered Sawyer a tight smile. "Let's move on. If we get bogged down in what we think we should have done, we won't be focused on what we should do next."

"Thank you, ASAC Harper," he said.

"Let's make that Pauline. Doesn't take as long to say."

Everyone around the table laughed.

"Thank you, Pauline," the chief said. "I'm Everett."

"Okay, Everett. So what can we do for you? How do you want to proceed?" She looked at Noah and Kaely and then turned back to him. "We can call in the BAU, if you'd like."

Kaely felt her stomach tense. She just couldn't lose this case. Not now. She knew she could break it.

Sawyer shook his head. "No, thanks. I'd like to keep going with Agents Hunter and Quinn. I think Agent Quinn is uniquely qualified to get us the information we need. I have complete confidence in her. In both of them. They're a great team."

Harper nodded. "I agree."

Kaely was shocked to hear her say that. She'd expected her to recommend bringing in the BAU. The FBI took great stock in their capabilities—and they should. They were the best. Why would Harper urge the chief to keep her and Noah here? She studied the ASAC, but nothing in her manner revealed what she was thinking.

"I want to sit down with my father again," Kaely said. "He's talking to me. I believe I can get you the information you want."

"Actually, he's already asked for another meeting," Sawyer said.

"He has?"

191

Sawyer nodded. "Since it's become clear that our UNSUB is most likely someone inside the prison"—he glanced at Harper—"or someone closely associated with the UNSUB's contact, you're still our best hope to find the person we're looking for. When do you want to talk to your father again?"

Kaely breathed a sigh of relief. The case was still theirs. "I'd like to see him tomorrow. Today is too soon. He needs time to think about Marie Beck's death. I think this might be another misstep from our copycat." She looked at Sawyer. "You need to get that information to him. Please contact Warden Galloway. He can find a way to let Ed know what happened. I'm not sure he wanted Marie Beck killed. He never chose people he knew or had any connection to as his victims. First there was the note in the victims' mouths. Now this. If these moves belong solely to the UNSUB, it won't sit well with my father. I want to use his anger to make him turn on his protégé."

"That sounds good," Sawyer said. "But Warden Galloway wants Ed to stay shackled this time. And I agree with him. After what happened last time, we can't take chances."

Kaely felt their talk would go better with her father unshackled, but with Chief Sawyer and the warden in agreement, she had no choice. Besides, after the tragedy following the note Kenny received, Kaely was forced to go along with whatever guidelines the warden put down. "All right. Whatever you say."

"Okay. Good." Sawyer swung his gaze to Noah. "Tomorrow you'll start talking to some of the inmates, Agent Hunter." Then he turned to face Kaely again. "And we'll make sure your father is ready for an interview as well, Agent Quinn. Since Warden Galloway won't be on duty, you'll be coordinating with Deputy Warden Clark. We've set up an interview for both of you with Kenneth Beck this afternoon. He asked for you since he knows you. We think that, under the circumstances, it's best to agree to his request. He's been through a lot. I'm grateful he's willing to talk to us so soon after losing his wife."

"That's great," Kaely said. Kenny might be the best witness so far. He knew people at the prison. Knew her father. The police had interviewed friends and relatives of previous victims and hadn't been able to find anything helpful. No one had seen anything. No one knew anyone who might want the victim dead. Kaely would like to see those interviews, but if Sawyer wanted her to go over them, he'd ask. And he hadn't. Kaely had no authority to request the records, so her choices were limited. Kenny was her best chance to locate the UNSUB. Or at least find someone else who might have the information they needed.

"What time is he going to be at the prison?" Noah asked.

"We can't risk your being seen with him there," Sawyer said. "Too dangerous. He'll be at Nona's Coffee Shop and Bakery. Two o'clock." He looked at Kaely. "Do you know it?"

She shook her head. "No. Sorry."

"Okay," Sawyer said. "I'll text the address to you. After you talk to him, call me. Let me know anything you learn from him that helps."

"We will," Kaely said. "And will you keep us updated if you discover something helpful? I know you don't have to, but anything you can tell me that will help me with my father . . ."

"Of course," Sawyer said. "I'm putting pressure on Warden Galloway to set up those interviews with the guards as soon as possible. I'm confident they'll begin on Monday."

"Thank you."

Harper stood. "And we'll contact you if we find anything helpful as well." Then she walked away, heading toward the guy working on the laptop. It seemed their conversation was over.

"That's just the way she is," Sawyer said. "Don't take it personally."

Bell also got up and left. Kaely looked at Noah, who rolled his eyes.

"That guy wants to run the show," Sawyer said, too quietly for anyone else to hear. "Every time Harper pulls rank, his nose gets out of joint." He shook his head. "I think he's a smart man with good insight, but he's not really a team player."

"ASAC Harper seems competent," Noah said.

"She is. I'm thankful to be working with her." Sawyer pulled a copy of the newspaper Kaely had seen the day before from under the files in front of him. "Interesting article."

She sighed. "I suppose everyone here hates my guts."

He shook his head. "Actually, Harper addressed the team. Told them this wasn't your fault—and threatened the career of anyone who even entertained the thought of contacting the media. She's determined to find out who was behind this."

"We have an idea but no proof," Noah said.

"Wanna share?"

Kaely shook her head. "Not now. If the person is innocent, having the full power of ASAC Pauline Harper after him . . . I wouldn't wish that on anyone."

Sawyer laughed. "I understand." He stood and faced them. "Good luck with your father tomorrow." He lowered his voice again. "To be honest, we're not getting anywhere here. This guy is outthinking us, staying one step ahead. Harper and Bell are both frustrated, and so am I. I'm praying you two find something to help us."

"Well, we believe the killer is connected to the prison," Noah said. "Once we find out how he used the laptop, we'll be able to narrow down who he might be. If he did it directly, then he *has* to be on-site. I heard what Harper said about other possibilities, but I just don't think so. This person would have to have contact with Ed, the UNSUB, Kenny—*and* be able to get information out of the prison. Our UNSUB is inside Anamosa."

"I agree," Sawyer said. "But there are a lot of people in that prison."

"But not many who have access to the office where the computer was," Kaely said. "It's really important for us to learn how that message got there."

Sawyer nodded. "You're right."

Kaely sighed. "I can't stop thinking about Marie Beck."

"Best to take Pauline's advice. Hindsight is twenty-twenty. The best thing we can do for her now is find her killer."

Noah and Kaely shook hands with the chief and said goodbye, and then they were almost to the door when a woman stopped them.

"Agent Quinn, we received a call from someone who says she knows you. She's asking you to call her." The agent looked down at a piece of paper. "Do you know someone named Georganna Williamson? She says you knew her as Georganna Hobson."

Kaely felt herself sway. Noah grabbed her as she reached for the piece of paper. Georganna Hobson? Georgie.

TWENTY-EIGHT

Noah held on to Kaely all the way to the car. She'd been the last one to drive, and he held out his hand for the keys. She pulled them out of her pocket and handed them to him without any argument. Once they were both inside the car, he said, "Your face went completely white in there. What's wrong. Are you sick?"

Without saying a word, Kaely handed him the note she'd been given by the agent inside the CP.

He read it and frowned. "I'm sorry. I heard what the agent said, but I don't understand . . ." His eyes widened as he looked over the note once again. "Georganna?" He searched her face. "Is this . . . Georgie? The real Georgie?"

She nodded.

Noah was silent for a moment. Then he said, "So reality is invading unreality. Wow. That's . . ." He shook his head. "I don't know what that's like, I guess. But I mean, couldn't this be a good thing? You could be getting your friend back."

"I . . . I don't know. I mean, if I talk to the real Georgie, what will happen to the only Georgie I know?"

"Uh, can I remind you that the Georgie you know isn't real? How can anything happen to her?"

Noah was surprised to see tears in Kaely's eyes. "Why are you crying?" he asked as gently as he could. He wasn't sure how to handle this, but he felt the need to tread carefully. "Maybe you won't need her anymore, Kaely. Wouldn't it be nice to have a real friend?"

Kaely shook her head. "You don't get it."

"I'm trying to. You have to admit, this is a rather strange situation. I'm not sure what to say here, but I want to help."

Kaely touched his arm. "I'm sorry. I know that." She took the note from his hand, then folded it before sliding it into her pocket. She looked at her watch. "We have three hours until we meet with Kenny. I'd like to go someplace where we can talk for a while. Lay out the whole case. I need to see it."

"Sure. I think that's a good idea. I noticed a Thai restaurant not too far from here. How does that sound?"

"Good. I love Thai food." She took a deep breath, obviously trying to calm herself. "Again, sorry for the emotional reaction. I was just . . . surprised. I assume Georganna saw the article in the paper and realized I'm in town."

Noah started the car and headed toward the street in front of the CP. "You said her parents came between you two after your father was arrested?"

"Yeah. Like I told you before, they were wonderful people. Her house was my second home. I loved it there. They were such a happy family. So much joy. Georganna has two brothers. They were really funny, and they used to tease us. It was great." She was quiet for a moment. "I'm certain her parents were just concerned about her. If there had been more time, I think they would have relented. But we left for the safe house soon after, so they never had a chance to change their minds. Then, after my father was sentenced, we moved to Nebraska."

"There wasn't a trail, so they couldn't find you."

"Right." She sighed. "I'm not sure if I should return her call."

"Of course, it's up to you, but I hope you do. She went to a lot of trouble trying to get that message to you. If we leave here and you don't contact her . . ."

"I might regret it for a long time," Kaely finished for him.

She sighed again. "You're right. But for now, let's concentrate on finding our UNSUB, okay?"

"Sure. No pressure from me."

"Thanks, Noah. I really don't know what I'd do without you."

He didn't say anything. He was still shaken about the message Kaely had gotten from her invisible UNSUB in Darkwater. The comment had to have come from her own fears. But what did it mean? Was this some kind of self-fulfilling prophecy? He tried to push away his concerns so he could concentrate on the here and now. He realized that was getting harder and harder to do.

They were almost to the restaurant when Kaely's phone rang. She took it out of her pocket and smiled. "Jason."

"Tell him I said hello." Noah liked Kaely's younger brother. He was always so positive, and Kaely needed that kind of encouragement in her life.

"Hi there, brother," she said into her phone. She listened for a moment before saying, "I don't know if that's a good idea. This isn't the place for a family reunion. My meetings with Dad are only to learn how he's controlling a vicious serial killer."

Obviously, Jason wanted to come to Anamosa while Kaely was here. Interesting. It seemed as if the past was converging on her. Noah hoped she'd tell him to come. He could use some backup with Kaely.

"Well, it seems as if you're determined, so come on." Kaely gave him the name and address of their hotel. "You can probably stay with me," she told him, "but let me check on that." She paused a moment. "I'll have to contact the FBI and tell them you're coming."

After a few seconds of silence, she said, "Okay. I understand. There's another hotel right across the street from us." She turned toward Noah. "What's the name of that place?"

"Northbrook Inn." He was surprised she didn't know. Kaely's eidetic memory was extraordinary. They saw that hotel every time they left their own building. Forgetting the name of the hotel was one more sign she wasn't firing on all cylinders.

After talking to Jason a few more minutes, Kaely ended the call and slid her phone back into her pocket.

"He's coming, then?" Noah asked.

She nodded. "I wish he wouldn't. This isn't the time for a visit. I'm not here for that. I'm not sure he'll understand."

"Jason's pretty easygoing. I think he'll respect what you're trying to do."

"Well, he didn't respect me enough to tell me he was visiting our father."

"You know why he didn't."

"Yeah, I do. I haven't said anything to him yet, but we'll talk about it when he gets here."

"By the way, what's the latest update on your mom?"

Kaely's mother had been diagnosed with cancer, but the last time Kaely had talked with her, an alternative treatment seemed to be having good results.

"She's still doing great," Kaely said with a smile. "Her doctor expects a complete recovery."

"I'm thrilled to hear that." Why hadn't she told him sooner? As soon as he asked himself the question, he knew the answer. It was because he'd drawn back from her over the last few months. She probably hadn't felt comfortable sharing anything so personal. Great. Now he felt guilty.

"She's started going back to church," Kaely continued. "She's found a small congregation near her house where the people have really welcomed her. She was bitter about the way our church acted after my father was arrested. They turned their backs on us."

"I'm sorry about that. That's not how churches should be."

"You said you went to church with Tracy before she died. How did they treat you?"

Noah shrugged. "They were great. Brought over enough food to keep me eating for months. I had to use a friend's freezer to store some of it. They did everything they could to help me." He shook his head. "I was the one who walked away from them. It wasn't anything they did. I was angry because Tracy believed so strongly that God would heal her. And then He didn't."

Kaely was quiet for a moment. "Those kinds of situations are hard to understand."

"I'm so sick and tired of hearing that." Noah hadn't meant his tone to be so harsh. Kaely turned her face away from him. He'd upset her. This wasn't the time to express his anger toward God.

"I'm sorry," he said. "Still have some issues." He tried to tamp down his irritation. Christians always seemed to have the answers—until life went south. Then all they could say was *Some things are hard to understand.* What a cop-out.

"I'm sorry," she said, her voice soft. "I seem to be apologizing a lot today." She fastened her dark eyes on him. "We live in a fallen world, Noah, with an evil enemy who seeks to destroy us. But the truth is he really can't. Maybe it seems to you that Tracy lost her battle. In a way you're right, but you have to remember that Tracy isn't dead. She's in heaven, healed and whole. Her prayers were answered. Maybe not the way you wanted, but still, the enemy didn't win. He lost."

She paused. "I know you miss her. You know, this life goes by so fast. Like the blink of an eye. But eternity is . . . forever. Maybe that doesn't help you, but it's the truth." She touched his arm again. "God didn't kill her, Noah. He loves her, and He loves you. I can't tell you what happened, but I can say you're mad at the wrong person. It's the devil who kills, steals, and destroys. God welcomed her into heaven. Tracy is happier than she's ever been."

Maybe Kaely was right. Maybe the anger he'd had toward God was misplaced. He'd never thought about how his pain might not be His fault.

He stared straight ahead. He couldn't think about this now. He almost found it amusing. Kaely didn't want to think about Georgie, and he didn't want to think about Tracy. How long could they ignore what confused and hurt them? The job couldn't always come first. Eventually they'd both have to deal with some harsh truths—or they'd never be completely whole.

TWENTY-NINE

Noah pulled into the parking lot of the Thai place he'd seen. On the way there, Kaely had called Solomon to tell him Jason was determined to come to Anamosa. When she'd hung up, she told Noah that although Solomon wasn't crazy about the idea, there was no way he could stop Jason. The FBI was just watching over him, not putting him in custody.

Noah didn't say anything, but he honestly felt Jason would be safer here with him and Kaely.

Soon they were sitting at a corner table in the restaurant, both munching on crab Rangoon. He ordered the Nam Tok Beef and Kaely asked for pineapple fried rice. The food was exceptional. About halfway through their lunch, Kaely took out a notebook.

"Okay," she said, "let's start from the beginning. Someone buries six new bodies next to nine older ones in an abandoned rail yard in Des Moines, the city where the so-called Raggedy Man killed fourteen women. The older bodies appear to be his work, which brings his total to . . . twenty-three."

Kaely stumbled over her last words. It was obviously difficult for her to face the evil acts committed by her father. Noah really couldn't imagine how it felt to have a dad who was a serial killer. His father was . . . a father. Kind, caring, funny. He still questioned Noah about his car, making sure he was taking care of it. "Have you changed your oil lately?" he'd ask when they talked on the phone. "Remember to have it checked regularly.

And keep a tire pressure gauge in your glove compartment." Although he didn't say *I love you* often, he constantly showed Noah love through his actions. Just thinking about his dad made him a little homesick. Time for a visit.

Kaely had fallen silent, probably thinking about the women who were dead because of Ed Oliphant.

Noah gently picked up the thread. "We know our UNSUB has had some kind of contact with your father because of the wire angel in the victims' hands as well as knowing where his other bodies were buried. Only your father could have told him those things."

Kaely took a deep breath. "Right. The wire angel component was never released to the public. But of course, some people knew about it. Law enforcement involved with the case. Anyone connected to the court who could access the records. But no one knew about the field except my father. That sealed it."

"Somehow the UNSUB knew you would come to Iowa," Noah said. "That means we have to be suspicious of everyone connected to the case."

Kaely sighed. "I honestly don't believe Sawyer or John Howard could be working with my father."

"What about Tobias Bell?"

Kaely was quiet as she considered his question. "He's got an ego, but I find it hard to believe he's involved."

Noah shrugged. "So maybe your father refused to answer any questions because he figured Sawyer wouldn't have any other options but to control you?"

"Maybe," Kaely said, slowly drawing out the word. "But it's a long shot."

Noah nodded. "I don't see any other explanation."

"Let's put that on the back burner for now," Kaely said, frowning.

"Kaely, why a wire angel?" Noah asked. "Did Ed ever explain that?"

She shook her head. "I have no earthly idea. He never made anything like that at home. He had a small workshop in the garage, and I saw rolls of wire there, but it never occurred to me that was unusual. Kids don't pay attention to stuff like that. And since authorities never released the part about the angels, we wouldn't have been alerted anyway."

"You know, it's almost a miracle that no one leaked that information to the public."

Kaely nodded. "I agree, but there really wasn't any reason for it. In the end the district attorney's office had all the evidence they needed. Like I told you, thankfully, my father pleaded guilty, saving us from going through a trial."

"Do you really think he did that for your benefit? Because your mom asked him to? Doesn't sound like something a man who didn't care about his family would do."

"My *mother* thinks he did it because she asked him to. Maybe he did, but to be honest, I don't buy it. I think he did it because he knew they had him. What was the point?"

"But don't serial killers usually like attention? Wouldn't a trial have given him more media exposure?"

Kaely frowned at him. "Can we get back to this case?"

"Sure. Sorry." Why was she deflecting? Was she really convinced her father had no feelings for her? He wasn't so sure.

"The UNSUB buried the last victim in that rail yard closer to the surface," Kaely said. "He wanted her to be found. He was ready to reveal himself."

Noah nodded. "But the people who found her probably bumped up his timeline."

Kaely was quiet for a moment. "He plans so carefully. I wonder how that affected him."

Noah popped a piece of beef into his mouth and thought about what Kaely had just said. "Well, it didn't seem to knock him off course. He already had someone else in his sights. He killed the woman they found in front of the gas station. The ME said she was murdered on Tuesday night, and she was found Wednesday morning."

"Yeah, he seems under control, but then he kills Marie. That couldn't have been planned. Somehow, he found out Kenny had talked to us. This was some kind of punishment."

Noah nodded. "He does go off script, then."

Kaely stared down at her food. "Which makes it hard to anticipate his next move."

"What else do we know for certain?"

Kaely took a deep breath. "We know our UNSUB has had contact with my father. He knows who this guy is." Kaely hit her fist on the table. "He's just as responsible for these deaths as if he were killing the women himself." She fastened her gaze on Noah. "It makes me so angry."

"I know. But anger won't get him to talk to you."

"I realize that." Kaely took a drink of her water. "It's so hard to sit across from him, Noah."

"I know."

She stabbed a piece of pineapple with her fork. "Okay, back to the case. Like I said, we know for sure that my father is communicating with the UNSUB. And now we also know our copycat is either inside the prison or has close contact with someone there. He knew about Kenneth Beck. Was able to find his wife. Your upcoming interviews will be so important. You may actually talk to our UNSUB or an individual who's working with him. If the computer tech decides the message on the laptop was written by someone who actually entered that office, then we've narrowed it down more. Someone who has access to that locked area is involved."

"Of course, it's possible our UNSUB may have found a way to get around the security system."

"True. At this point we can't rule out any possibilities. I understand the secure wing is pretty new. What about technicians who helped set it up? Of course, with the password changing frequently, that probably isn't realistic." She pointed her fork at him. "When you're doing your interviews, be really careful. Don't tip your hand."

"You're worried."

"Yeah, the message on the computer tells me he knows things he shouldn't know unless he—or she—is watching us. Even if the message was sent from somewhere offsite, how did the UNSUB know we would be assigned that room? Just the fact that it was the only one available doesn't seem to be enough. It still bothers me."

Noah put down his fork. "You said 'she.' I thought most serial killers are men."

"They are. But some have been women. Aileen Wuornos. And Jane Toppan."

"Who?"

"Toppan killed dozens of people in the late 1800s. Then there was Nannie Doss. She murdered five husbands, a mother-in-law, her sisters, two of their children, and her own mother."

"Yikes. I guess you could include the Charles Manson women in that list." He studied her for a moment. "Why did you bring that up? Do you think our UNSUB could be a woman?"

Kaely shrugged. "I don't know."

"You're still thinking about Dr. Engle. You think a Christian woman is murdering women?"

"Anyone can call themselves a Christian," Kaely said, darkly. "My father went to church. Dennis Rader was a church leader."

"But could she overpower them?"

"With a stun gun? Sure." Kaely rubbed the back of her neck. "Maybe I'm reaching, but Engle is the only person we know who's actually talking to my father, and she could have easily obtained access to that laptop."

"Yeah. I guess we can't rule out anyone, and her office is right down the hall."

"Look, I'm not saying it's her, but we need to figure out who it could be. Fast. A prisoner? One of the guards? Warden Galloway, Dr. Engle, Deputy Warden Clark?" She pointed her finger at Noah. "That one guy. You know. The guard who looked so menacing? He saw us talking to Kenny. He should be the first interview on your list of guards. What was his name? Raymond Cooper?"

He nodded. "But he couldn't gain access to that secure area, right? Nor could another guard or an inmate. Unless, as you suggested, they gained access to the special code."

Noah watched as she tapped her fingernails on the tabletop after she pushed away most of her lunch. He hoped they'd find something soon to bring this case to an end. He wasn't sure Kaely could hold it together much longer. But what could he do about it? He didn't know, but he couldn't just stand by and watch her come apart. He was convinced she shouldn't have come here. The FBI might be her life, but they'd asked too much of her this time. He was learning that the indestructible Kaely Quinn was a myth. In the end, she was just a flesh-and-blood woman, as easily broken as anyone else.

THIRTY

Kaely and Noah got to the coffee shop before Kenny did. Noah offered to get them both coffee. Kaely decided to be adventurous and asked for a caramel frappe. It was delicious. She hadn't been able to finish her lunch because her stomach was tied in knots. Thankfully, the icy coffee drink easily slid down her throat, for some reason soothing her.

She was having a tough time concentrating. Maybe she was just tired. She'd decided to get to bed early tonight since after they talked to Kenny, they'd be through for the day. She felt a little guilty about interviewing him so soon after his wife's murder, but the police detectives wouldn't allow them to interview family members of any of the other victims.

She also felt guilty about Marie Beck's murder even though Pauline Harper had tried to convince the team—especially Sawyer—they couldn't have moved fast enough to stop it. Marie was found in a parking lot not far from where the last victim had been found, her body dumped behind a church. When the church janitor emptied the trash last night, he'd found her. She'd been killed just like the others.

Kaely had just taken another sip of her frappe when Kenny walked in. He was wearing a cap pulled low as if trying to hide his face. Probably afraid for his life. Poor guy.

He went to the counter and ordered an iced coffee. Then he came to their table. "Thanks for meeting me here," he said. "I can't take a chance of being seen with you at the prison." He sat down across from her and Noah. "Of course, there's not much more they can do to hurt me. They've taken Marie. If they kill me, they might be doing me a favor." Tears filled his eyes, and he reached for one of the napkins in the dispenser on the table. "Sorry," he said.

"Nothing you need to apologize for," Noah said. "We can't help feeling as if some of this is our fault. Obviously, someone saw you talking to us."

Kenny shook his head. "It isn't your fault. Please don't think that way. The only person at fault here is the person who murdered my Marie."

"Kenny, do you have any suspicions? Someone you think might be involved?" Kaely asked.

Kenny's eyes darted around the room as if trying to make sure he wasn't being watched. Finally, he nodded. "Look, you might think this sounds crazy, but there's this guard. Raymond? He's the one who wanted me to hurry up and get all that stuff for you to look through."

"Raymond Cooper?" Kaely said. "I remember him, and we've since seen him hanging around. He gives me the creeps. You think he might be involved?"

"I . . . I don't know. But like I told you, he spends a lot of time with Dr. Engle." He shrugged. "It's just . . . odd." The tightness in Kaely's stomach increased. "Are you saying you think they're in this together?" That would explain a lot. There had been quite a few serial killer couples. Is this what they were dealing with? If so, the profile Kaely had been shaping in her mind was completely wrong. Just like everything else she'd done lately. Why couldn't she get a handle on this UNSUB? Why was she having so much trouble concentrating?

"Is the only reason you suspect this Raymond person and the doctor because they spend time together?" Noah asked. Kaely could hear the doubt in his voice. He was right. That wasn't enough of a reason for Noah and Kaely to suspect them.

"No, not really. It's the way they act when they're together. As if they don't want to be overheard. I walked past the doctor's office not long ago. The door was partly open, and Cooper saw me. If looks could kill, I would have dropped dead. He got up and closed the door as quickly as he could."

"Did you hear anything they were saying?" Kaely asked.

Kenny shrugged. "I heard their voices, but I wasn't paying attention. Didn't know I needed to."

"I understand." She couldn't help but be a little disappointed. Kenny's information wasn't really helpful. "We'll look into it. Maybe he's not the person we're looking for, but he could be working with our killer." She paused for a moment before saying, "Kenny, do you mind if I ask you about what happened the night Marie was killed?"

"No. I want to help."

"Tell me how you think the killer was able to get to her."

"She . . . she was going to the store. We had planned to watch a movie, and we were out of popcorn." His voice choked. "Marie loved popcorn. I should have gone for it, but I wasn't feeling well. My sinuses were giving me fits."

"And she just didn't return?" Kaely had read the police report that morning and knew all the details, but she was hoping Kenny might add something they'd missed. Something that would help them.

He nodded. "When she didn't come home right away, I tried to call her on her cell phone. No answer. After about an hour, I got in our other vehicle and went looking for her. When I found her car in the grocery store parking lot, I went inside, but I couldn't locate her. Even had a store employee call for her over the intercom." He sighed shakily. "I went back to the car, but she still hadn't returned. That's when I called the police. But it never occurred to me even once that her disappearance had anything to do with the Copycat Killer." He shrugged. "Your mind just doesn't go there, you know? Something like that can't happen to you or someone you love. It always happens to someone else."

"The police didn't find anything when they went to the scene?" Kaely asked.

"No. Nothing. Everything was gone, along with her purse and her phone. They were able to identify her only because Marie had her ATM card in her pocket. She'd withdrawn some cash earlier in the day."

No purse at the scene. No phone. He was taking trophies. That was a good thing. Find the trophies. Find the UNSUB.

Kaely's phone rang, and she pulled it out of her pocket. Jason. "I'm sorry, I need to take this," she said. "I'll be right back."

She answered her phone and asked Jason to wait, then walked outside. "Sorry," she said. "Talking to a guy whose wife was killed by our UNSUB. I feel so sorry for him."

"I can talk to you later," Jason said.

"It's okay. He isn't really giving us anything that will help. When will you be here?"

"Tomorrow afternoon. I've made reservations at the hotel across from you."

"Still not sure this is a good idea. Like I told you, I'm not having a kumbaya moment with Dad. I'm trying to stop a serial killer."

"I get it. But has it occurred to you that I might be able to help? That maybe he'll tell me something he won't tell you?"

"No, Jason. Don't bring up our UNSUB with him. You could ruin everything. I'm working hard to develop trust. If he thinks I sent you in to talk to him—"

"Okay, sis. I get it. Chill out. I'll keep my visit family oriented. I've been told you found out I've been to the prison before. I think Dad and I have a pretty good relationship."

Kaely wanted to laugh. Ed Oliphant couldn't have *good relationships*. He was showing Jason whatever he thought his son wanted to see. But Kaely couldn't tell her brother that without hurting him, so she kept that knowledge to herself.

"Wish you'd told me about your visits."

"Sorry. I just didn't want to argue with you."

"We'll talk about it when you get here."

"Will you be armed?"

In spite of herself, Kaely laughed. "We'll see. I'm meeting with Dad tomorrow afternoon, so I'll phone you when I get back to the hotel. Let's plan on going out to dinner."

"Sounds good. At some point while I'm there, let's drive into Des Moines and eat at Mort's."

"Went there right after we checked into the field office. Great minds think alike. That sounds wonderful. Let's do it."

"Awesome. And, sis?"

"Yeah?"

"I can't wait to see you again."

Kaely smiled to herself. "Me too. Love you, little brother."

"Same to you."

Jason said good-bye and hung up. Kaely put her phone in her pocket and went back into the coffee shop. When she got to the table, she found Kenny telling Noah about his wife. She could tell Noah was moved. These two men had been through the same kind of loss. Kaely sat down and listened, but she didn't say anything. This was something they understood in a way she couldn't.

"She had sable-brown hair," Kenny was saying. "And the greenest eyes I've ever seen. She had a way of smiling that made everyone around her feel better." He blinked away tears. "How am I going to live without her? And how can I live with the knowledge that my job cost Marie her life?" He shook his head and stared into his coffee cup. "She didn't want me to work at the prison. Thought it was too dangerous. She was afraid I'd be hurt . . . or killed. How could I know that she would be the one most affected by my decision? If only I could take it back."

"Kenny, it's obvious you loved your wife," Noah said. "You've got to understand that unless you took that job knowing it would lead to her death, you can't blame yourself. You chose a job. You didn't choose to lose Marie."

Kenny looked up at Noah. Kaely could see that Noah's words had brought some comfort. They'd also helped her see her own role more clearly. If she'd had any idea Marie was in danger, she would have moved heaven and earth to protect her. No matter how many times she went over it, she couldn't see a way she and Noah could have done anything differently. The people at the CP had been responsible for protecting Kenny and his family. She and Noah weren't given the authority to do so.

"Why Marie?" Kenny asked, his question directed at Kaely.

"I don't know," she answered truthfully. "But I imagine it was a warning of some kind."

"To me?"

"Not necessarily. It might have been directed toward someone else. Sending a message that if they told us too much—if they revealed what they knew—the same thing would happen to someone they loved."

Kenny's face paled. "Marie died as a warning? That's all her life meant to some . . . twisted psycho?" He stared past Kaely as if he saw someone standing behind her. "She meant a lot more to me than that." He looked back and forth between them. "Please, let me help. Give me a way to help catch him. I need to do this for Marie."

Kaely understood his anger, but he could cause more trouble for all of them if he tried to inject himself into the investigation. "Please, Kenny," she said softly. "Go home. Bury your wife. Mourn. Give it some time. When you're better, contact us. If we're still here, we'll let you know if there's something you can do. But I hope by that time, we'll have him. Then you can watch him get thrown in jail, where he'll spend the rest of his life."

"Do you think he'll come to Anamosa?"

Kaely was pretty sure Kenny would be out of a job if that happened. "I have no idea. Let's not get ahead of ourselves. One step at a time, okay?"

"Okay. But I can't go back to work right now. Not until you catch this guy." Kaely felt compassion for the grief-stricken prison guard, but there really wasn't much she could do to help him.

"I'm sure you have friends," Noah said. "But if you need to talk . . ." He pulled out his wallet and took out a card. "Call me."

"Thanks, Agent Hunter. And I'm sorry about your wife."

"I appreciate that." Noah smiled at Kenny and turned to look at Kaely. "Who called?"

"Jason. He'll be here tomorrow afternoon. He'll rent a car at the airport and then check into the hotel across from ours. I'll call him when we get back to our hotel. Then we can all get together for dinner."

"Sounds good."

"I'd better go," Kenny said. "I have a lot of things to do. Planning a funeral is . . . tough. I wasn't prepared. Never thought I'd be doing this now."

He stood and shook hands with both of them. "Thank you

for working so hard to find this piece of scum. And again, if I can do anything to help you, call me. Day or night."

"We will. Thanks, Kenny," Noah said. "We'll be praying for you."

"Thank you. That means more than you know."

With that, Kenny left. Kaely watched him through the glass windows that surrounded them. "Poor guy," she said as Noah sat down.

"I know."

"You're going to pray for him?"

Noah grunted. "I can pray if I want to."

"Of course you can," Kaely said. She smiled as she took another sip of her coffee.

THIRTY-ONE

So . . . what do you think?" Noah asked Kaely after getting another cup of coffee.

"I think we need to follow up on Raymond and the doctor. She's certainly smart enough to be our UNSUB. Maybe Raymond is carrying out her instructions."

"Obviously our UNSUB was watching Kenny's home and followed Marie to the store," Noah said. "The police and the FBI will have followed up on that. Asking neighbors if they noticed anything. Is it too much to hope someone saw the UNSUB?"

"Maybe. I'd love to know."

"But we can't ask the FBI about it because we're only supposed to be working inside the prison." Noah knew he sounded glum.

Kaely pulled out her phone and scrolled through her numbers before selecting one and making a call. "Chief Sawyer," she said, nodding at Noah. "We just met with Kenny. He mentioned a couple of people you might want to follow up on."

Noah listened as she brought the chief up to date on Raymond Cooper and Dr. Engle. Then she said, "I wonder if you found anything helpful when Kenny's neighbors were questioned."

Noah grinned. She was giving him something and hoping he'd reciprocate. But would the chief really share information with them about the investigation? Kaely was quiet for a while. Finally, she said, "Thank you. Talk to you soon." Then she hung up and shrugged.

"Nothing. One lady walking her dog saw Marie leave the house. Another neighbor knows when Kenny left to go check on Marie because he accidentally set off his alarm when he unlocked his car. I guess he does that frequently. She was watching her favorite TV show, so she was able to give the police a pretty precise time. The store confirms that Kenneth showed up there when he said he did and asked them to page his wife. The police have ruled him out as a suspect." She sighed. "Unfortunately, no one noticed anything else. No car that shouldn't have been there. No one who might have followed Marie."

"People don't pay attention," Noah said. "The UNSUB could have been there, but unless people have a reason to watch for something unusual, they don't see anything. Our guy could have waited until the dog walker turned the corner before taking off after Marie."

"That's what I was thinking." Kaely looked at her watch. "I'd like to head back to the hotel, if it's okay with you. I want to prepare for my interview with my father tomorrow."

"Kaely . . ." Would she get angry if he asked what she intended to do tonight?

She frowned at him. "What?"

"I'm concerned. Are you going to profile our UNSUB?"

She looked away from him. Noah noticed she was chewing on her lower lip, a clear sign that she was thinking. Then she took a drink of her coffee. Stalling. When she put down her cup, she finally met his gaze. "I don't know. I'd like to try."

"I told you I don't want you to do that."

Kaely smiled. "The UNSUB isn't actually there, you know." The smile slipped from her face. "It's true I let my own concerns filter into the last profile, the one in Darkwater, but I won't let that happen this time."

Noah ran a finger against the side of his cup. How far could he push this without watching her shut down? "Look, I just don't want you to risk it, okay?"

Kaely started to say something, but Noah shook his head. "No. Listen to me. If it should get out of control again . . ." He reached over and took her hand. "I'm worried about you, Kaely. Please."

"I really appreciate your concern. But I told you I'd let you know if I decide to work a profile, and I will. I promise." She pulled her hand away from his. "Remember, you're right next door. If I need you, I'll call for you."

"Let me be there with you. I won't interfere."

For a moment, he thought he'd gotten through to her, but then he saw a familiar look on her face. Resolve. She had no intention of giving in. Kaely Quinn was determined to face her demons alone. Noah sighed inwardly. There was no way their relationship could ever become anything more than what it was, a friendship along with a strong undercurrent of something else. Something more powerful that would never be explored unless Kaely lowered her defenses.

"All right," he said, an edge to his voice he hadn't intended. "We'd better go."

She didn't say anything, just picked up her cup and headed for the door.

Noah lagged behind, watching her walk out of the shop. Then he took his own cup to the counter and asked for a refill. He knew Kaely was waiting on him, but he didn't care. He wasn't at her beck and call.

His last victim had been carefully selected to let Kaely Quinn know he was close to her. He wanted to watch her squirm.

Blame herself for talking to one of the guards at the prison. Putting someone's wife in danger.

But now the game was going to change. He would be shadowing her closely. Waiting for an opportunity to do something unexpected. A line from an old movie came to mind. He would make her an offer she couldn't refuse. And when he did, she would come to him willingly.

And then he would kill her.

When they got back to the hotel, Kaely went to her room, first telling Noah she intended to order room service for dinner. She needed an evening alone. He seemed almost dismissive, but she knew he was worried about her. Although she trusted Noah, she had to take back her life. She'd allowed this assignment to shake her, and she couldn't afford to be less than her best.

"Maybe you should have taken him up on his offer."

Kaely looked at the couch to see Georgie wearing an accusatory expression.

"No. I don't need that. I'm okay."

"You're not sure that's true or I wouldn't be here."

Kaely shook her head. "Time for you to go." She watched, waiting for Georgie to disappear. Strangely, she continued to sit there, staring at her.

Finally, Georgie said, "So are you going to meet with me?"

"Meet with you? It seems I'm doing that now."

"You know what I mean."

"The real you?" Kaely sighed as she sat down on a chair. "I don't know. What should I do?"

"I thought you wanted me to leave. Now you're asking for advice?"

Kaely glared at the image of Georgie, who seemed unshaken by her obvious disapproval. "Yes, I am. What do you think?"

Georgie hung her head for a moment. When she looked up, Kaely was surprised to see tears in her eyes. But of course, she knew why they were there.

"You're afraid you'll disappear if I talk to the real Georgie," Kaely said softly. It wasn't said as a question. The thought had been in Kaely's mind ever since she'd received Georganna's message. She reached into her pocket and took out the note with her phone number. She stared at it for a while and then put it back into her pocket. She still wasn't sure what to do.

"I'm not going to call . . . just yet," she told Georgie, whose expression hadn't changed.

"Don't profile the UNSUB tonight. You don't have control. You know you don't."

Kaely shook her head. "You're wrong." She was angry. "I'm not crazy. I don't care what Dr. Engle thinks or what Noah thinks. I don't even care what you think." She found herself standing but didn't remember getting up. "I'm tired of everyone trying to take care of me. First it was Solomon, then Noah. Even you. It's got to stop."

"Why are you so upset?" Georgie asked, her brown eyes sparkling with concern.

"Get out!" Kaely shouted.

When Georgie disappeared, sadness washed over Kaely. Then tears rolled down her cheeks, which made her even angrier. Why was she crying again? Why couldn't she control these stupid emotions? Something Dr. Engle said floated into her thoughts. *What you've been through . . . having your life ravaged by finding out who your dad really was. It had to be devastating. Children who suddenly discover their parent isn't the person they thought they were . . . that they're capable of great evil*

. . . It can cause a child to fracture. To create unhealthy ways to protect themselves."

Was she fractured? Could the doctor be right? She thought she'd created Georgie because she wanted someone to talk to. But could the truth be that Georgie existed to protect her?

Even as the thoughts came to her, she rejected them. No. She was fine. She didn't need Dr. Engle's input. The truth was she didn't need anyone except God. She reminded herself that she was a skilled, trained behavioral analyst for the FBI. She was strong and self-sufficient. She'd be fine.

She found her notebook and a pen. Then she sat down at the table in the room and began to write down everything she could think of that pertained to this case. No matter what Georgie said, tonight she was going to attempt to talk to the Copycat Killer.

THIRTY-TWO

He picked up the phone and called his disciple. After he gave his instruction, he heard only hesitation. "Are you refusing my order?" he asked. "Do I need to remind you that I know where your family lives?"

"No, I'm not refusing. I'm sorry. But I don't want to get caught."

"You won't if you do this right." He ran through the plan he'd designed.

"All right. I'll take care of it."

"You'd better. And remember, I have ears inside the prison. If you try to betray me—"

"I won't. I promise."

"Don't forget, you have a lot to gain from this. The money I give you will get rid of all that debt and help you keep your house. I'm sure your wife and kids will appreciate that."

"I know. You're right."

"Okay. Do it tonight. And make sure it's done correctly. I want him dead."

"I understand."

"Toss this phone. Use one of the others I gave you. And remember, we only connect by phone. Never in person."

"I know. And I'll take care of the phone."

He hung up. He was excited to see this part of his plan finally happen. Tonight, after all these years, justice would begin. He felt tears forming in his eyes. Stunned, he lifted his finger and wiped away the dampness that trickled down his cheek. He couldn't remember the last time he'd really cried. When tears weren't used to manipulate someone. Maybe as a child, but never as an adult.

He shook his head. The anger that had fueled him ever since he'd found the truth overpowered all his other emotions. But he had been denied long enough, and he had more to do before the wrongs in his life would finally be set right. Now he was passing judgment on those who had taken what belonged to him.

His soft laughter was tinged with hate and bitterness—and anticipation. *They'll never see me coming.*

Ed opened his eyes, awakened from a deep sleep when someone called his name. Somehow, light flooded his cell, almost so bright he couldn't see. Was it morning already? He sat up and swung his feet over the edge of his bed, realizing that the light wasn't coming from the sun. His cell had no windows. How could this happen? But he wasn't afraid. Quite the opposite. The light was warm. Comforting.

Then suddenly his past played in front of him like a television show. His childhood. The abuse he and his sister had endured. The grief that had shattered him into a million pieces, the only love he'd known ripped from his heart.

Tears streamed down his cheeks, and he pushed himself out of his bunk and fell to his knees.

The same voice that called his name said, "'God so loved the world that He gave His only begotten Son, that whoever believes in Him should not perish but have everlasting life.'"

Ed cried out as the Deliverer touched his tortured soul. "Oh, God. Forgive me." He couldn't believe that the One who had seen all the evil he'd done loved him anyway. Between sobs, Ed whispered the words his son had taught him. What Jason had called the sinner's prayer. And at that moment, he felt God breathe life into him. The light in his cell entered his body, and Ed Oliphant felt the joy of becoming a brand-new creation.

Noah couldn't relax. He couldn't shake what Kaely had told him about the last time she'd profiled an UNSUB. That he'd told her she was going to die. And soon. Noah went to the refrigerator and took out the sandwich and beer he'd ordered earlier. He sat down on the couch and put his food on the coffee table. He unscrewed the top of the beer and took a long drink. It was true he hadn't had much to do with God since Tracy died, but that had started to change. Even though Kaely admitted she had a lot of healing still to do, he could see something in her that he wanted.

"So, God," he said aloud but in a low voice, "why does this threat from an invisible UNSUB scare me so much? Either Kaely is coming up with this stuff on her own, which is deeply troubling, or . . ."

Like Kaely, Tracy had believed in demonic influence, which Noah had always dismissed with skepticism. After a while, she quit mentioning it. But he hadn't forgotten her words. "We're in a battle, Noah," she'd said. "Good versus evil. Denying evil exists won't make it go away."

At the time, it seemed ridiculous. But Tracy wasn't a ridiculous person. She was smart. And realistic. He couldn't keep ignoring what she'd said. He trusted her.

He took another chug of his beer and sat the bottle down. Kaely was truly frightened by what she'd heard, so how could the words have come from her? What possibility did that leave besides demonic influence?

He quickly finished his meal and then put his tray in the hallway. He was pretty sure Kaely was going to work a profile tonight. He glanced at his watch. A little after ten. Had she already started? The possibility chilled him. Somehow, deep inside, he knew she shouldn't do this.

He planned to follow his gut, but before he did, it was time to take care of something he'd put off for too long. He needed to be completely prepared, and he could almost hear Tracy pleading with him on her deathbed. Tonight, her most ardent prayer would be answered.

Noah sat down on the couch and bowed his head.

Kaely finished her notes and spread them out on the table, glad she'd taken the time to change into sweats and eat a bite from room service. She could hear Georgie still whispering in her ear, but she ignored her pleas to stop. This is what Kaely did. More women were going to die if she didn't confront this UNSUB. Mr. Hoover looked up at her from the chair where he'd curled up to sleep. Then he put his head down and nodded off again.

She hadn't even begun her profile when she felt something dark and malevolent forming in the chair across from her. She started to talk to it, but for some reason her vocal cords felt almost frozen. She tried to get words out, but they were only gasps that didn't make sense. Fear began to roll over her when suddenly her phone rang. She'd meant to turn if off but had forgotten. She grabbed for it as if it were a life preserver and she was drowning in a sea of shadows. Just as quickly as the image across from her appeared, it vanished.

Kaely felt a release and stood up. Deciding she needed some air, she grabbed her cell and walked onto the balcony, quickly closing the door behind her so Mr. Hoover wouldn't follow her.

When she answered the phone, she listened to the man on the other end. When he finished, she acknowledged the message and hung up, then put the phone in her pocket and dropped to her knees. She couldn't stop sobs from pushing their way up from somewhere inside the deepest part of her. They came in waves.

When she heard the sliding doors from the next unit open, she was also aware of Noah's voice, but she couldn't make out his words. Only seconds later, he came up behind her and picked her up before going inside.

"Shut the door," she sputtered. "Mr. Hoover."

Noah managed to lean against the glass door and slide it shut. Then he carried Kaely to the couch and put her down. He sat down next to her, and she leaned her head on his shoulder, her sobs uncontrolled. It felt like emotional vomiting, but she let it come until nothing was left.

Noah took a napkin from the coffee table and wiped her face. "Can you tell me what's wrong?" he asked, gently.

She could hear the concern in his voice, and it made her feel safer. "The . . . the prison called. The deputy warden, Clark." She took a deep breath. "It's my dad. Someone knifed him in his bunk. They don't think he's going to make it."

"Where is he?"

"At a hospital near the prison. We need to go right away."

"Okay," Noah said. She could tell he was concerned about her ability to go anywhere right now, but he shouldn't have worried.

Kaely pushed herself off the couch. "Give me just a minute to wash my face, change clothes, and get my weapon. I won't take long."

"Kaely," Noah said, "what you're wearing is fine, and you

don't need to be armed. You're going to the hospital as a daughter. Not as an FBI agent. Just get your ID, your phone, and whatever else you really need."

She hesitated for a moment before saying, "You're right. Sorry." She looked down at her sweats. "Let me at least put on a pair of jeans. And get my purse."

"Okay. I'll get my jacket, and then we'll go to the car together."

She started to walk away but then stopped and turned back to look at him. "Thanks, Noah. I know I've said this before, but I don't know what I'd do without you."

He didn't respond, but the words echoed in his heart. No matter what happened from here on out, he would never leave her side.

THIRTY-THREE

When they got to the hospital, the woman at the front desk sent them to ICU, where they stopped at the nurses' station. A kind woman in scrubs led them to a small room with a few chairs, a table with a lamp, and a magazine holder on the wall. Two watercolors in pastels were also on the walls, which were painted a soft yellow. The entire room was designed to look peaceful. Kaely had seen her share of rooms like this—where families were sent to hear bad news.

"If you'll wait here, I'll find the doctor," the nurse said. The expression in her brown eyes was soft and sympathetic. Even though the patient was a monster. "He can tell you more about your father's condition."

Kaely thanked her. Noah sat down beside her and took her hand. She wanted to assure him she was okay, but the truth was she was far from okay. She felt embarrassed to react this way about a despicable serial killer, but when Clark had told her what happened, Ed Oliphant somehow became her dad again.

A memory she'd pushed back into the dark recesses of her mind suddenly came alive and took over. Jason was staying the weekend at a friend's house, so her dad had suggested a father-daughter weekend. He took her fishing. She remembered how proud he'd seemed to be when she pulled in a big catfish, and that night he fried the fish on their camp stove. Along with the fish, they'd eaten her mom's homemade potato salad and baked beans and her delicious orange cake. Kaely could

228

never figure out why food tasted better outside. It didn't make sense, but at the time she decided it was the best meal she'd ever had.

They'd camped by the lake under the stars. He'd told her ghost stories that weren't too scary, and they'd made her laugh.

She'd talked about school. Everything she liked. Everything she didn't. And all the things that scared her. And he'd listened. Really listened.

Then before they went to sleep, they talked about songs they liked. Her dad didn't know much about the music she listened to, and she knew even less about the songs he grew up with. She fell asleep listening to her father singing "In the Dark of Night," an old song from the thirties he'd taught her. She could still hear his voice. *In the dark of night, I'll be there. I love you so, and I'll never let you go. In the dark of night, I'll be there.*

How could she have forgotten that camping trip? She kept trying to remind herself who he was—The Raggedy Man. A person she didn't know. Even with all her training, in her heart she still couldn't understand how the father she trusted—she loved—could have been a vicious fiend who killed people for pleasure. She just couldn't make sense of it.

Just then a man with a stethoscope around his neck came into the room. He pulled the door closed and sat down across from them.

"I'm Dr. Brightman," he said. He fixed his gaze on Kaely. "Your father is in critical condition. He was stabbed several times as he slept. He's in surgery now, and the surgeons are doing the best they can. But the damage is severe."

When he paused for a moment, Kaely knew the words coming next.

"I'm afraid the prognosis isn't good. With the seriousness

of his wounds and the amount of blood he lost, frankly, I'm surprised he's still with us." He clasped his hands together. "I think you have to prepare yourself for the worst."

Kaely listened to him, but it was as if she were somewhere far away. Not in the room with anyone else. *In the dark of night, I'll be there. I love you so, and I'll never let you go. In the dark of night, I'll be there.*

She realized Dr. Brightman was waiting for a response.

"Thank you, doctor. I understand. May I see him when he's out of surgery?"

He nodded. "He'll be asleep for a while after we bring him back here. But if—"

When he hesitated Kaely realized he didn't want to use the word *if*. He didn't want to add more pain to an already distressing situation.

"When he wakes up, we'll get you immediately," the doctor finished.

Kaely thanked him again, and he got up and left the room. Why had she asked if she could see her father? What could she say to him?

"Let's pray for him," Noah said when the door closed. "And for you."

Kaely blinked at him several times, not sure she'd heard him correctly. "Pray for him? What do you mean?"

Noah gave her a wry smile. "Prayer is a way of talking to God. I thought you knew about it."

"Very funny. Why are you praying—again?"

He looked away from her for a moment, then turned back and gazed into her eyes. "Let's just say that God and I have an understanding now. I promised to stop being angry with Him for something He had nothing to do with. And He promised to forgive me and help me figure out this crazy life."

Kaely frowned at him. "You don't have a crazy life."

"Yeah, I do. You see, I'm hopelessly in love with a crazy woman, and I can't help it. That's why I need God."

Kaely reached up and touched Noah's face. "This crazy woman is totally in love with you too. She has been for a long time. I'm sorry I never said anything. I was afraid."

Noah laughed softly as he blinked away tears. "*You* were afraid? I was terrified."

"If you think I'm going to get in a contest with you to see who was the most frightened, forget it." Her voice trembled, but she didn't care. "I think this is the moment when you're supposed to kiss me."

"There you go, telling me what to do again."

"You're right. Now do what I say."

"Yes, ma'am."

Noah put his fingers under Kaely's chin. Then he leaned in and put his lips on hers, softly at first but then with more emotion. Kaely cried at the yearning and the beauty of the moment. She had waited so long to feel his kiss. It was beyond anything she had imagined.

When they parted, he noticed her tears. He wiped them away with his finger. "I love you, Kaely. And I won't walk away. Ever. I promise."

"Even if I do some boneheaded thing and put myself in danger again?" She was a little breathless.

"Even then. But don't do it, okay?"

She smiled at him. "I'll try. I promise."

"I guess that's the best I'll get."

She nodded. "It is. But now when I think about putting my life on the line, I'll remember I have two of us to think about."

He took her hands. "Thank you." Noah closed his eyes and lowered his head. Then he prayed aloud for her father before praying for her. As he spoke to God, Kaely felt a peace wash over her. When Noah finished, she opened her eyes.

She felt better. More focused. She suddenly remembered Jason.

"Oh, Noah. I have to call my brother." She pulled out her phone. He was probably asleep. His flight was booked around noon, and he planned to be at the hotel by three at the latest. Would their father still be alive by the time he got here? She quickly tapped his number from her contacts list. He answered almost immediately, and she explained what happened.

"I'll see if I can get an earlier flight, maybe yet tonight," he said. "I'll be there as soon as I can."

"I forgot to ask before. Is Audrey coming with you?" Kaely really liked Jason's wife. She was such a positive person. A strong Christian.

There was a brief silence before Jason said, "Well, I was going to wait to tell you when I saw you, but maybe I should explain why she can't come."

"Is everything okay?"

"Yeah, sis. But Audrey's been throwing up a lot. I'm sure she won't want to get on a plane. They make her ill anyway."

"Throwing up? Is she sick?"

"No, Kaely. Think about it."

Kaely suddenly realized what her brother was trying to tell her. "Oh, Jason. You're having a baby?"

Jason chuckled. "Actually, Audrey's having the baby. I'm just around to hold her head while she pukes and make her peanut butter and pickle sandwiches in the middle of the night."

"Did you say peanut butter and pickles?"

"Yeah. It's a thing, I guess. They're really not that bad."

Kaely laughed, although it felt a little out of place in the current situation.

"I'm sorry, sis. Should I come to the hospital when my flight gets in?"

"No. Take a cab and check in at your hotel, then call me. I'll give you an update. If Dad's still here, I'll come and get you."

"Okay. I'll be praying for you and Dad. And if you get the chance to talk to him? Tell him I love him, okay?"

Kaely promised to do it, but the vow stuck in her throat.

"I'd better go," Jason said. "I'll call you and let you know how soon I can be there."

"Okay. Love you."

"I love you too."

"I can go get him if you need me to," Noah said when she'd hung up.

"Thanks, but I want to do it. I think . . . I think we need some time together."

"I understand."

She leaned back in her chair. She hoped Jason would make it here before their father died. If he was conscious, maybe someone should tell him he's loved. Kaely just wasn't sure she could do it.

"Kaely, did you try to profile our UNSUB?" Noah asked.

Kaely's first reaction was to draw back from his question. But it was time to trust. It might be hard for her, but she believed God had brought her and Noah together. Even though it might be difficult to tell another human being the complete truth, she had to try. She took a deep breath and said, "I was about to. Then the phone rang."

"I want you to wait until we can figure out what's gone wrong with your process. We'll do it together. Please. Use the old-fashioned way of profiling. At least for now."

She chuckled. "I don't think the behavioral analysts at Quantico would appreciate you saying their methods are old-fashioned."

"You know what I mean."

She nodded. "Yeah, I do." She sought his eyes. "When I sat down to profile our UNSUB, things got weird, Noah. Even before I really got into it." She wrapped her arms around herself, recalling the darkness that had tried to form across from her. "You win. I won't try it again until things go back to normal."

"Thank you."

Although neither one of them said it, Kaely was aware that something evil had tried to invade her profiling procedure in Darkwater, and now it was. At some point, she would have to confront whatever—or whoever—it was.

THIRTY-FOUR

When Kaely woke up, she was surprised. She'd put her head on Noah's shoulder, certain she couldn't sleep. But now she struggled to sit up straight, and her neck was stiff.

"Glad you nodded off," he said.

"Didn't intend to. Any news?"

He shook his head. "Not yet. Jason called while you were asleep. I didn't want to wake you, so I answered your phone."

Kaely had left it on the side table next to her chair so she'd hear it if it rang. "Wow. I must have really conked out." She picked up her phone and put it in her purse. "What did he say?"

"Somehow he was able to get a flight out." Noah looked at the clock on the wall. "He's in the air right now. Should be landing here in about thirty minutes. Said he'd rent a car at the airport and drive to the hotel. When he gets there, he'll call you." He frowned at her. "Are you sure he shouldn't come straight to the hospital?"

"I don't know. I didn't think my father would be alive by the time he got here. But you might be right. I'll check on Dad and make a decision."

"Okay. By the way, did you know you sing in your sleep?"

"No. That's interesting. How was I?"

"Actually, you're pretty good." He had a twinkle in his eye. "You might have a career as a singer if you ever leave the FBI."

"Shut up," she said, sure she was blushing. "What in the world was I singing?"

"As odd as it sounds, I think it's a song by an old group from the thirties. 'In the Dark of Night.'" He grinned. "I wouldn't have guessed you'd know a song that old. You're definitely an enigma wrapped in a riddle."

"Ha-ha. But you knew it too." She'd been certain that was the song he'd mention. It kept playing in her head on some kind of weird loop. "My dad sang that song to me a long time ago. For some reason I can't get it out of my head."

He slowly moved his arm from around her. "Sorry. I think I lost feeling in this arm about an hour ago."

"Oh, Noah. Why didn't you wake me up?"

He smiled. "Don't be silly. It was the best two hours of my life."

"You're a very sweet man. Do you know that?"

"I've been told."

She was so glad he was here. His strength made her feel stronger.

He shifted in his chair and appeared to study her. "Seems to me you're experiencing a lot of emotions about your father. Want to talk about it?"

She nodded. "It's so weird. I've been angry for so long. I've tried to look at him clinically, through my training, but down deep is rage . . . and confusion. For some reason, now all I think about is some stupid camping trip we took when I was twelve." She looked up at him. "I feel ashamed for caring, Noah. He's hurt so many people."

Noah lifted her chin with his fingers. "But he's still your dad, Kaely. I don't think you can just forget something like that, no matter how much you want to."

"Seems you're right. But it's confusing."

"I know." He kissed her lightly. "We'll figure it out together."

Before Kaely could respond, the door to the room opened,

and Dr. Brightman stepped inside. Kaely steeled herself for bad news.

"Your father made it through surgery. The surgeons did their best, but his organs are beginning to fail. His injuries and the loss of blood he experienced before he was found just caused too much stress on his body. I don't think he'll be with us much longer. I thought he'd sleep for a while, but he's awake." He nodded toward Kaely. "He's asking for you."

Kaely felt numb. Why did her father want to talk to her? What could she say to him? How should she act? And could she deliver Jason's message? That he loved him?

"Can I go with her?" Noah asked.

Dr. Brightman shook his head. "I'm sorry. It's family only in ICU."

Kaely grabbed Noah's hand. "I'll be okay. Don't worry."

"All right. I'll be here when you get back."

She leaned over and kissed him. "I know."

Kaely got up, grabbed her purse, and followed the doctor. She could feel her heart pounding in her chest as they walked past the nurses' station outside the ICU, and then the doctor opened a metal door and ushered her into where there were several separate rooms off a hallway. Kaely could immediately tell where her dad was. Two armed officers stood outside his door. The doctor stopped to tell them who Kaely was, and they nodded. She noticed the curiosity in their expressions. The daughter of the infamous Raggedy Man. She ignored them and followed the doctor into the room.

She gasped when she saw her father. He was so pale. His hands and feet were bound, and he had an IV. Some kind of tubing lay on his chest.

"We removed his breathing tube temporarily," the doctor said. "He tried to pull it out himself. He insists on talking to you. But we need to put it back as soon as possible. His lungs were compromised by his injuries."

"Okay," Kaely said. Her father was staring at her. She dropped her purse onto a chair and then walked toward the bed, still not knowing what to say or what to do. She wasn't an FBI agent trying to trick him now. She was a daughter standing next to what could be his deathbed. She'd hated him for so long. Could she be the daughter he needed during his last moments? She didn't know.

His eyes were fastened on hers, and Kaely could see a hint of desperation in them.

"Hi, Dad," she said in a low voice. "Jason will be here soon. I just found out Audrey's pregnant. You're going to be a grand-father."

A tear rolled down her father's face, and for some reason it stoked her anger. How many parents would never hear those words because of Ed Oliphant?

He opened his mouth and tried to speak, but only raspy sounds that made no sense came out.

"The breathing tube made his throat raw," Dr. Brightman said. He lifted a cup from a tray near the bed. It had a small pink plastic spoon inside. Ice chips. The doctor spooned a small amount into her father's mouth. He had a hard time swallowing them, but he nodded his thanks to the doctor.

Then he turned his attention back to Kaely. "Not . . . not who he says . . ." He croaked the words. "Said he would kill . . . You need . . . need . . ."

"Who stabbed you, Dad?"

He shook his head. "No, no. Ray . . . mon . . ."

An alarm went off from a nearby machine, and her father's eyes closed. Dr. Brightman leaned over him. "You need to leave now," he said to Kaely. The door to the room opened, and two nurses pushed in a cart with a defibrillator. One of them took Kaely's arm and pulled her into the hall. "Stay here, hon," she said. "We need to help your father right now." She gestured toward one of the personnel behind the counter of the nurses' station. "Emily, take her back to the waiting room."

Kaely jerked her arm away. "I know where it is, thanks." She whirled around and hurried down the hall. Why was she upset with the nurse? It wasn't her fault.

Kaely had to face the truth. Her father would probably be gone before the sun rose on another day.

She wanted to feel something normal, like any other daughter might when losing a parent. Sadness. Grief. But she felt nothing but resentment.

THIRTY-FIVE

When she opened the door to the waiting room, Noah stood. "You're back so fast. Is everything okay?"

She told him what happened. "They're working on him now. But, Noah, he said Raymond Cooper stabbed him. And that he's not who he says he is."

"We need to call Chief Sawyer right away."

She sat down, lost in thought. Something was wrong. She was sure of it.

"I'm sorry about your dad," Noah said.

"That's not what's bothering me."

"What's wrong?"

"I just don't see Raymond as our UNSUB. Our killer is crafty. Smart. Raymond . . ."

"We haven't even interviewed him, Kaely." He frowned. "A quick conversation isn't enough to form a solid judgment."

"Maybe not, but several things lead me to believe he isn't a serial killer."

Noah sighed. "Okay, I'll bite. What did you see in that brief moment we met him that leads you to such a conclusion?"

"First, he's married. Wedding ring. And he has a baby. Spit up on his uniform."

"And how in the world do you know it was baby spit up?" Noah said, frustration in his voice. "Maybe it was chicken soup."

"On his shoulder? That's not where people spill things."

"Is that it? Still not enough to rule him out."

"His eyes were red. He was tired. He'd been up late. Probably with the baby. He doesn't fit the profile."

"The profile you haven't done yet?"

Kaely grunted. "The profile of a serial killer. The profile in my head. And there's something else."

Noah just raised his eyebrows and waited.

"While he talked to us, he kept touching his wedding ring."

"I did notice that. But I just assumed he was nervous."

"About what?"

Noah blinked several times. "I . . . I don't know. Maybe he wasn't used to talking to FBI agents."

"But he oversees killers, rapists, and thieves every day?" Kaely shook her head. "No, it was something else. He's worried about something, and it has to do with his family. Besides, he's not intellectually capable of being our UNSUB."

"Yeah. He didn't seem like the brightest crayon in the box."

"Excuse me?"

Noah blushed. "Sorry. I opened my mouth, and my mother tumbled out."

Kaely laughed softly. "Your mother sounds wonderful."

He nodded. "She is. You'll like her."

"I'm sure I will."

Noah was quiet for a moment. "What if he had help? Could Dr. Engle be pulling his strings? Kenny said he thought something was going on between her and Cooper."

"That's exactly what I was just thinking. We haven't had time to investigate him, but I think Cooper is more of a lackey." She met his gaze. "But maybe not for Dr. Engle. What about Warden Galloway?"

"Or Deputy Warden Clark? They all have access to the room with the laptop."

She nodded. "If Raymond stabbed my father, someone was giving him orders. I think all three should be investigated."

"You're right."

"I left my phone and purse in my father's room. Lend me your cell, and I'll call Sawyer about what Dad said."

"Let me do this. What if the doctor comes back with news?"

She sighed. "Thanks. I hadn't thought of that."

It was almost four o'clock in the morning, so Sawyer was probably asleep. If they couldn't get him, they'd call the CP. Someone would be there. Law enforcement was working around the clock. But Noah got through to Sawyer, and as he brought him up to date, a nurse came into the room.

"Your father is still with us," she said before Kaely could ask. "Come with me."

Kaely signaled to Noah that she was going, and he nodded.

They were walking to her father's room when the nurse handed her a small envelope. "Someone left this for you at our information center downstairs. It was sent up here."

Kaely nodded absentmindedly and put the envelope in her back pocket. She'd open it after she saw her father. When she went into his room, the breathing tube was back in his throat, so he couldn't talk to her. The nurse walked out, leaving them alone.

He was looking at her with a pleading in his eyes, and she forced herself to walk over and take his hand. As he closed his fingers over hers, a wave of nausea washed through her. "Dad, Jason asked me to tell you he loves you. He should be here shortly. I know he wants to see you."

He squeezed her hand so tightly it hurt, and she wrestled it out of his grip. "Everything will be okay," she said, trying to keep her voice steady. "Noah is on the phone right now with law enforcement. They'll pick up Raymond Cooper. Please try to relax."

He shook his head, his face tight. Then his fingers curved, and his hand moved as if he were writing something. Kaely went to her purse and pulled out the notepad she always carried, along with a pen. She didn't think her father could write with his hand tied down, so after glancing at the door, she unfastened the strap. Then she handed him the pen and held up the pad for him. He struggled to put the pen on the paper, and his hand shook as he wrote. After a few seconds, his eyes rolled back in his head, and the pen dropped from his fingers. The alarm sounded again, and Kaely quickly slid the small notepad into a side jeans pocket.

She knew her father was dying, but she didn't know what to do. She grabbed his hand one more time and leaned down next to his ear. She did the only thing she could think of. She began to sing. "'In the dark of night, I'll be there. I love you so, and I'll never let you go. In the dark of night, I'll be there . . .'"

The corners of her father's mouth turned up. He'd heard her. She could hear the crash cart rumbling down the hall, and a few seconds later several nurses surrounded her father's bed. "You need to leave again," said the same nurse who'd brought her there.

"I know." She looked at her father's face one last time and then left and walked down the hall. Once the police officers guarding his room couldn't see her, she leaned against the wall. She'd just spent the last few moments she'd ever have with her father. Why had she sung that song to him? She couldn't tell him she forgave him. Nor could she tell him she loved him. Somehow, though, she was convinced he'd heard just what he needed to hear before he died. But the song wasn't for The Raggedy Man. It was for the father who took her camping.

As she waited for the news she knew was coming, she reached

into her back pocket, searching for her notepad. She wanted to know what her father had written in the last minutes of his life. Instead, she pulled out the envelope the nurse had given her. Maybe she should open it. It might be important.

After reading the note inside, she nearly cried out in shock. Then she stuffed the note and envelope back in her pocket and stared toward the room where Noah waited for her. A few seconds later, after lifting the car keys out of another pocket, she turned and walked the other way. She was thankful Noah had asked her to keep the keys when they arrived. If she'd had to ask him for them . . .

She got onto the elevator, and once in the lobby, she walked out into the night.

Noah glanced up at the clock again. Kaely had been gone almost forty minutes. He was surprised she hadn't at least checked in with him. Kept him up to date on her father's condition. He'd heard another alarm and seen a crash cart go by, but maybe it wasn't for Ed.

Noah was just about to go check on her when Dr. Brightman walked into the room. He looked around and frowned.

"Where is Miss Quinn?" he asked.

It seemed so strange to hear Kaely called *Miss* that it threw him for a second. "I think she's with her father."

The doctor looked surprised. "I just left Mr. Oliphant's room. She isn't there."

"She must be in the restroom, then. She should be back soon."

"If that's true, she's been there a long time. We sent her out of the room a half hour ago."

"I'll look for her, doc," Noah said. "When I locate her, should I have her find you?"

He nodded. "Tell her to go to the nurses' station. They'll page me."

"Okay."

Noah followed the doctor out the door and headed toward the bathrooms. A family came down the hallway toward him, a nurse with them. He turned to watch them enter the waiting room. Someone else was facing an emotional battle. Hospitals didn't give him warm, fuzzy feelings. He'd spent enough time in them as a patient the past few months. And then there were all the days he'd spent with Tracy.

When he reached the bathrooms, he knocked on the women's door and called out Kaely's name. No response. He called again and was just thinking about going in himself when a woman came out. She looked annoyed.

"Ma'am," Noah said, trying to appear calm and mannerly, "is a woman with dark red hair in there? I need to talk to her."

"No one in the bathroom but me," she huffed. "Not very relaxing to have someone knocking on the bathroom door while you're inside."

"I'm sorry. I really am. But it's important that I find my friend. Her father is in intensive care."

"I'm sorry, but still—"

"You're sure no one else is in the bathroom?"

The woman sighed. "I told you I was the only person inside. Now if you'll excuse me . . ."

Noah watched as the woman walked away. Once she was out of sight, he pushed open the door and walked in. She was right. No one was there.

Confused, he went to the nurses' station. "Excuse me," he said to a nurse who seemed very interested in whatever was on his computer screen. After a few seconds, he looked up.

"Can I help you?"

"My friend—Ed Oliphant's daughter—do you have any idea where she is? I can't find her. Dr. Brightman said she wasn't in her father's room."

The nurse got a strange look on his face. "No, she's not in there. Just a moment."

He stood and went to where two other nurses talked to him in low tones. Then one of the other nurses rose from her seat and joined Noah. He recognized her as the nurse who had come for Kaely earlier.

"I believe she went downstairs," she said.

"I don't understand. Why would she go downstairs? Is there a cafeteria or something down there?"

The nurse shook her head. "The cafeteria is on another floor, but it's not open yet. I assumed she was leaving because . . ." She closed her mouth quickly, but Noah knew what she was going to say.

"Ed died, didn't he?"

"I can't discuss his condition with someone who isn't family." Noah could see the conflict in her face.

"You don't have to. It's obvious." He frowned. "But why wouldn't she come and get me? I don't understand."

"Maybe it had something to do with the envelope she got?"

"What envelope?"

The nurse leaned closer, as if trying to keep her words between them. "I have no idea. It was left downstairs for her at the information desk. They sent it up here, and I gave it to her. She put it in her pocket without opening it. When I saw her head for the elevators later, she looked upset."

"Thank you." Noah turned toward the elevators, but she called him back, looking around as if trying to see if anyone was listening. Then she lifted something from beneath the counter. "Here's her purse," she said as she handed it to him. "She left it in her father's room. And please tell her to contact the morgue. They'll need to know where to send the body, assuming she wants to claim it."

He nodded. The nurse was confirming that Ed had passed away without actually saying the words. "I'll tell her. Thank you."

He got on the elevator and punched the button for the first floor. What was going on? Did Kaely need some fresh air after her father died? But why would she leave the building without letting him know?

As he scanned the first floor, he noticed the information desk. He went up to an older woman with frizzy gray hair and sleepy eyes who looked like she'd rather be home in bed.

"I'm sorry to bother you," he said to her, "but someone dropped off an envelope for a friend of mine. It was sent upstairs to ICU. Do you know anything about it?"

She nodded. "Yeah, a man gave it to me. Said it needed to go to an Agent Quinn. Said she was visiting her father in ICU. I told him he could take it up to the ICU nurses' station, but he refused. Just walked off and left it on the counter." She shrugged. "I guess he was in a hurry."

"Can you describe him?"

She thought for a moment. "I . . . I'm not sure. It was so fast."

Noah tried to keep himself from becoming aggravated with the woman. "Was he white? Black? Hispanic?"

"Oh, he was white. Had one of those sweatshirts. You know, with the hood? I don't know the color of his hair. Couldn't see it."

"Do you remember the color of his eyes?"

"He wore sunglasses. I thought it was odd since it's the middle of the night."

"Tall, short, fat, thin?"

She blew out a quick breath of air. "I'm sorry. I just wasn't paying attention. I had no idea I was going to get the third degree about it."

Noah could almost guarantee the woman had been dozing when the man arrived. He wasn't going to get anything useful out of her. He thanked her, trying not to sound sarcastic, then ran toward the entrance of the hospital. Once he was outside, he looked around, hoping to see Kaely sitting on a bench. But she was nowhere to be seen. He jogged through the parking lot toward where they'd left their car. It was still there, but the driver's side door was wide open, the car keys on the seat. No one was inside.

Kaely had disappeared.

THIRTY-SIX

It didn't take long for the police to arrive, but a little longer for Chief Sawyer to pull into the parking lot with Bell right behind him.

"What happened?" the chief asked when he approached Noah.

As Sawyer and Bell listened intently, he told him the same story he'd shared with the police officers who'd arrived first.

"I called Jason several times. He should be in town, but he's missing too. His phone just goes to voice mail. I also called the hotel where he planned to stay. He hasn't checked in yet."

"I assume you tried to call Agent Quinn?" Bell asked.

Noah pulled Kaely's phone out of his pocket. "It was in the purse she left in her father's room in ICU. I gave it to one of the policemen."

"Great. Do you have any idea what was in the envelope she got?" Sawyer asked.

"An idea? Yeah. I think it was a note. And whatever it said made her leave the hospital without talking to me. My guess is that someone has Jason, and Kaely's trying to save him. The message was most probably a threat. You know the drill. *Don't contact the authorities or your brother dies.* Not the first time we've seen this."

"And Ed told Kaely that Raymond Cooper stabbed him?" Sawyer asked. "Is he our UNSUB?"

"Kaely is convinced it's not him. I don't think it's him, either."

"What exactly did she say?" Bell asked.

"That her father said Raymond Cooper stabbed him and that he's not who he says he is."

"I don't understand," the chief said.

"Sounds to me like he was saying Cooper *is* our UNSUB," Bell said.

Noah shook his head. "I really don't think so." He thought about going into why Kaely didn't believe Cooper was their man, but he wasn't sure how to bring up baby throw up.

"Well, we need to follow up on him anyway."

"Look, maybe you should talk to Kenny," Noah said. "He said he overheard Dr. Engle and Cooper talking. It sounded suspicious. He wondered if they might be in on this together. Ed spent a lot of time with Dr. Engle, and she probably knows more about him than anyone."

The chief nodded. "Okay." He turned his attention to Bell. "Has anyone figured out how our UNSUB was able to send a message to that laptop at the prison?"

Bell nodded. "It was done by someone who had direct contact with the computer."

"Then we still don't know who our UNSUB is," Sawyer said. "And he just might have Agent Quinn and possibly her brother as well." He shook his head. "This is unacceptable."

"At least we know it has to be someone who has access to the restricted area of the prison," Noah said. "Kaely and I both think you need to question not just Cooper but Dr. Engle, Warden Galloway . . . and the deputy warden. Clark."

"We're already looking closely at him," Bell said.

Noah frowned. "Do you mind if I ask why?"

"Getting to Ed in that cell was too easy. We're not saying Clark was in on it, but since it happened on his watch, we've got to wonder. At this point we have to check out everyone."

An idea popped into Noah's head. "You know, Jason was

supposed to rent a car at the airport. You might want to contact the rental companies there. Maybe if we can track the car . . ."

Chief Sawyer gestured to one of his detectives and asked her to check it out. The woman walked a few yards away and immediately got on her phone. "If we can find the car Jason rented, at least we can get an idea of where he was when he was abducted. If he was."

"I'm telling you, that's what happened," Noah insisted. "It's the only option that makes sense."

"Look," Sawyer said, "Agent Quinn is smart. I can't believe she didn't leave some kind of clue behind. A way for us to locate her."

"Not if she thought it might cost her brother his life." Even though Noah believed what he'd just said, he had to agree with Sawyer. Had he missed something?

Just then one of the officers from Des Moines Identification came up to them. They were going over the parking lot with a fine-tooth comb. Noah didn't have much confidence they would find anything since so many cars came and went from the large, busy hospital, but he noticed the evidence bags the officer held had several items. Bits of glass. Dirt. Even a feather. Noah stared at it. It was large. He wondered what kind of bird had feathers that big.

The officer, who wore gloves, held up a small notepad. "I'm not sure what this is," he said. "Looks like some kid's drawing, but you might want to check it out. It was under Agent Quinn's car."

The chief, also gloved, took the pad from the officer's hand. He shook his head. "Doesn't look like this has anything to do with her disappearance, but bag it anyway. You know the drill."

"Wait a minute," Noah said. "Can I take a look at it?" The officer held up the pad so Noah could see it. It looked like the notepad Kaely always carried with her. He stared at the strange scribbles. First a numeral one or a letter *l*. Then the letter *S*, but the end of the *S* wasn't completed. It was almost straight. It was followed by a backward numeral four. Then there was something that looked like a cursive capital *J*. The message ended in a long squiggle that made it seem as if the writer couldn't finish whatever he was trying to communicate.

"You think this means something?" Sawyer asked.

"I don't know, but one thing I'm sure of. If Kaely was being abducted, like you said, she'd do everything in her power to leave us a message. Kaely always carries a notepad, and I'm certain this is hers. I'm going back to ICU, and I'd like to take this with me. See if anyone who worked with Ed recognizes it. I'll bring it back."

The chief nodded at the I.D. officer, who put the pad in a clear bag, making sure the scribbles showed through. Then he handed it to Noah.

Noah ran toward the hospital entrance and punched the buttons on all the elevators until the doors of one opened. Then he hit the button for the ICU floor, ignoring people heading toward his elevator. Kaely was in trouble, and he couldn't waste a second.

When he reached the nurses' station, he asked if any of the nurses had seen Ed write something. No one had.

"I need to see his room," Noah said.

"I'm sorry," a nurse he hadn't seen before said. She appeared to be in charge. "The body hasn't been removed yet. And you're not family."

A wave of anger coursed through him. He took out his creds and flashed them at her. "I'm with the FBI, and I want in that room. His daughter, FBI Agent Quinn, has been abducted, and time is of the essence."

The nurse hesitated a moment, but then she came around the long counter and motioned for him to follow her. "What are you looking for?" she asked.

He stopped in the hallway and took the evidence bag out of his jacket pocket. "I know this looks like silly scribbles, but I'm wondering if it's a message Ed was trying to write before he died. Do you know anything about it?"

She shook her head. "I seriously doubt he made this. His hands were tied down. Hard to write like that. Besides, he was highly medicated."

"Just let me inside the room"—he looked at her name tag—"Carol. As I said, Agent Quinn is missing. This was found under her car. I think it could be a message for us. Please help me."

Carol nodded. "Okay." She opened the door to Ed's room. No one was guarding him now. Ed wasn't going anywhere. His body was covered with a sheet.

"Can you check his hands?" Noah asked.

Carol seemed reluctant to touch his body, but finally she lifted the sheet on the side closest to them and looked at his hand— one of the hands that had choked the life out of so many women. It was clear touching Ed Oliphant bothered her. Noah couldn't blame her. Ed's hand was still bound by a strap. Carol shook her head. Then she walked around the bed and raised the sheet again. She frowned and looked at Noah, who hurriedly joined her. Ed's right hand was unbound. Still didn't prove anything, but it gave Noah hope.

"What's that?" Carol asked. She bent and lifted something from the floor, then handed it to Noah.

"It's Agent Quinn's pen," he said.

"How do you know it belongs to her?"

Noah took the blue pen from her. It had words written on its side. *They shall mount up with wings like eagles.* And the end had been chewed. It was definitely Kaely's. "Her brother gave her several pens with Scripture on them." He nodded toward a dispenser for latex gloves on the wall. "May I have one?"

"Sure."

Noah pulled one out and put it on, then holding the pen in his gloved hand, he placed the bagged notepad back in his pocket. "I know Ed wrote this. I wish I could figure out what it says."

Carol let go of the sheet and covered Ed's unbound hand. "I hope you find your answers," she said softly. The toughness she'd exhibited earlier seemed to melt away, and she smiled. "And I wouldn't worry too much about your partner. Obviously, she has a relationship with someone who can protect her."

Understanding she meant God, Noah nodded as if he agreed, but he couldn't help but think about Tracy. She hadn't been *protected*. He'd known for a long time that he wouldn't survive if he lost Kaely too. It would be too much to bear. He had to find her. No matter what it took.

He thanked Carol and strode into the hallway. He waited until he couldn't be seen by anyone at the nurses' station and then bowed his head and pleaded with God to keep Kaely safe. "And show me where she is," he whispered. "Help me find her. She trusts you, God. And I'm trying to."

Noah headed to the men's bathroom. Inside, he put the bag with the scribbled message on the counter, then took out his phone and snapped several pictures, still holding the pen in his gloved hand. He put the bag back in his pocket, along with his phone, and jogged to the elevators. When he got to the parking lot, he found Chief Sawyer speaking to one of his detectives. Bell was standing a few yards away, talking on his cell phone.

Noah waited until Sawyer finished and the detective had walked away. He ran up to the chief and carefully explained what had happened upstairs. He held out Kaely's pen. The chief called for an I.D. officer, who brought over another evidence bag. He held it open, and Noah dropped the pen inside and took off the latex glove, stuffing it into his pocket. Then Noah gave him back the bag with the pad.

"I have no idea what Ed was trying to write," he told the chief, "but I'm going to work on it. I know this is important."

Bell came up to them. "Do you have the notepad?" he asked the chief.

Sawyer held up both the pad and the pen. Noah explained where he'd found the pen. "The strap on Ed's right hand was unfastened," he told Bell. "The pen was under the bed. I believe it's clear that he wrote that note and that Kaely left it for us. That means it's important."

"Looks like gibberish to me," Bell said. "But we'll do what we can with it."

The detective charged with contacting car rental companies came up to the chief. "We found the car Jason Oliphant rented," she said.

"Where was it?" Sawyer asked.

"In the long-term parking lot at the airport. Way in the back where no one else was parked." She frowned at them. "I think we should prepare ourselves. The officers who located it say there's blood inside. A lot of blood."

THIRTY-SEVEN

Although Bell told Noah to go back to the hotel and get some sleep before they gathered at the Command Post in a couple of hours, Noah had no intention of closing his eyes. He went back only to take a quick shower, change clothes, and check on Mr. Hoover. After feeding him, Noah left the doors between his and Kaely's suites open. He made some coffee and then sat down on the couch, pulling up the image of the note he had on his phone. Then he sent it to his email and went over to the table, where he'd put his laptop.

He quickly hooked it up to the printer he'd brought with him and printed out the image. He took it back to the couch and stared at it. Kaely wouldn't have left it behind unless it would help them find her. Why had the Copycat Killer taken her and Jason? It didn't make sense. This wasn't his MO. Anytime a killer changed his method, it was important to figure out why. It was obvious now that the Scripture he'd put in his victims' mouths was meant for Kaely. Maybe for Jason too. Was this some kind of twisted revenge? But why? Ed's kids weren't responsible for their father's actions.

He took out his phone again and pulled up the verse from Deuteronomy on a Bible reading app. *For I, the Lord your God, am a jealous God, punishing the children for the sin of the parents to the third and fourth generation of those who hate me.* Noah was pretty sure this guy was intent on some kind of justice. He stared at the words *punishing the children for the sin of the parents.* But if the Copycat Killer was imitating The

Raggedy Man because he looked up to him, why would he see
Ed as someone committing sin? Wouldn't that mean he was
committing sin as well?

And the most confusing question? Why get Raymond to kill
Ed if Ed is some kind of hero to this nut? *Punishing the children
for the sin of the parents.* For some reason the phrase kept running through his mind. What was he missing? It felt as if it were
right in front of him, but he couldn't see it. Was he just too tired?

Mr. Hoover came striding in from Kaely's room. He didn't
come straight to Noah. Instead, he walked around as if looking
for something. Kaely. Noah fought back tears.

"She's not here, Hoovy. But we're going to get her back. I
promise."

The cat sat down and stared at him for several seconds. Then
he walked over to the couch, jumped up, and settled next to
Noah.

Noah ran his hand over his soft fur. Would he be able to
keep that promise? Was Kaely still alive? Mr. Hoover put his
paw on Noah's leg. Noah didn't try to wipe away the tears that
washed down his cheeks. "Please God," he whispered. "I don't
know what to do. Please, please help me. We both need her."

Kaely kept trying to free herself, pulling hard against the
cords that kept her bound to the rickety chair. He'd put a hood
over her head before he drove her to this place in his car, right
after she met him by her own car in the hospital parking lot.
She'd had no choice but to follow his instructions since he said
he had Jason. Maybe she hadn't profiled him completely, but
she knew his threats were real. She couldn't take any chances
with her brother's life.

From what she could tell, they were inside an old house, in

the basement. The windows, small and close to the ceiling, were covered with something. Black paper? She wasn't sure. She wanted to get a better view of the entire area, but her chair was tied to a large support beam in the middle of the room, and she couldn't scoot very far. He'd also secured her wrists with plastic handcuffs.

She noticed a large mound of dirt near the outside wall, but that was about as much as she could see. Why was it there?

Jason was in a bad way. Like her father, he'd been knifed, and although their abductor had cleaned and dressed the wound, her brother was weak. He'd lost a lot of blood. He was lying on an old mattress on the floor, his right hand tied to a pipe with a rope.

"His fault," she'd been told. "He didn't have to fight me."

If only she could get free, she'd help her brother and then either kill or arrest the man who'd brought them here. She didn't care either way. She and Jason were alone now. She'd heard his car start up and take off. She had to find a way to free herself.

But the more she struggled, the more she realized that, without help, she and Jason were at the mercy of a madman.

———

A little after eight in the morning, Noah joined the rest of the team at the Command Post for a strategy meeting. SAC Howard was there, but the meeting was brought to order by Pauline Harper. Where was Sawyer? Noah looked around, finally spotting him across the room. He was talking on the phone. Odd. Usually when a session like this was called, it was a priority. Other things were put aside until the meeting was over. The call must be important.

"First of all," Harper said, "I want to tell you that the BAU has been called in. We're bringing the full force of the FBI into this investigation since one of our agents has been abducted."

She ran over all the facts they had so far. Nothing new. Her coffee brown eyes swung to him. "Special Agent Hunter, I'd like to hear exactly what happened last night at the hospital."

Noah cleared his throat. "Agent Quinn visited her father's room twice. After the second visit, she left the hospital without telling me. I found our car still in the parking lot with the driver's side door wide open and the car keys in the seat. Then after questioning some of the staff, I learned she'd received an envelope left for her at the information desk in the lobby."

Harper held up her hand. "I believe we sent people in to question the person who received the envelope, and we also viewed the CCTV footage?"

A man Noah didn't know responded. "The woman working the front desk couldn't give us a good description of the man who left the message. She seemed . . . a little sleepy. All she could tell us was that he was a white man wearing a hoodie and sunglasses. We looked at the video. This guy knew there were surveillance cameras. He purposely kept his face hidden. The same is true of what the cameras caught of him in the parking lot. Agent Quinn's car was just out of range, so we have no recording of what happened to her out there. Not sure he knew his abduction wouldn't be seen, but with a disguise, he probably didn't care."

"Can you describe his body type?" Noah asked.

"Yes. Slight. We asked the woman at the desk if the person who left the envelope could have been a woman. She admitted it was possible. She mentioned that if it was a man, he had a rather high voice."

"Then it couldn't have been Raymond Cooper," Noah said. "He's big. Really big. With a very deep voice."

"We know Cooper's not behind this," Chief Sawyer said, walking up to the desk.

"But is he working with someone who is?" Noah asked.

"He was." The chief sighed. Noah noticed how tired he looked. Sawyer had been out of commission about a year ago with a heart attack. He hoped the older man wasn't pushing himself too hard. "But he's not now," Sawyer said. "He was found dead about an hour ago."

Noah was taken aback. He hadn't seen that coming. "What happened?"

"He phoned his wife early this morning and said he was sorry for everything he'd done, including stabbing Oliphant. He told her he did that because she and their baby daughter were in danger from the person he was working for, and he had to protect them. Then he asked her to leave the house and go stay with her mother. He let her know he loved them, then ended the call. He must have shot himself in the head not long after. A park employee found his body in Gray's Lake Park."

"Then someone else is definitely behind this. Someone who used Cooper to carry out his wishes," one of the police detectives said.

"Or hers," Noah added. He told them about Kenny seeing Cooper and Dr. Engle talking, with Cooper acting suspiciously.

"We'll look into it," Harper said. "We're still following up on Deputy Warden Clark."

"What about Warden Galloway?" Noah asked. "He told us he was going to have one of the guards keep an eye on Kenny. I think it might have been Cooper. He'd have a lot of influence over him, and the UNSUB would probably be someone Cooper was really afraid of. Otherwise he would have simply called the police or—"

"Notified the warden?" Harper said. "Good thinking, Agent

Hunter. And Galloway would certainly have access to the laptop." She nodded toward the police detectives sitting together. "Can you get on that? I want to know the whereabouts of both wardens. Have we located this Dr. Engle?"

"We've tried to reach her, but she's not answering her phone," one of the detectives said.

"Send someone to her house. We need to find her. Now."

Harper leaned on the tabletop. "We need a lead, people. So far, we have no direct evidence. Nothing to help us locate our UNSUB. We've got to find our agent and her brother fast, before it's too late." She stood. "You're dismissed for now. Get on your assignments. Report to me when you have something."

Everyone around the table but Noah got up and left. Harper frowned at him. "Something else, Agent Hunter?"

"Well, I don't really have an assignment, do I? I was sent here to help Agent Quinn. Obviously, that's not happening now."

She sat down. "Did you finish your assignment at Anamosa? Did you interview the prisoners? The guards?"

"Not really. I was supposed to start seeing inmates today and then talk to some of the guards tomorrow."

"Then go back there. See if you can find anything helpful. See if Dr. Engle is at the prison. It's a long shot, but we've got to do everything we can."

"Okay. But I need someone to let me into the area of the prison where she has her office. I don't have the latest code, and prisoners and guards aren't allowed in . . ." He ended his sentence in a whisper, suddenly feeling frozen to his seat.

"Are you all right, Agent Hunter?" Harper asked.

He shook his head. "Have you been able to reach Parry Clark?"

Harper stood and called out a name. The detective she'd told to find him hurried up to the table.

"Have you talked to Deputy Warden Clark?" she asked.

He nodded.

"Get him back on the phone, now. Then give the phone to Agent Hunter."

The detective looked confused, but he pulled out his phone and selected a saved number, then responded when his call was answered.

"Yes, sir. I know it's early, but we're trying to save two lives." The agent was quiet for a few moments. "That's okay, sir. Special Agent Noah Hunter would like to talk with you." The detective handed the phone to Noah.

Noah had no time for niceties. He went right to the point, asking the question he needed to ask. When he heard the answer, it was as if all the blood in his body had just dropped to his feet. He handed the phone back to the detective, not bothering to say good-bye to Clark.

The detective thanked the warden and hung up.

"Agent Hunter, I need you to tell me what's going on," Harper said.

Noah stared at her, his mind clicking, moving several pieces of information around until they formed a clear picture.

He stood, facing her. "I believe I know who our UNSUB is."

THIRTY-EIGHT

lthough the room was mostly dark, some light peeked around the corners of the paper covering the windows. Kaely guessed it was probably around nine or ten in the morning. By now Noah and the team at the CP would know they were missing. She prayed they'd found the notepad she'd thrown under her car before her abductor forced her into his vehicle. It wasn't much, but it was the only thing she could do. She would have dropped the note this killer sent her as well, but she hadn't had time. His note and the envelope were still in her jeans.

She'd been in such a hurry to leave that she'd left her purse in her father's room with her phone in it. Of course, her abductor would have taken it from her if she'd had it with her.

How would they find her and Jason? Unless her father had managed to tell them something that led them in the right direction, the FBI was at a dead end. Were she and Jason were going to die? Even though she couldn't see a way anyone could locate them in time, she prayed that God would lead law enforcement to this place before it was too late.

Kaely kept pulling against the plastic handcuffs. They could be broken. Not everyone knew that, but she did. Unfortunately, she needed her hands in front of her to break the clasp, and the way he'd fastened her chair to the beam made it impossible for her to get into the right position.

She decided to redirect her efforts to the chair. She jumped up and down, trying to break it. It wouldn't take much for it come apart. She'd just heard a crack when another sound reached her ears. A car engine. He was back. Where had he gone? The prison? Was he trying to make the team think he'd been there the entire time? Or was this his partner? She couldn't be sure. She stayed still. The last thing she needed was for him to realize she'd been trying to escape.

The garage door slammed shut, and footsteps sounded across the floor above her, ending at the entrance to the dank basement. The door opened, and he walked down, holding on to the loose railing attached to the unstable stairs. This whole structure was falling apart. Kaely doubted he owned the house. It was most probably deserted. Even if her team had somehow discovered who he was, if nothing connected him to this place, how could they find them?

Kaely fought against despair. She had to figure a way out of this herself. She couldn't count on anyone else, not even Noah. Their salvation was left to her . . . and God. She had to believe He'd help her, that He would deliver her and Jason. He had always been there for her, in the big things and in the small things. Why would He desert her now? He wouldn't. She took a deep breath and filled herself with all the faith she could muster. She had no intention of breaking down in front of their captor. Right now, she just wanted answers.

He walked over and stood in front of her, grinning. "How does it feel to be the weak one, Kaely? Or should I say Jessica?"

"I'm not Jessica anymore," she said as calmly as she could. "I'm Special Agent Kaely Quinn, a trained FBI agent. And the best trained law enforcement officials in this country are looking for me. You're no match for them."

He walked over and slapped her face. Hard. Her cheek stung, and she felt warm blood in her mouth. She looked at him and smiled. "Feel better?"

His expression was one of controlled rage, but he stepped back. "Don't you want to know why?" he asked. "Why I brought you here?"

She heard Jason moan. He was coming to. She prayed he wouldn't say or do anything that would cause this man to hurt him more.

"I don't really care," she said, lying. "I just know you'll spend the rest of your sad life in prison."

He stepped toward her again. She braced herself, but he didn't hit her. Instead, he leaned down and put his face just inches from hers. "You still don't see it, do you? Didn't you ever feel as if you'd seen me before? As if you knew me?"

She shook her head. "No. I have no idea what you mean."

"Look at my eyes. My nose. Don't they seem familiar?"

What was he talking about? He really was nuts. "No. I have a great memory. If I'd seen you before, I'd remember."

He pushed back the hair that covered his ears. "What about these?" he asked. "They look just like my father's."

Kaely gasped involuntarily as the pieces began to fit together.

"Finally," he said, that irritating grin still plastered on his face. "Nice to meet you, sis."

"I . . . I don't understand."

He grabbed a chair similar to the one she was tied to. Then he pulled it over and planted it in front of her before sitting down.

"Seems Daddy liked to sow his seed in different places," he said. "My mother met him at a local café. He could be charming, you know."

Kaely knew her father had cheated on her mother numerous times. Somehow, he was able to keep his affairs and his victims separate. She had never understood why women had responded to Ed Oliphant. He certainly hadn't been attractive, but he had possessed a certain kind of energy. Something powerful he was able to turn on when he wanted to. For some reason, certain women had been drawn to him.

"After she found out she was pregnant, he dumped her. When I was old enough to ask about my father, she told me he was killed in Iraq. That he was a decorated soldier. She even showed me photos of a man in a military uniform. I believed her story my entire life—until she was killed in a car crash four years ago. She didn't have the chance to get rid of the lockbox where she kept articles about good old Ed. At first, I couldn't figure it out. Had she known The Raggedy Man?

"Then, at my mom's funeral, my aunt decided I should know the truth. The photos of the soldier who was supposed to be my father were of an old school friend of my mother's. My aunt told me my father was an infamous serial killer." He sighed and leaned back in his chair. "As you can imagine, I was shocked. Horrified."

"So you decided to become just like him? That doesn't make sense."

"Ah, but it does." He fastened his dark eyes on hers. "You see, I'd had these impulses for years. Ever since I was a young boy. Now I knew why."

"You're a psychopath. Just like him."

Kenny shrugged. "I guess so. Seems it can be passed down in families, huh?"

Kaely shook her head. "No. There's no proof of that. I'm certainly not like you. And neither is my brother."

"That just means I'm more like Daddy than you are."

"So you located him and got a job at the prison."

He nodded. "He was pretty upset when I told him who I was. Didn't want anything to do with me. Then I started doing favors for him—put money in his account, made sure he got the largest piece of meat at dinner, things like that. Finally, he gave in. Started talking. Eventually I got him to tell me all the tricks of his trade."

Kaely frowned at him. "Why would he share that? I don't believe you."

"But he did. Especially after I threatened you, our brother, and your mother."

Kaely shook her head again. "No. First, my father didn't care anything about us. He didn't have the capacity. Second, he could have gone to the warden and told him about your threats."

"Wrong, sis. He cared enough that I could take advantage of it. And, you see, I had someone helping me. Ed knew if he tried to turn me in, you were the first person on my list my protégé would kill. But since he didn't know who it was, he couldn't safely stop me. If he went to the warden, you'd get a bullet in your head. Or maybe you'd be killed in some slow, painful way."

He frowned. "Wait. You just said our father *didn't* care, not he *doesn't*. He's dead, then?"

He hadn't known Ed was gone. At least, he must be dead by now. She wondered how Kenny would react to his death. "My father died early this morning. He spent the last moments of his life trying to let the police know you were the one who killed those women."

His eyes widened as soon as she said her father was dead, probably not hearing anything else she said. "Good," he said, a smile on his face. My associate accomplished his mission after all, then—although he was supposed to finish Ed off right away, not let him linger." He paused for a moment. "Will you mourn him?"

"No. Will you?"

"No. And I'm sure he died afraid I would kill you. Which I will, of course. I never really wanted my associate to do it."

Kaely still wasn't sure why he wanted her dead, but she had no intention of arguing with him. She needed to slow down his plan. Give the team time to find her and Jason—if they could.

Staring at the man who threatened her life, she knew she had to forget he was her half brother. He might be a damaged soul, but this was no time for compassion.

She intended to take Kenneth Beck down—however necessary.

THIRTY-NINE

arper called everyone back to the table. She waited to speak until they were all settled and quiet, all eyes on her. "Agent Hunter is pretty sure he knows who we're looking for," she said. She nodded at him.

Noah stood. He picked up a copy of Ed's note and then grabbed a pen. "First, remember that Ed was dying and doped up." He pointed at the paper. "This isn't the letter *l* and this isn't an *S*. I assumed the bottom of the *S* just wasn't completed, but I was wrong." He took his pen and wrote over the scribbles, creating a capital letter *K*. Then he moved on to the next scrawl. "Not a backward numeral four. It's the letter *e*." He pointed to the next scribble. "This almost looks like a cursive capital *J*. But it's not. It's the letter *n*. This last mark means nothing. Just Ed's pen going off the page because he was weakening."

Harper spoke. "K . . e . . . n . . ."

Noah nodded. "Kenny. Our UNSUB is Kenneth Beck."

Harper shook her head. "Your interpretation of the note is interesting, Agent Hunter, but it's not enough. We can't go after Beck based on this."

"That's not all I have. The records we were going through were moved to a secure wing of the prison. You've got to have a code to get inside. Access is denied to prisoners and guards, so inmates won't have a reason to take a guard hostage. It's designed to keep the guards and the prison staff safer."

"So?" one of the detectives said. "How does that point us to Kenneth Beck?"

"Beck tried to implicate Cooper and Dr. Engle. He said he walked past the doctor's office and saw her with him. But Cooper couldn't get into that area. And neither could Beck. They're not allowed in there. They don't even have the code to get in."

"Then where does this therapist meet with prisoners?" Harper asked.

"In a room where guards can keep an eye on her. Kaely . . . I mean, Agent Quinn interviewed her father there. The office Dr. Engle has in the section I'm talking about is where she meets with administrative staff but mostly writes reports and keeps her records, things that shouldn't be available to the prisoners. Like I said, the security in that area is new. I think Beck just forgot about that when he made his comment to us. Deputy Warden Clark confirmed my conclusion. He said there was no way Dr. Engle would have met alone with Cooper in her office. And Beck couldn't have been walking around back there. It's impossible."

"But how could Beck access the laptop?" Harper asked.

"I don't know. But somehow he did."

Harper frowned and stared at the note Noah had written on, turning the squiggles from Ed Oliphant into Kenny's name. Noah couldn't tell what she was thinking. Finally, she said, "If we pick him up, and you're wrong . . . This man has been through a lot." She shook her head. "How could he be our UNSUB when his own wife was a victim?" She focused her attention on Noah. "I think you're wrong. Maybe Mr. Beck misspoke. Maybe he saw Raymond Cooper and Dr. Engle somewhere else."

"What if he killed his own wife to cover his tracks?" Noah said.

The silence around the table was mute witness to the kind of cold-blooded inhumanity that would be capable of something so horrendous.

Finally, Noah said, "It's hard for me to believe too. I talked to the man after his wife was murdered. I could swear he was devastated."

"So, are you changing your mind?" Bell asked.

Noah shook his head. "No. Agent Quinn taught me psychopaths are good at acting. Pretending to be whoever they think you want them to be. Just because he seemed grief-stricken doesn't mean he was."

"But we checked him out carefully," one of the detectives said. "And we found nothing in his background to make us think he was involved. Everyone we talked to said he and his wife had a perfect marriage. And his alibi checked out. He was at home with her and then left to find her when she didn't come back from the store. His neighbors saw him."

"Was he seen around the time the ME placed time of death?" Harper asked.

The detective looked uncomfortable. "Well, no. But Marie Beck was seen leaving the house. She was alive when Beck was with her." He shook his head. "I think you've got this wrong."

"But it's not impossible?" Noah said.

The detective hesitated. "No, not impossible."

"Okay," Harper said. She swung her gaze to Chief Sawyer. "Can you send some officers out to pick him up? Take him to the station. We'll question him there."

The chief nodded.

"*If* you find him," Noah said, "I'd like to be there when you talk to him." He looked at the detective. "Is there a life insurance policy?"

He shrugged. "I don't know."

"Can you find out?" Noah asked pointedly. Although Noah didn't say it, he was shocked that the police hadn't performed a more thorough investigation when it came to Beck. They'd

glossed over him because he was a victim in their eyes and because they were working so hard looking for other leads. Noah
was pretty sure that was exactly what Beck had counted on.
There wasn't much anyone could do about it now. The scowl
on Chief Sawyer's face made it clear he wasn't happy about
the investigation either.

"Agent Hunter, I'd still like you to go to the prison and finish
the work you were sent here to do," Harper said. "This is just
a possibility, and we need to cover all our bases."

"Please," Noah said. "Agent Quinn is . . . is very important
to me. I want to do everything I can to find her."

Harper paused for a moment before saying, "I understand.
But you need to make sure your tasks at the prison are finished.
I want to know if anyone else there was involved."

"I'll do it. As soon as I know Agent Quinn and her brother
are safe."

Harper started to say something else, but stopped, sighed,
and dismissed the meeting. As the people left, Noah asked
Harper if he could stay at the table.

"I want to make some notes. See if I can connect the dots.
Make sure we're on the right path."

"Something else Agent Quinn taught you?"

He nodded.

"Fine. If you come up with anything to help us, let me know."

"Okay. And thanks."

Harper nodded and walked away. Noah grabbed a pad of
paper and began to write.

"So why did you have to kill all those women?" Kaely asked.
Even though she was stalling for time, she really wanted to
hear the answer.

"I needed to show Daddy I was better than he was. Teach him that rejecting me was a mistake."

Now Kaely could see his real face. Psychopaths didn't do well with rejection. Their anger can spiral into a desire for revenge, and obviously, that's what happened to Kenny.

"But what about Marie?" Kaely asked even though she already knew the answer. The evil in this man was mind-blowing, but Kaely fought to stay in her FBI persona. She couldn't allow herself to be affected by him or what he'd done in the name of her father. Two serial killers in one family. How could this be?

"Kaely, are you all right?"

She looked over to see Jason awake, struggling to sit up. He looked around. Stared at Kenny.

"What's happening?" he asked.

"Nothing. We're okay," she said. She locked her eyes with his. "I need you to stay calm, Jason. And quiet. Do you understand?"

Although the expression on his face made it clear he didn't, he nodded. Jason trusted her, and she knew he would do what she asked him to do.

"Don't you want to introduce me?" Kenny said. "Tell him how our little family has grown? By the way, I fixed him up the best I could. Couldn't have him die before he knew why."

Kaely fought to swallow her anger. He'd saved Jason so he could kill him after his ego was fed.

"Tell me about Marie," she said, forcing the words out.

Kenny shrugged. "Marrying her was just part of the plan. If you saw me as a victim, then you wouldn't look at me as your . . . What do you call them? UNSUB?"

"You married a woman just to kill her?" Kaely said, unable to keep the disgust out of her voice. "Did she love you?"

"I guess so. She was fine. Tried to be a good wife. I miss her . . . a little. She was a good cook. And she kept a clean house."

"You sound like you're talking about the maid."

He nodded. "That's what she was. Of course, there were side benefits." He winked at Kaely, and she felt sick. "By the way, did everyone like my little touch with the car alarm?" He laughed. "I set that thing off over and over so it wouldn't look strange the night I supposedly left for the store. I wanted the neighbors to notice the time. I needed an alibi. Of course, Marie was already dead by then."

"But one of them saw her leave."

"She saw *someone* who looked like Marie get in her car. I left that car at the store and then caught a cab home, still dressed like a woman. Had him drop me off in the alley behind the house. No one saw me go inside. Then, when I looked like myself again, I got into my other car, setting off the alarm so everyone would swear I was home the entire time."

"The messages stuffed in your victims' mouths were for me, I assume," she said, trying to change the subject.

"Yeah. My own personal touch. Daddy didn't like that. Made him pretty angry. I'm not sure why."

"You messed with his MO. Changed his signature. Serial killers are pretty committed to their habits. They don't like to see them altered."

"Obviously. But I needed to give you a clue, didn't I? Too bad you didn't pick up on it, at least enough to stay away." His smile was sickly sweet and didn't reach his eyes.

"How did you know I'd come?" Kaely asked. That question had bothered her from the beginning.

Kenny laughed. "I didn't. I told Ed to keep quiet when they questioned him. Refuse to talk. I was pretty sure someone would think of you. But if they didn't, we were prepared to have Ed ask for you." He peered closely at her. "From everything I know about you, I was convinced you wouldn't be able to stay away.

You have an overdeveloped sense of justice. How could you not try to stop someone copying your father's killing spree?"

Kaely was shocked by his explanation. He was right. Even if she'd had to get involved on her own, she would have.

"And the laptop?" she said. "That threw me."

He snorted. "So easy. I offered to help the outgoing activities consultant carry out his stuff. Watched him punch in the code. One night when Dr. Engle was in her office, I went in, added the message, and left. The place has only one working camera, and I know how to avoid it. Anyone would just assume Engle went out and came back. Visited one of the snack machines or something." He scooted forward in his chair. "But I think that's enough talking for now. We have some business to attend to."

"One more question," she said. *Is all this stalling going to help? Does anyone know where we are?* "How did you get Raymond Cooper involved in this thing?"

Kenny leaned back, and Kaely almost sighed with relief. "Oh, so you figured out good old Raymond was my helper. His house is in foreclosure. I promised to give him the money to pay it off. For his family. He wasn't exactly sure what I was up to. I gave him a little cash up front—not enough to solve his problems, but enough to interest him. Then I sent him out to take pictures of you, your brother, and your mother. I made sure they were time stamped so Daddy would know they were taken by someone besides me. He needed to know I could take any of you out with one word. And did you like our little act? I pretended to be afraid of Raymond, so you'd think I was too much of a wimp to kill anyone. Raymond played his part beautifully."

"Yes, he did," Kaely said. "It never occurred to me that you were capable of such evil. But did Raymond know you were trying to make us suspect him?"

Kenny shrugged. "I made sure he had alibis. He was never a serious suspect."

"You thought this whole thing out thoroughly, didn't you?"

Kenny laughed. "Yes, and it worked. Once he knew you and your brother were in danger, our father finally told me everything I needed to carry out my plan." He took a deep breath and blew it out. "But, like I said, Raymond wasn't supposed to let Daddy hang around. I guess he didn't have the guts to finish him off. At least you got to say good-bye."

Ignoring the last little dig, Kaely said, "Where were you going to get all this money?"

"I guess I can tell you since you won't be leaving here alive. A nice little insurance policy worth a half-million dollars."

Something came to life inside Kaely. That was it. How Noah and the team would tie Kenny to the murders. If they could figure out whatever her father had written on the notepad she left, they'd surely check for an insurance policy. Then they would know. But that still didn't lead them here. How could they possibly make it in time?

Kaely looked at Jason. He was watching her as if she had the power to save them. But she didn't. The words of the UNSUB she'd tried to profile in Nebraska came back to her. *"You're going to die. It will not happen here, in Darkwater, but it will happen. And soon."* Was this it? Was this the day she would die?

FORTY

As Noah worked on his notes, his stomach clenched with disgust. This guy was a real lowlife. But try as he might, he couldn't figure out Beck's motive. Could he simply be such a fan of Ed Oliphant that he was willing to become his disciple? Yet it was clear he hadn't pleased Ed. First there was Ed's reaction when he found out about the Scripture placed in the victims' mouths. Then the note he wrote as he was dying. If Kenny was his protégé, why would he try to stop him?

It appeared to Noah that something had gone wrong. But what? And why? And why did Beck turn against his hero and have him killed? He felt a little sorry for Cooper, but he could have stopped Kenny at any time. At some point he knew what Kenny was up to, and so the deaths of innocent women were on his head too. It was clear that it had gone too far, past what Cooper could endure.

The detective who admitted they hadn't followed up the way they should have with Beck walked up to the table. "Half-a-million-dollar life insurance policy on Marie Beck. Kenneth has one on his life too. Probably just to keep from looking too suspicious. And Marie had a nice trust fund from her deceased parents. She couldn't inherit it until she turned twenty-five, which happened a couple of months ago. My guess is he's been planning to empty their bank accounts and disappear as soon as the insurance paid off. He asked the insurance company to get him the money as quickly as they could. Told them he needed it for Marie's final expenses. Obviously, that's not true."

"I'll bet he used the promise of money to keep Raymond Cooper on the hook."

The detective nodded. "We did some checking on him too. His family was close to being evicted from their home."

"Well, that explains it." He nodded at the detective. "Thanks."

Although he could have walked away, the man just stood there. "I messed up," he said. "This is my fault."

Noah wanted to yell at him, but he managed a smile. "Hey, we're all human. Kenneth Beck looked like a victim, and we were all on overdrive, looking for our UNSUB. You guys were doing your job, and you had a lot on your plate. You would have found it."

"Yeah, we had someone looking into Beck, but it didn't have the kind of priority it should have. We were just too slow." The detective walked away, his head down, not looking at anyone else in the CP. Noah sighed. Working in law enforcement was tough. So much rested on shoulders that didn't belong to superheroes, just regular human beings who make mistakes. Some days you were tired, sick, hurting, and dealing with loss, but you still had to operate perfectly. Never missing a beat, knowing one misstep could cost a life. It wasn't surprising that suicide rates were high among law enforcement officers.

About twenty minutes later, Harper came back to the table, an odd look on her face. "We heard from the lab. They went over everything collected from the hospital parking lot last night. Most of it is nothing. Dirt that could have come from anywhere. Gum stepped on so many times there's no way to get DNA from it. Besides, it's too old for what we need. A few other items that don't help us. But there is one really odd thing."

"What's that?" Noah asked.

"A feather."

"Oh. I remember seeing a feather in one of the evidence bags. Lots of pigeons and crows around the area. Not sure how that can help us. That's a large one, though."

Harper shook her head. "Believe it or not, it's an eagle's feather."

The hair on the back of Noah's neck stood up, and goose bumps erupted on his arms. "Did you say an eagle's feather?"

Harper nodded

The words on Kaely's pen filled his mind. *They shall mount up with wings as eagles.*

Chief Sawyer came running toward them. "We found it," he said, breathless. "An eagle preserve, on the outskirts of town, in an area that's been purchased for a new apartment complex. The last houses there have been vacated and are slated to be torn down soon. If Beck got a feather caught in one of his tires and it dropped off in the parking lot . . ."

"That's a leap, chief," Harper said.

"But that feather was found right next to Agent Quinn's car. And one of those empty houses would be the perfect place for Beck to take her and her brother." He looked at Noah. "I think that's where they are."

Noah jumped to his feet. "I do too." He thought about the pen. Kaely wouldn't have known about the eagle's feather, but Someone else did. Noah saw it as a sign. His voice cracked with emotion. "Let's go get them."

Kenny leaned back in his chair with his eyes fastened on Kaely's. Jason was sitting up, still in obvious pain but at least conscious.

"How in the world do you think you're going to get that insurance money?" Kaely asked. "The FBI is probably already onto you."

Kenny's laugh was hollow and cruel. "I doubt that. They're not looking at me. I'm a victim, remember? And Cooper isn't going to say anything. Besides, the insurance company is expediting the funds. In a few days I'll have the money, and then I'm gone. Your friends won't discover the truth in time."

"You'll never be able to move that much money. The FBI will track you."

"I don't owe you an explanation, but I told you, I've been planning this a long time. I have a bank account already set up, and I have a brand-new identity. When the insurance company pays, I'll transfer the money immediately. Your beloved FBI will never find it."

"I wouldn't count on that."

Kenny stood. "Oh, I certainly am counting on it. I learned someone with money can hide it in one of several countries—and live cheaply."

"Half a million dollars won't last forever."

He laughed again, and it still sounded hollow. Void of emotion. "Maybe. But my wife's recently inherited trust fund certainly will. I chose Marie for a reason. Actually, a few million reasons." He nodded toward the stairs. "I have something to do, but I'll be back."

"Why do you want to kill us, Kenny?" Kaely asked. "If we really are related, that makes me your sister. Jason is your brother. We've never done anything to hurt you. Seems my—our—father is the one you should be angry with. And you've already killed him."

Kenny's face turned dark. "I did more than kill him. I showed him I was as good as he was. Better." He glared at her. "He didn't acknowledge me as his child, so I'm going to take away the other children he cared so much about. That will make me his *only* child."

His smile chilled Kaely down to her toes. She thought she understood the minds of psychopaths more than most people, but she was still shocked by his hatred.

"My father didn't really love any of us, Kenny," she said. "We have a lot in common. Jason and I were rejected by Ed Oliphant too."

Kenny stepped closer, his face again only inches from hers. "'For I, the Lord your God, am a jealous God, punishing the children for the sin of the parents to the third and fourth generation.'"

She could feel his sour breath on her face.

"I'm going to end your life. Just the way our father killed all those women. Then I'm going to bury you in this house." He pointed to the area of earth Kaely had noticed earlier. "This house is going to be bulldozed in a few days. You won't be found for a long time. If ever." He turned and hurried up the stairs.

Kaely didn't know where he was going or when he would return, but she was pretty sure they didn't have much time. She began banging her chair against the concrete floor.

"Kaely, be quiet," Jason said, his voice faint. "He'll hear you."

"I hope not. We're running out of options. I've got to get us out of here."

She pulled herself up as far as possible, but the cords binding her to the beam kept her from gaining much traction. This was the best she could do. She had to make this effort count. With all her might, she struck the chair against the floor one more time. She was elated to hear another crack. A leg of the chair had splintered, and a few more thuds caused it to fall off. Kaely and what was left of the chair fell over, snapping the cords that held her to the beam.

She scooted as far as she could to get away from it, then wriggled until she could pull her bound hands over the top of the shattered chair. That gave her the ability to force her arms down and literally step over them, which put her hands in front of her. From this position she was able to use a technique that broke the plastic loop cuffs. However, one of the straps cut into her arm, and it began to bleed.

Ignoring the pain and blood, she scrambled to Jason and untied the rope holding him to the pipe. It hadn't been tied well. He could have easily escaped himself if he hadn't been injured.

"I need you to stay here," she whispered. "Pretend to still be tied up. When he comes down the stairs, the first thing he'll see is you. That will give me a few seconds to surprise him. Understand?"

Jason nodded, but he was so weak Kaely feared he might not make it. He needed help—and fast. It looked as if he was going into shock, and shock could be deadly.

"Hang on, Jason. Think about that baby. Your new son or daughter. Okay?"

He nodded and then closed his eyes. Kaely put the rope back, making it look as if it were still attached to the pipe. Then she scooted across the floor, looking for something she could use as a weapon. When she heard steps on the floor above her, heading to the basement door, she desperately grabbed the broken chair leg. It had splintered on the end and was sharp enough to cause injury. Holding it with one hand, she crawled over to the stairs. Then she hid behind them, waiting for Kenny to come down.

"You only have one chance at this," Georgie whispered in her ear. "Bring him down now. If you don't overpower him—"

"Go away," Kaely whispered through clenched teeth. But Georgie was right. If she didn't stop Kenny now, he would kill them. And what he said was most probably true. Their bodies might never be found.

FORTY-ONE

Noah had talked his way onto one of the SWAT vans, and now they sped to where they believed Beck had taken Kaely and Jason. He found himself silently bargaining with God.

I know Tracy's death wasn't Your fault. I'm sorry I was angry with You. Please forgive me. But if Kaely is still alive, I'm begging You to keep her safe, Lord. I can't lose her now. I just can't. If You keep her alive, I'll spend the rest of my life following You.

It felt as if it were taking forever to get there. A team had gone ahead to scout out the area, but revealing themselves too soon might make Beck kill his captives before they could breach the perimeter. Although they weren't sure they would have the chance to reason with him, they'd also brought along a hostage negotiator. They had to be prepared for anything.

As the minutes ticked by, Noah could only hope in a God he'd once turned his back on. Was He still listening? Would He protect the woman Noah loved with all his heart and soul?

Kenny was halfway down the stairs when he stopped. Did he realize she'd escaped? She waited for the right moment. He took two more steps, almost to the bottom of the stairs. When his foot reached the floor, she came out from behind the stairs and swung at him with all her might, hitting him in the face and knocking him down.

His look of surprise was genuine. He'd obviously never

considered that she might get free. She raised the chair leg once again. She had to knock him out and then tie him up so she and Jason could get out of the basement and find help. But as she brought the leg down, Kenny raised his hands and grabbed it. Then he got on his knees, and they both fought for the only weapon Kaely had. Kenny was much stronger than she'd counted on. His slight build was deceiving. She could see the well-developed muscles in his arms.

Although she held on with all her might, Kenny was fueled by psychopathic rage. She was no match for him. He ripped the chair leg out of her hands, causing several deep wounds in them. Then he hit her once in the face, knocking her to the floor. He stood over her, grinning. She could only watch as he raised her makeshift weapon and brought it down with great force.

The advance team communicated that, so far, they'd gone to three empty houses near the eagle preserve. They would have approached each building from behind, using trees and bushes to shield their efforts, careful not to do anything to cause suspicion, their vehicles out of sight. But they'd seen no signs telling them anyone was in those houses—or even had been there recently.

Only two houses remained—a white ranch-style home with green trim and a two-story house with a large porch. The ranch would be next.

"Give me your binoculars," Noah told one of the SWAT team members. When he got them, he trained his sight on the two-story structure.

"What are you looking for?" the officer asked.

Noah handed him the binoculars. "Look at the windows in the basement of that two story."

The officer stared through the binoculars for a few seconds and then lowered them. "I'd say someone's trying to hide whatever's in that basement."

"That's where they are," Noah said. "Now let's hope they're still alive."

While the SWAT officer communicated with the advance team, Noah stared at the house, trying to squelch the nearly overwhelming urge to get out of the SUV and crash through the front door. He knew he had to wait for SWAT to do their job, but the waiting was torture. Had he lost Kaely?

When Kaely came to, she was lying on the floor. She couldn't see anything and finally realized her face was covered with blood. She blinked several times, trying to clear her vision. She looked down to see that her hands and feet were bound with red ribbon. Her head hurt so much she cried out in pain.

"You caused yourself that injury," a voice said.

Kaely turned her head even though it hurt. Kenny was sitting in a chair next to her, watching. "Where is Jason?" she asked.

Kenny gestured toward the makeshift grave he'd dug earlier. "He's just waiting for you."

"No!" Her tears mixed with her blood as she struggled to sit up, but Kenny pushed her down with his foot.

"I asked our father why the red ribbon and wire angel," he said, his voice matter of fact as if they were talking about the weather. "He wouldn't tell me. I don't suppose you know?"

"He never told anyone," Kaely said, her voice raspy and her lips cracked with dried blood. A part of her was ready to give up. Jason was dead. There was no way for the FBI to find them. Maybe it was time to see what heaven was like. Drifting away sounded wonderful. But something rose up inside her. She just couldn't give Kenny the satisfaction of killing her.

He held up a piece of wire twisted into two figure eights, resembling an angel with wings. "Fifty years from now, maybe they'll knock down the apartment complex they're building here and find you with this in your skeleton fingers. What a story that will be. You'll be famous."

"Kaely, you're a fighter." Georgie stood next to Kenny. "Don't give up. You can't. Not now. Show him who you are."

"'By the pricking of my thumbs, something wicked this way comes. Open, locks, whoever knocks,'" she whispered.

"What?" Kenny said.

"You're going to die. It will not happen here, in Darkwater, but it will happen. And soon."

"No," Kaely said. "No."

"Sorry, Special Agent Kaely Quinn, but your time is up."

Kenny got out of the chair and knelt beside her. His hands circled her neck, and he began to squeeze. Kaely fastened her eyes on Georgie. But Georgie was gone. Someone else stood there. Dressed in white, he smiled at her. She smiled back as she began to lose consciousness.

Noah waited in the SUV, trying desperately to stay out of the way, but his patience was wearing thin. It felt as if they'd been inside the old house for hours, not minutes. Finally, the SWAT commander stepped out and waved an all clear, meaning the scene was secure. Rather than wait for the SUV to drive up to the house, Noah jumped out and ran toward the front door, tears making it hard to see where he was going. When he reached the porch, he stared the commander in the face, unable to find the words he wanted.

"They're both alive," he said, "but barely. We've called for ambulances. They're on the way."

Noah had to grab on to the porch railing to stay on his feet. "Can I see her?"

The commander hesitated a moment before saying, "All right, but don't touch her."

Noah nodded and forced his feet to move. As he entered the old house, he encountered officers standing near a door that had to be the entrance to the basement. They didn't say anything as he pushed past them and ran down the stairs. When he saw Kaely lying on the floor, he wanted to pull off the red ribbon binding her hands and feet. But he knew he couldn't. The EMTs would probably do that and save them for the ME. Not that it was necessary anymore. A few feet away from Kaely, Kenneth Beck lay in a pool of blood, his eyes wide open, looking at nothing. He wouldn't be taking more lives.

Noah went to Kaely and knelt next to her. "Can you hear me?" he asked. Her face was covered with blood, one eye was swollen shut, and she had bruises on both sides of her face. Noah wanted to kill Kenneth Beck all over again for the agony he'd inflicted.

She opened her only good eye and nodded slightly, but then winced.

"Kenny is dead," he said.

"I know," she mumbled, almost in a whisper. "Where is Jason?"

"He was dumped into this hole," a SWAT officer standing nearby said. "I guess Beck was going to bury him, but we pulled him out." He moved over some, and Noah saw Jason. His eyes were closed.

"Is he . . . is he still alive?" Noah barely choked out.

"He's still breathing, but we need that ambulance ASAP."

As if someone heard him, the whine of sirens began to fill the air. Noah put his head near Kaely's. "Help is here, Kaely. Just hold on. You and Jason are going to make it, you hear me?"

"Yes, I hear you." With much difficulty, Kaely turned her head to the side. "Where is he?"

"Who?"

"The man. There was a man here. Dressed in white. I saw him, Noah. He was right here."

Kaely took a deep breath and passed out.

Noah hung his head and cried.

FORTY-TWO

Two weeks had passed since Kaely and Jason were rescued from the clutches of Kenneth Beck. She was feeling fine—a few headaches but nothing serious. The wounds on her face and hands were healing as well. Jason had gone home. It was a miracle that Kenny thought he was dead and hadn't tried to finish the job he'd started.

As Kaely waited in the small café, her stomach was tied in knots. How would this go? Could she handle it?

Then she saw an attractive woman coming toward her. She had beautiful chestnut hair, large brown eyes framed with dark lashes, and a perfectly shaped nose. A smile played on her lips as she came to the table and sat down.

"It's been a long time," she said softly. "Thank you for seeing me. I wasn't sure you would."

"I wasn't certain I would either. I'm sorry to have to ask you to drive all the way to Anamosa. I just didn't have the time to drive to Des Moines this afternoon."

Georganna leaned toward her. "I was happy to do it." She looked into Kaely's eyes. "We tried to find you after you moved away, but we couldn't."

"We stayed in Des Moines for a while," Kaely said, trying not to sound bitter. "As long as we could. But it became impossible. We had to leave." She paused. "Your parents wouldn't let you see me."

"Kaely, my parents loved you. They still do. But they were shocked. They needed time to digest what happened. And with the media trucks in front of your house . . ." She sighed. "Maybe they made a mistake, but it wasn't because they didn't want us to be together. They were just trying to protect me. I'm sorry."

Although Kaely hadn't planned on getting emotional, her eyes filled with tears. "I understand," she whispered.

Georganna reached over the table and took her hand. "I'm not sure you do, but I think we can deal with it, don't you? We're finally back together. My parents would love it if you came to dinner before you go back to St. Louis. You can meet my husband too. Is that possible?"

Kaely brushed a tear from her cheek. "I wish I could, but I'm leaving tomorrow, and I have something planned for tonight." She smiled. "How about I come back in the next couple of months and take you up on your offer?"

Georganna returned her smile. "I think that would be wonderful."

Noah slept until almost eleven. For some reason he was still exhausted. It was as if the release of all the tension and stress from trying to find Kaely had zapped his strength. He forced himself out of bed and made some coffee. He'd already packed almost everything for the trip home.

Kaely had two appointments before they left. Noah glanced at the clock. She was having an early lunch with Georganna Hobson Williamson now. Georgie. He was proud of Kaely for deciding to face her. Kaely was determined not to hide from the past any longer. Dr. Engle had convinced her she could find real healing only by confronting what hurt her.

He couldn't stop thinking about something Kaely told him, that someone else was there with her and Kenny. A man dressed in white who smiled at her. Gave her comfort. Was she hallucinating? Was this another Georgie type sighting? Nothing would shake Kaely's belief in what she saw, and Noah had no intention of challenging her. He'd seen too many odd things lately. He chose to believe that God had answered his prayer. That was all he cared about.

He was hungry and decided to order breakfast. He had plenty of time. Kaely was going to the prison after her lunch with Georganna. Dr. Engle had promised to tell her some things about her father now that she was no longer bound to protect his secrets. Noah shook his head. He could hardly believe they'd considered her a suspect, but at the time they were desperate. They couldn't reach her that Sunday morning because she'd turned off her phone while she attended an early morning meeting at her church, and she'd kept it off after the church service began. Not really the actions of a deranged serial killer.

Although Noah and Kaely had talked some, for the most part he'd held off telling her everything he wanted to say. She'd needed the time to heal. But he intended to. This evening they were having an early dinner at Mort's in Des Moines before they drove the rest of the way home.

As he picked up the phone to call room service, he wondered if tonight would change the rest of his life. He hoped so with all his heart.

Kaely headed to the prison after her lunch with Georganna. Although at first seeing her had been a little uncomfortable, they'd soon fallen into a relaxed banter. Kaely felt as if it had been only a day or two since the last time they were together, not two decades. She smiled to herself. She and Georganna had vowed to stay in touch. Kaely had meant her promise to come back to see Georganna's parents and meet her husband. If a month ago someone had told her she'd be vacationing in Des Moines, she would have called them insane.

After arriving at the prison, she checked in, and then a guard came to escort her to the area where the staff offices were located. The guard let their presence be known, and a few seconds later, Melanie came down the hallway and let her through the locked door. She smiled as Kaely stepped inside.

"Good to see you," Melanie said.

Kaely had visited the doctor several times since she was rescued from Kenneth Beck. She hoped Melanie would never know that at one time she and Noah truly had suspected she was working with the Copycat Killer.

Kaely followed her into her office, and Melanie closed the door behind them. Kaely sat down.

"Coffee?"

"No, thank you."

Melanie poured herself a cup and then sat down across from Kaely. "Are you feeling any better since the last time we met?"

"I'm good. Still some headaches, though."

"And inside?"

Kaely shrugged. "Not sure. Still trying to deal with things, I guess."

The doctor smiled. "That's honest. No attempt to hide from your emotions." She shook her head. "You've endured a lot."

Kaely sighed. "True, but I believe God is bringing me through it. You've helped me a lot."

"Good. Just make sure you stay truthful with Him—and yourself."

"That's my intention."

"Anything you want to discuss before we move on and talk about your father?"

Kaely hesitated a moment. She was concerned about something. Could she share it with this woman?

Melanie just sat there, silent. Waiting.

Finally, Kaely said, "I know research doesn't back murderous traits being passed down from parent to child, but . . ."

"But it still worries you?"

Kaely nodded. It was stupid, and she knew it. But the possibility had haunted her ever since she was a teenager. Knowing she was related to Kenneth Beck had reignited her fears.

"Can you name one child of a serial killer who followed in his or her father's footsteps?" Melanie asked.

"I can name two. Francis Weaver and Michael Kallinger."

"Francis was Ward Weaver's stepson," Melanie said. "And Michael Kallinger killed along with his father. He was trained to do it." She appeared to be studying Kaely. "But you know that. What about Melissa Moore and Kerri Rawson? They didn't turn into serial killers."

Kaely knew the doctor was referring to the children of Keith Jesperson and Dennis Rader.

"No, I realize they didn't."

"Kaely, are you truly afraid you're going to suddenly start killing people?"

Kaely shook her head. "No, of course not. But . . ."

"But what about your children."

"Yes."

"You know the psychopathic trait isn't hereditary. What is this really about?"

Kaely leaned back in her chair. "I guess I could use that cup of coffee after all," she said.

Melanie went to the coffee maker, giving Kaely a chance to think. Why *did* this bother her so much? What the doctor said was true, yet for some reason she'd never been able to shake her fear. Two uncertainties had followed her for years—the fear that she would give birth to someone like her father and the fear of dying young. The second worry had dissipated when she saw the man in white watching her when Kenneth Beck put his hands around her neck. She was convinced she'd seen an angel. The Scripture was true. *He shall give His angels charge over you, to keep you in all your ways.* One of the pens Jason had given her displayed that promise. She'd looked at it so many times, but now it was alive to her. Real.

The other fear was that her children could turn out like her father. What kind of mother would she be if she saw Ed Oliphant whenever she looked at her child?

As the doctor poured the coffee, Kaely prayed she could find a way to leave her apprehension behind.

FORTY-THREE

After Melanie gave Kaely her coffee, she sat down, smoothing her dark blue skirt and crossing her legs. "Anything else?"

Kaely sighed. "I haven't talked to you about what happened in St. Louis."

Melanie frowned, lines marring her smooth skin. "St. Louis?"

Kaely took a deep breath and told her about the case in St. Louis and the deep betrayal of a friend. Melanie didn't say anything, just listened. Kaely was grateful. She'd held on to her jumbled emotions a long time and needed to get them out.

When she finished, Melanie said, "I know this sounds cliché, but how did that make you feel?"

"I was hurt. Angry. Afraid to trust anyone."

Melanie nodded. "Perfectly normal. Almost everyone deals with the fear of trusting people. But your background makes it harder. Children are supposed to trust their parents. They are their foundation. To find out who your father really was traumatized you, so you're much more sensitive to betrayal. That's why it's hard for you to get past the situation in St. Louis."

"I'm doing much better after talking with you, but I still can't seem to shake this deep-seated fear. I've prayed and prayed, but it's still there."

Melanie smiled. "God isn't always on our timetable. You know, sometimes handing our problems over to Him and waiting on His response is all we can do. Some things we can't fix on our own no matter how hard we try." She uncrossed her legs and leaned forward. "You seem like the kind of person who wants to find solutions to everything. When you can't, I think it frustrates you."

Kaely nodded. "You're right." She brushed away a curl too close to her eyes. "But while I'm waiting on God to deliver me, how do I have close relationships?"

"Are you thinking about someone specific?"

Kaely hesitated a moment before saying, "Yeah. Yeah, I am."

"Have you prayed about it?"

"Yes. But I'm not getting an answer."

"You may already have it." Melanie smiled again. "Be quiet for a moment and listen to your heart. Turn off your mind."

Kaely felt a little frustrated. If the answer was inside her, she would already know what to do. But as she sat in the silence, she realized she could do only one thing. Only one path led to peace. Odd how she hadn't picked up on that before. As she'd said, she'd spent a lot of time praying. Even more time trying to figure things out, but maybe she hadn't spent enough time just listening.

"I can tell by the smile on your face that you have an answer," Melanie said. "Does it bring you peace?"

Kaely nodded. "The truth is I have to take this chance. I'm even willing to be hurt, but I don't think I will be. I'm tired of being afraid. And alone."

"Good." Melanie stood and retrieved a file from her desk. "I told you I'd share some things about your father now that he's gone. Do you want to talk about anything else before I do that?"

"I don't think so."

"Okay." Melanie opened the file. "What do you know about how your father grew up?"

Kaely shrugged. "Not much. He didn't talk about his child-hood. I understand his mother and sister died when he was young and his father abandoned the family. I know he lived with his grandparents for a while." She fastened her gaze on the doctor. "I'll warn you right now, I don't give much credence to the *abused child to serial killer* explanation. Lots of abused kids grow up to be useful people. They don't allow their pasts to determine their future."

"Like you?"

"I wasn't abused as a child."

Melanie sat down, crossed her legs again, and leaned back in her chair, the file balanced on her lap. "You don't think having a father who goes around killing women behind your back is being abused? Has it been easy dealing with his choices?"

"No, of course not."

"Sounds like abuse to me. And wouldn't you say you've reacted to it? Becoming an FBI behavioral analyst to combat the evil your father created? I would say your life changed in response to your father's decisions."

Kaely sighed. "Yes, I know that. But I guess I never thought of my father's choices as abuse. I suppose you're right." She was silent as she studied Melanie. "I suspect there's a point here?"

"The point is this. I'm not going to offer excuses for what your father did. But I am going to tell you about things that drove him, that contributed to his illness. As I said, I don't expect you to think they excuse what he did, but I believe you have the right to know all this. And in your position, your calling, knowing might even be helpful."

Kaely crossed her arms over her chest. Defensive move. She didn't care. She wasn't looking for help from her father's past, no matter what he'd been through. There weren't enough reasons in the world to explain his actions. "Go ahead," she said, reluctant.

Melanie opened the file. "Seems Ed was raised by a cruel

father who beat him and his sister regularly. He locked them in a closet for hours if they did anything he thought was wrong, and he burned them with cigarettes. His parents spent almost every penny they could get on drink, drugs, and cigarettes. Hardly anything for their children."

She closed the file. It seemed she knew its contents by heart. "Ed and his sister, Missy, weren't allowed any toys, but your father fashioned one for Missy. An angel made from wire. Missy loved it. She carried it everywhere with her. Talked to it."

Melanie hesitated. This seemed difficult for her. "One day their father beat Missy so badly that she died. She was only nine. Ed was twelve and watched it happen. He'd wanted to step in and protect his sister, but he'd been afraid. For some reason, his mother tied Missy's hands and feet with some ribbons her grandmother had given her. Red ribbons. They put her in a plastic bag and buried her deep in the backyard of their rental home. While Ed's father was looking for the bag, Ed put Missy's wire angel in her hand. His way of saying good-bye to the little sister he loved.

"Then they moved to where no one knew Missy had ever existed, Ed's father threatening him with a similar beating if he ever told anyone what happened. Not long after that, his mother killed herself, and then his father took off. Ed did live with his grandparents, who'd been told Missy died from an illness, until he could go out on his own. But he never told them or anyone else what his father had done." She frowned. "Ed and his family moved so many times, always to rental properties, that he couldn't remember where his sister was buried. Maybe the FBI could do some research and find her remains."

"I'll try. I'd like to see her have a proper burial." Kaely turned over the information the doctor had given her, but it didn't make sense. Even to a profiler who was trained to understand the psychopathic mind. "But . . . but if he went through that kind of pain, why would he do the same thing to innocent women?"

"I can't explain it completely," Melanie said. "In his tortured mind he was recreating the most traumatic moment of his life. His actions were a sign of his mental illness. I also believe it was inspired by the Enemy, making him relive it over and over. He followed that evil voice . . . as long as he could." Melanie sighed and stroked the outside of the folder. "I've read quite a bit about Ed since he came here, Kaely. I wonder if you know how he was caught."

Kaely nodded. "Of course. He was profiled by an FBI behavioral analyst who suggested my father may change costumes after it was reported that a little girl saw him and referred to him as a raggedy man."

Melanie nodded. "He changed costumes after the media started calling him The Raggedy Man, then?"

"Well, not right away, I guess. I mean, he needed time to come up with something new."

Melanie paused, staring down at the file in her lap.

"If there's something you want to say, please just say it," Kaely said tersely.

"I'm sorry. I wasn't trying to be enigmatic, but I was just wondering why you've never seen it."

Kaely held back an exasperated sigh. This is why therapists tended to irritate her. She looked out the window. What was Melanie referring to? Then an idea she'd never considered jumped into her mind. "The media reported that the profiler suggested the killer might change his disguise to someone in law enforcement, and my father was wearing a policeman's uniform when they caught him—*after* the profiler was quoted. Why would he change to exactly what the profiler suggested?" Kaely stared at Melanie as she tried to grasp the meaning of her words.

"Because he wanted to be caught, Kaely. Needed to be stopped."

Kaely snorted. "Needed to be stopped? Why? He didn't care about anyone, including his victims."

Melanie took another sip of coffee before saying, "He didn't care in the way some people would, of course. But he did in the only way he could. His emotions, his ability to love had been . . . seared when he was young. Almost like an electrical line with a short circuit. Some psychopaths will argue that they do love. Is it the kind of love we're taught? The kind of love we learn from God? No."

She paused for a moment. "Maybe what he felt was closer to affection for a possession. I don't know, but in his way, your father cared about you. And when your life and the life of your brother were threatened, he did what he could to save you. Have you asked yourself why he cooperated with Beck? I don't think it was until he was stabbed by Raymond Cooper that he realized Kenneth really intended to kill the both of you no matter what he'd promised. Once he knew you were in danger, he tried to tell you who the Copycat Killer was."

"If you knew what was going on, you had the responsibility to say something," Kaely said. "You're required to report criminal activity that might involve harm to others."

"Your father never mentioned his relationship with Kenneth Beck. I asked him about the Copycat Killer, and he threatened to end our sessions if I brought him up again. Later, however, he did say something I didn't understand at the time. But I do now."

"And what's that?"

"He told me he was sorry for all the pain he'd caused his children. And he was determined to protect them now." She sighed and looked toward the windows, beyond which trees covered the ugliness of prison walls. "I wondered what he meant, but I had no clue it was related to the Copycat Killer."

Kaely took a deep breath and let it out. "I can understand that."

"Kaely, I talked to your father about Christ. He listened, but I'm not sure how much of it he received. He didn't talk a lot about God. Could be many reasons for that, but I'm not going to speculate about it. He did mention that your brother had also talked to him about salvation."

Melanie picked up her coffee cup and took another sip. Kaely was surprised to see that she was emotional. She'd cared about Ed.

"Yeah, I'm aware of that. Jason did everything he could to win Dad to the Lord, but there was never a commitment."

"Ed told me once that he wasn't good enough for heaven." She sighed deeply. "I did my best to convince him that heaven isn't for perfect people. It's for forgiven people. I'm not sure he ever believed me."

"Why are you telling me this?"

Melanie put down her cup and clasped her hands together. "Ed knew how to receive Christ. I told him. Jason told him. I'm hoping that in those last hours of his life, he cried out to God. I wanted to give you some hope."

"Well, let's *hope* his victims made it to heaven," Kaely said bluntly. "But we don't know, do we?"

"No. No, we don't." She smiled. "You'll have to find a way to deal with your anger toward your father. Stay honest. Tell your new therapist that you're angry."

"I'm sorry," Kaely said. "You've been great. I don't mean to be objectionable."

Melanie chuckled. "You're not the least bit objectionable." She got up and walked to her desk. Then she pulled open a drawer and took out a small box. After shuffling through it, she removed a card and took it to Kaely before sitting down again. "This is a therapist in St. Louis. I'd like you to see her when you get home."

Kaely glanced at the name and address. Carolyn Hutson, and her office wasn't far from hers. "Okay. Thanks."

Melanie put the file on a table next to her. "Before you leave, may I pray with you?"

Kaely was surprised by the request, but she nodded. Melanie scooted forward in her chair, and Kaely did likewise so she could take her hands. As Melanie prayed, she didn't plea for help. But her prayer was full of power, a declaration of the authority believers experience in Christ. Kaely was so moved by the overwhelming presence of love in the small room that she could barely catch her breath.

When she finished, Melanie smiled at her. "Just let God keep working in you. He wants you to be free from the past. You have a wonderful life in front of you, you know. Fight for it."

Kaely stood. "I will," she choked out.

Melanie walked her to the door. "I'm sorry for everything you've been through and so glad you and your brother recovered from your injuries. If you ever need someone to talk to, call me. I'll be glad to listen."

"Thank you." Kaely stuck out her hand, and Melanie took it. "I really do appreciate your time. You've helped more than I can say."

"Good. Let me walk you out."

A few minutes later Kaely was being escorted out of the prison. When she reached her car in the parking lot, she got in, then put her head on the steering wheel and cried until she couldn't cry anymore. But it wasn't from sadness. It was release. And joy.

FORTY-FOUR

It wasn't quite time to leave for the drive to Mort's, but Kaely was already packed and ready to go. She sat down on the couch to relax a bit. This would be her third trip to the restaurant during her trip to Iowa. She and Noah had taken Jason and Audrey there before they left for home. Audrey had braved a flight to be with him in the hospital.

Kaely couldn't stop thanking God that her brother had survived the awful knife wound Kenneth Beck inflicted. She was also thankful Beck had thought Jason was dead when he dumped him into the hole he'd dug for both of them. Jason admitted he was actually conscious for some of it.

"I kept trying to help you, sis," he'd said. "But I was too weak. Then when he pushed me into that hole, I passed out again. I didn't regain consciousness until I woke up in the hospital."

"If you'd angered him, he would have killed you, Jason. I'm so glad you didn't do anything to set him off."

"And I'm grateful the cavalry showed up just in time," Jason had said, looking at Noah. "A few minutes later . . ."

Noah had been pretty quiet while Kaely recovered. She'd seen him like this before, when he had something on his mind. She had no idea what it was, but she wasn't worried. She trusted him.

She couldn't stop thinking about what Melanie said, that her father might have accepted God's forgiveness before he died. She had no way to know what happened, but she wasn't going to dwell on it. It was better to simply put him in God's hands and leave him there.

After having his body cremated, she'd looked for a cemetery where his remains could be buried. Of course, there was no funeral. Couldn't be one. But it seemed no one even wanted The Raggedy Man buried in their hallowed ground. Kaely had no intention of taking his ashes home with her, though. Finally, one small cemetery, owned by a church, accepted his remains.

"We're not his judges," the pastor had said. "Our job is to love. If Christ loves the world, then we should as well. And that includes your father."

They would allow her to pay only for the cost of having the ground opened and closed, wanting to be a blessing to Kaely and her family. She paid them the small amount they asked for and then sent a larger check after the burial. Kaely and Jason talked about going to the cemetery, but the media was inflamed over the death of the infamous Raggedy Man. Somehow, they'd figured out where he was buried and were scouting out the small cemetery, no doubt hoping to see his son and daughter there—all much to the chagrin of the church. The pastor and his parishioners had actually been called traitors by a columnist in one of the local papers.

Kaely called the pastor to apologize for the attacks, but he'd just chuckled. "People of faith have endured a lot harsher persecution than this. It will pass. Something else will happen in our town, and the media will trot after that. We'll be forgotten."

Kaely's eyes misted thinking of the kind pastor and his long-suffering congregation. She had driven past the cemetery once, early in the morning before the media vans arrived. She spotted the newly turned earth and was touched to see flowers on the grave. She was certain the church had placed them there. No one else in Des Moines would be brave enough.

She believed her invisible friend, Georgie, was gone for good.

She didn't feel sad. Georgie lived inside her. Always had. But now Kaely had moved into a healthier relationship with God. He was the first person she needed to talk to. Kaely's faith was growing, and she was getting better at hearing that still small voice inside of her.

She glanced at her watch. Almost time to leave. She got up and checked her image in the mirror. She liked the way her dark red hair looked with her black dress. She wore a simple silver choker with a small pearl around her neck and pearl earrings she'd also packed.

She laughed as she noticed Mr. Hoover sitting on the floor behind her, staring at her disapprovingly.

"I know," she said, "but we're going home. Life will get back to normal."

Noah had taken care of the persnickety cat while she'd been in the hospital. Even though she'd been gone only a few days, Noah said the big cat had been restless, lying by the door, waiting for Kaely to come back. She'd missed him, too, showering him with affection when she returned. Mr. Hoover put up with it for a while, but then he'd finally reclaimed his imperious attitude. As she stared at him now, she realized they were a lot alike. The abandoned cat and the emotionally abandoned girl were both learning to trust again.

"If you're good, I'll bring you something from supper," she said. "How about a shrimp?" Mort's was known for their shrimp cocktail. Kaely could hardly wait to bite into a huge chilled shrimp dipped in spicy shrimp sauce. "I might be rethinking that," she said, smiling at Mr. Hoover, who made it clear he wasn't that interested in what she was saying.

Kaely jumped when Noah knocked on the connecting door. "Come in," she said. She couldn't hold back a small gasp when he walked into the room. He was wearing his black suit with a white shirt and a silver tie that brought out his gray-blue eyes. His longish black hair, which was usually tousled, was combed into submission. She was struck by how handsome he really was.

"You clean up great," she said. "But we're both wearing black. Do you think people at the restaurant will assume we've come from a funeral?"

He grinned. "No, they won't see anything but how beautiful you are."

She gulped at his compliment. "Let me find my purse, and then I'll be ready to go."

"I'll carry our bags down to the car," he said.

Kaely went into the bedroom to grab something she'd picked up after her meeting with Melanie. She didn't want to take her clunky leather purse with her tonight, so she'd visited a local clothing and accessories store to buy something more appropriate. The small, black satin clutch purse was perfect. Its rhinestone-studded silver clasp matched her necklace. She checked again to make sure everything she needed was inside. Then she looked around the room one more time to make sure she wasn't leaving anything behind.

She came back into the living room and walked over to Mr. Hoover. "Sorry, we've got to travel again, but you'll be home tonight," she told him as she reached into the carrier and stroked his thick, soft hair. She had really fallen in love with him and completely understood the loyalty pet owners had for their fur babies. He'd made her feel less alone, and that was a tremendous blessing.

"Ready?" Noah said as he walked through the door.

Kaely straightened and nodded. "Can't wait. I already know what I'm going to order."

Noah grabbed cat carrier. They left the room and got into their car. Noah offered to drive, and Kaely accepted. She appreciated the chance to relax for a while. It didn't take them long to get on the road and head toward Des Moines. On the way Kaely told Noah about her meeting with Melanie.

Noah was silent for a while after she finished.

"Did I say something that upset you?" she asked.

He shook his head. "No, I . . . I guess I'm feeling some compassion for your father. What a horrible way to grow up."

"It's true, Noah. But turning that experience into a reason to kill . . ."

"I know, but children can break, Kaely. And I've become convinced that the devil uses broken people for his purposes." He turned to look at her. "Have you thought any more about your profiling technique?"

"Yes, I have. I truly believe I'll be okay now. I have authority over the Enemy, and I just need to use it. I guess I couldn't accept the reality of what was happening. I mean, we read about the devil, but I don't think we're as vigilant as we should be." She smiled at him. "Thank you for trying to protect me. And don't worry. I don't intend to use it until I'm sure everything's under control. And that you feel all right about it."

"Thank you. I'm relieved to hear that."

"You're welcome."

He glanced at her again. What was on his mind? Kaely got a little nervous, preferring he keep his eyes on the road.

"So finding out about your father's childhood didn't change the way you feel about him? Not even a little?"

Kaely sighed as she thought about all the years of anger, resentment, and rage she'd experienced because of her father's evil deeds. Yet her feelings *had* changed some. Now there was sorrow. For everyone involved. "Yeah, some. But I'll always be sorry for the destruction he caused."

"Anything else from your meeting today with Dr. Engle?"

Kaely had been thinking about her discussion with the doctor ever since she left the prison. Not just because of the depiction of her father's upbringing. It was more than that. She wasn't sure exactly what happened in Dr. Engle's office, but when Melanie prayed, Kaely felt as if the dark emotional blanket that had covered her for years had finally been lifted. When she drove away, that's how she felt—free. The fear of dying young was gone. And the words of the invisible UNSUB who told her she was going to die soon had become nothing more than an attack from the Enemy. It wasn't true, and she wasn't afraid of it anymore.

"She gave me a card that belongs to a therapist in St. Louis. I intend to call her after we get home. I want to make sure I heal completely. I think regular counseling sessions might help—as long as they're God-centered."

Kaely remembered something else Melanie had said. That if she ever needed a person to talk to, she would be there. Kaely looked at Noah. She might call the doctor someday, but now she had someone she could talk to about anything. Someone who had stood by her despite her quirks, her mistakes, and her fractured soul. He'd seen the best and the worst she had to offer. And he was still here.

She smiled to herself. Georgie hadn't left because she'd met with the real Georgie. Her imaginary friend was gone because Kaely had Noah. She didn't need to invent someone to share her life with anymore. She loved Noah Hunter, and she wanted to spend the rest of her life with him. But although he'd professed his love for her, was he ready for some kind of future? She didn't know.

Kaely settled back in her seat, still thinking about everything that had happened earlier in the day.

"Here we are," Noah said, waking her up.

She sat up, surprised that she'd fallen asleep. She looked out the window and realized they were pulling into the parking lot at Mort's.

"You were sleeping so peacefully, I didn't want to wake you," Noah said, smiling.

Kaely straightened, then pulled down the visor and looked into the mirror. She ran her hands through her hair to reshape it and smoothed out her dress.

"Don't worry. You look beautiful,"

Kaely laughed. "Thankfully, I didn't drool."

"It wouldn't have mattered."

Kaely felt herself blush. She didn't say anything, but she loved hearing Noah compliment her.

They checked on Mr. Hoover. He was sleeping peacefully in his crate. The evening air was cool, so they cracked the windows and left him where he was.

The outside of the restaurant was decorated with small sparkling lights. They covered the outdoor seating area, making it look magical. Beautiful.

"Could we eat outside?" Kaely asked. "It's such a nice night."

"Sure, I think so. Stay here. I'll ask them if they can change our reservation to one of these tables."

Kaely wasn't certain why she needed to wait in the parking lot, but she stood there until Noah came back, a smile on his face. When they stepped onto the patio, a restaurant employee led them to a beautiful table facing a garden. A water fountain gurgled and sparkled in the dusk. There were lights in the water. Soft music played in the background. It was perfect.

Kaely and Noah sat down, and after the waiter took their drink orders, he left. Kaely thought it rather odd.

"Shouldn't we get menus?" she asked Noah. "I thought I knew what I wanted, but now I'd like to look over all the options."

"I'm sure he'll bring them when he comes back," Noah said. His voice shook a bit.

"What's wrong with you? You seem nervous."

"I'm not nervous. I'm—"

She and Noah both turned toward the door to the restaurant as it opened. Several waitstaff descended down the stairs. One of them carried a cake with candles, the flames dancing in the slight breeze. Then they all began singing "Happy Birthday."

Kaely's mouth dropped open. "I completely forgot. Today's my birthday."

When they'd finished the song, patrons sitting near them applauded. Then their waiter carefully sat the beautiful cake on Noah and Kaely's table. It had fluffy white icing with yellow flowers and *Happy Birthday, Kaely* written in green icing. Amid the flowers was a small box with a yellow bow.

Kaely thanked the staff for their efforts, and several of them wished her a happy birthday before they left. Their waiter stayed at the table.

"I'll bring your menus shortly," he said, a smile on his face and sending a knowing glance to Noah.

As he walked away, Kaely smiled. "This is the nicest birthday I've ever had. Thank you so much. I can't believe you went to all this trouble." The truth was she was embarrassed by all the attention, but she loved that he'd cared enough to set this up. She would never forget it. "Do we eat dessert first?" she asked, laughing.

"Not quite yet," he said, the tremor still in his voice. Then he stood and pulled the small box off the cake. When he opened it, he took out a smaller, black velvet box.

"Kaely, I know how hard life has been for you. I've watched you fight through situations that would have destroyed anyone else. Yes, some things about you drive me crazy. Like the way you run into danger without a second thought. At one time I was willing to walk away because I was afraid you'd break my heart if I got close. But then I realized you *are* my heart and that I want to be part of your life. Forever."

Kaely gasped as he came closer and got down on one knee. One of her favorite songs played in the background—a Keith Urban love song.

"I adore you, Kaely Quinn," Noah said, tears making his eyes shiny. "I've never known anyone like you, and I simply can't live without you."

He opened the box, and she saw the beautiful ring inside. "I'm not asking for a commitment tonight." He closed the box and handed it to her. "I'm willing to wait until you're ready. But someday, I'd like to marry you."

Kaely didn't worry about her makeup as tears fell down her cheeks, and she stared at the box in her hands. Then she lifted her eyes. "Noah, I think I fell in love with you the first day I met you. I just couldn't admit it. I'm sorry for everything I've put you through, and I will try harder to keep myself safe. For you." She smiled. "I don't know when I'll be ready, but I'm getting stronger. Better. When I'm sure I can be the kind of wife you need, my answer will be yes. As long as you're willing to put up with me and a cranky old cat—"

"I love that cranky old cat. And you."

Noah got to his feet. Then he pulled her up and kissed her like she'd never been kissed before.

As Keith sang in the background, Kaely Quinn was sure she was about to step into a life more challenging and exciting than anything she'd ever known.

And she was okay with that.

ACKNOWLEDGMENTS

Thank you again to Supervisory Special Agent Drucilla L. Wells (retired), Federal Bureau of Investigation, Behavioral Analysis Unit. She brings a sense of reality to this series. I've said it before, but without her, these books wouldn't be possible.

Thanks to Tim Diesberg, former IDOC Anamosa State Penitentiary, for "walking" me through the prison. I love using real places in my books when I can, but without someone like Tim, it's not possible. He was understanding and patient with my dumb questions. Although most of the information I used is real, the secured area reserved for staff was built from my imagination. I'm explaining this because I don't want Tim's friends to accuse him of making up stories. That's *my* job!

My thanks to Felicia Bowen Bridges, author of the award-winning INTERNATIONAL MISSION FORCE series, for answering questions about how state labs and medical examiners work. She was a great help.

Thank you to my friend Carla Hoch for giving me more

information about dead bodies than I'll ever need. I think the nightmares are starting to subside. (Just kidding. Kind of.)

Once again, thank you to Raela Schoenherr for allowing me to write this series. I'm sad to see it end but excited about our new adventure. Thank you for your continued support. And a big thank-you to Jean Bloom for her editing help.

Nancy Mehl is the author of more than thirty books, including the ROAD TO KINGDOM, FINDING SANCTUARY, and DEFENDERS OF JUSTICE series. She received the ACFW Mystery Book of the Year Award in 2009. Nancy has a background in social work and is a member of ACFW. She writes from her home in Missouri, where she lives with her husband, Norman, and their puggle, Watson. To learn more, visit www.nancymehl.com.

Sign Up for Nancy's Newsletter!

Keep up to date with Nancy's news on book releases and events by signing up for her email list at nancymehl.com.

More from the KAELY QUINN PROFILER Series

The daughter of an infamous serial killer, Kaely Quinn has established a new life for herself in St. Louis with her undeniable talent as an FBI Behavioral Analyst—though her methods may be perceived as unorthodox. With the help of her partner, Noah Hunter, Kaely must hunt down the world's most dangerous madmen before anyone else—including herself—is killed.

KAELY QUINN PROFILER: *Mind Games, Fire Storm, Dead End*

You May Also Like . . .

On a mission to recover the Book of the Wars, Leif and his team are diverted by a foretelling of formidable guardians who will decimate the enemies of the ArC, while Iskra uses her connections to hunt down the book. As they try to stop the guardians, failure becomes familiar, and the threats creep closer to home, with implications that could tear them apart.

Kings Falling by Ronie Kendig
The Book of the Wars #2
roniekendig.com

When elite members of the military are murdered on the streets of Washington, DC, FBI Special Agent Bailey Ryan and NCIS Special Agent Marco Agostini must work together to bring the perpetrator to justice. As the stakes rise in a twisted conspiracy and allies turn to enemies, the biggest secret yet to be uncovered could be the end of all of them.

End Game by Rachel Dylan
Capital Intrigue #1
racheldylan.com

When cybercriminals hack into the U.S. Marshal's Witness Protection database and auction off personal details to the highest bidder, FBI Agent Sean Nichols begins a high-stakes chase to find the hacker. Trouble is, he has to work with U.S. Marshal Taylor Mills, who knows the secrets of his past, and the seconds are slipping away before someone dies.

Seconds to Live by Susan Sleeman
Homeland Heroes #1
susansleeman.com

BETHANYHOUSE